MW00676941

EYE OF THE BEHOLDER

ALSO BY JEFF PATE

Winner Take All

JEFF PATE

EYE OF THE BEHOLDER

A CLARK HAGER NOVEL

Harlan Publishing Company
Greensboro, North Carolina
USA

HARLAN
PUBLISHING

Eye of the Beholder is a work of fiction. Any references to real people, events, establishments, organizations, or locales are intended only to give the fiction a sense of reality and authenticity. Other names, characters, places, and incidents portrayed herein are either the product of the author's imagination or are used fictionally.

Harlan Publishing Company
5710-K High Point Road PMB 280
Greensboro, NC 27407 USA

Visit our web site at: http://www.harlanpublishing.com

FIRST EDITION

Library of Congress Control Number: 2001086097

ISBN: 0-9676528-3-9

First Printing: April 2001

Author's note and acknowledgments

The last year has been such an adventure for me—with the release of *Winner Take All* and seeing the book achieve more than I ever imagined, to now as I cross my fingers, hoping my newly-acquired fans will like *Eye of the Beholder* as much. I've met many people along the way, and I hope I can continue to bring you entertaining books.

I want to say thanks to all my friends and family, who played a big part in making the first one a success. Additionally, I wouldn't have accomplished so much this year without the help and support of booksellers and community relations managers at the many bookstores I visited. They enthusiastically took a chance on me when some wouldn't. Thanks.

Special thanks go to my parents Ken and Bettie Pate. They've been behind me through all the ups and downs with this fledgling career and never discouraged me. Mom and Dad, I hope I've made you proud.

To Kevin and Betsy (my brother and sister) and their families: thanks for spreading the word about my books. It made a difference.

Finally, thanks to my editor Sara Claytor who has gotten a bad rap for mistakes made that were my fault. We did it again, Sara. I hope this one is an 'A'.

Jeff Pate

January 2001

As always, for Lauren

This book is dedicated to Pam Hackenberg, who passed away in December after a two-year battle with Cancer. Pam, you will always be loved and your vivid spirit inspires us all.

"Believe only half of what you see and nothing you hear."

—English proverb

CHAPTER

1

July

DARKNESS SURROUNDED HER. She was trapped inside a forest of trees gently swaying in the warm summer breeze. A storm was coming—she could tell by the sudden drop in temperature—but a storm was the least of her worries. She had to get away—away from that monster. She couldn't see much past her face, only the trees, with their branches hanging low like in fairy tales, poised to grab her from this path. But there was no real path, only the one she'd managed to follow without stumbling or colliding head-on into a tree.

The leaves crackled with the sound of footsteps, slow and deliberate. He was coming. "I know you're here somewhere," the monster called in a pensive tone.

A shrill of adrenaline rushed through her body at the sound of his eerie voice, causing a shivering chill to soar up her spine. Instantly, she darted down the path away from her attacker.

"Ah hah!" he cackled, "I see you. You can't get away!"

As she ran, the branches reached out and scraped her face, tearing into her fragile skin, but she was unaware of the pain. She dodged in and out of the way of low hanging limbs and brushed by leaves and pine needles sweeping at her cheeks. Furiously zigzagging around the dark images, her hand scraped against the bark, peeling away the skin of her palms. Again, she felt no pain—only fear and terror.

Her chest was hurting now, both legs aching and about to explode. She had lost one shoe at the onset of her escape. Around another tree, she grasped a branch and turned around to view her pursuer. Breaths were difficult as her chest heaved back and forth. Her throat was on fire, and her toes cramped. She wanted to fall and rest. All she could do was cough, cough and cough, like she was choking on her own air. She was trying to breathe too fast—a normal response to sprinting what she thought was a mile.

Her hands were shaking, although she couldn't see to tell. She braced her hands on her thighs and felt her cool skin and remembered she was wearing no pants, nor panties—a sacrifice for the sake of her escape. Tears finally welled in her eyes as she, for the first time, consciously realized she was probably going to die. Her lips quivered and her tongue swelled thick and dry.

She heard him again—methodical steps in the leaves, with branches snapping under the weight of his body, grunting sounds like a hungry wolf in search of his dinner. Then she saw the black shape of the monster trudging around a tree, his arms pushing branches away from his body. Dressed all in black. No face. No features other than ones she remembered feeling while he lay on top of her.

He was hard, not muscular, but thin and wiry. And he smelled—intense body odor or something else—something unusual, like something she'd never smelled before in her life. But at the same time, it was as familiar as her husband's cologne. The pungent aroma first caught her attention when she got into her car just before the attack, only seconds before he appeared from the back and his grimy hand clamped over her mouth, the other holding the knife sharply against her throat. His voice was evil and raspy. *Don't even think about screaming, bitch!*

As she drove according to his command, she remembered his hands groping all over her body—her breasts, his fingers between her legs, his breath so hot and rank with alcohol. It made her sick, but she was too terrified to think of anything other than submitting to his will. She spat in disgust at her memory of him inside her, grunting as he was now, telling her she was loving it, and loving him inside her. Her stomach cramped—she was going to vomit, but she held it back, cupping her hand over her mouth.

The shadow figure stopped and faced her direction. Still he had no face, just the dark resemblance to something human, but she still wasn't sure. He had bitten her. On the shoulder she thought, and she felt a sore area just above her left breast. Did he see her? Or was he just standing there to rest or hear any movement from her?

She stood still. Her heart pounded in her chest and she took a deep breath—one that didn't come easily—and held it, trying to remain silent in the darkness.

A loud horrific and hilarious laugh sounded from the creature some fifty yards away. "I've got you now!" he shouted. "There's no escape, my lovely. I can't wait to hold you once again!" And he laughed again, his head rocking back and forth.

Suddenly a clap of thunder cracked and shook the earth. A bolt of lightning illuminated the monster's face, but it wasn't a normal face. It had a nose and mouth, but it looked like the face of the devil, with blood red eyes and a long red tongue that slithered around his thin red lips. He really was a monster. Or was it only her imagination? Or was she dreaming? *Please wake up! Please!*

She couldn't hold it. Not for a moment longer. The scream of terror was too much to confine in her mouth.

She shook and kept her mouth closed, her lips sealed, but trembling and her throat convulsing, wanting to release the fear locked inside. The scream lasted for at least a minute, she thought—seemed to echo throughout the woods. When she finished, she took off again, flailing at the limbs, shaking the leaves from the trees, and from behind her, she heard his breath. His heart was beating down on her, and she had to get away. *Keep running...just keep going. You can't give up. You can't give up.*

She scrambled up an incline, a steep hill covered with leaves. The wind whipped through the trees. Another crack of thunder exploded as the lightning bombarded the forest. She stopped, covering her ears, her hands trembling. She turned to face him. Her legs were dying, her entire body trembling out of fear and fatigue, but adrenaline rushed again. She was going to fight one last time—defeat this evil monster. There was no other choice. *Where is he?*

She squinted, trying to discern the black shape between the trees from the trees themselves. No shape or movement. Nothing. She drew a hard breath and her chest and throat were on fire, her heart thundering out of her chest. Wind squalled again; it was warmer now—not like before. The storm would pass, she thought.

Calmness settled in the forest, but she still looked for the black shape. Quickly she snapped her head in both directions and then behind in a feverish survey of her surroundings. The trees were placid. She took a deep breath. Something was missing. *Where is he?*

A warm breeze swept across her face—seemingly, a blanket of safety with the trees swaying. Looking around again, she saw nothing, felt nothing but her own heart still thumping at a less furious pace. Taking a deep breath, she knelt next to a tree and hugged the trunk, peering in the distance for some movement. The breeze blew gently again and it produced a familiar odor. This time, the wind was icy. She felt him, but where was he? She shivered from the cold and smelled him.

Get up! Damnit! Run for your life!

She braced and began to rise. No breath could come. The wind blew frigid once more. A lightning bolt crashed into the trees. As a hand clamped tightly around her throat, she felt the driving force of the knife thrust into her back.

Bite! Scratch! Claw! Punch! Kick! Scream! Please God! Please...

CHAPTER

2

THE TELEVISION SCREEN flickered white and gray. Luther Rivers sat with his feet propped on a desk surfing the three channels received by the portable, at the same time listening to a soul music radio station, which jazzed in the background. Nothing much going on that night for Luther. His only other activity was a service call on the 440 Beltline—a strange fellow in an old black Toyota with a flat tire and no jack. It was a seemingly forgettable job, but one he would remember because he'd cracked the knuckle of his right hand, splitting his skin and seeping blood. *You should've worn your gloves, Luther,* his wife would say.

He looked at his hand as an Earth Wind and Fire tune blared on the radio and checked his work on the bandage. The bleeding had stopped at least for now, but when he ran a finger along the edge of the wound, he winced in pain. Soreness had already set in.

Cuts, bumps, and bruises were all hazards in the world of driving a wrecker on second shift. For Luther Rivers, it was a job that not only paid fairly decently, but more importantly, it kept him off the streets where he could get into trouble. Trouble was something that seemed to follow the two-time ex-con just recently released from prison after doing seven of a ten year sentence for Robbery and Rape.

No more trouble for Luther. He didn't want to go back to prison again. The way it was in North Carolina now — "three strikes and you're out" — another charge and he would be a Habitual Felon — a "lifer." At almost forty, Luther had spent eleven years of his adult life behind bars, which wasn't as bad as some of his brothers, but still the same, his mama wanted her baby to be different.

Keep your nose clean, Luther. Don't be like your brothers.

Luther looked at the Budweiser clock on the wall and saw it was almost twelve, nearing the end of his three to midnight shift. Soon it would be "Miller time," but he would end it with "the Bull" instead. On his way home he planned to pick up a couple of 40s at the Circle K, pop one open and watch *In Living Color* reruns on Comedy Channel. Luther smiled and tasted the cold malty taste of the beer going down his throat. When the phone rang, he stopped smiling. His eyes shifted back to the clock and the red numbers showed *11:53.* "Damn!" he said knowing the call would delay his date with "the Bull."

"Capital City Towing," Luther said into the receiver.

"Have you got a tow truck available tonight?" a male asked. Luther thought he'd heard the voice before.

"You got it, man. What's the problem?"

"Well, uh, my wife called and said she broke down somewhere on Highway Seventy between Raleigh and Durham. Out in the middle of nowhere I'd guess from the way she was whining about it," said the man, who sounded white and a little pissed his old lady wanted him to take care of her business. "You think you can go down there and pick up her Mercedes. It's a silver E- 420."

A 'Benz, huh? Luther said to himself. Must be rich white folks. "I guess so, man. What she say was wrong with it?"

"How should I know?" the man snapped. "She just said it quit running and she told me to call a tow truck."

"She gonna be out there with the car?"

"Possible," the man said with a little chuckle, which he undoubtedly thought went unheard. "She called me from her cell phone and said she was gonna try to get a ride from a girlfriend. I don't know. I'm out of town and can't come and get her."

"That's cool, man. She gonna leave the key so I don't mess up the transmission?" Aretha Franklin's high-pitched voice brought Luther's attention back to the radio. He closed his eyes and hummed to himself.

"I told her to leave the ignition key under the mat and the doors unlocked. That okay?"

"Yeah, man. Where you want it towed to, and how you gonna pay for it if she ain't with the car?"

"Just take it back to your lot. I'll arrange for someone to get it when I get back into town. I'll pay you then, okay?"

"Sure thing, mister. What's the name?" Luther pulled a pen from his shirt pocket and wrote: *Benz 70 Raleigh — Durham.* "Go ahead."

"My name is Russell Craven," the man stated flatly and Luther scribbled with the pen: *Craven.* The man told him "thanks" and Luther hung up the phone.

Luther grabbed the keys to his wrecker and locked the door to the shop. While walking through the parking lot, he decided to go by the store and pick up at least a double-deuce for the ride. Just a warm-up for when he got home.

The warm summer air was thick and a slight breeze, infrequent, was a welcome feeling on Luther's sweaty neck. He pulled the damp shirt away from his skin to allow cooler air to filter down his chest. Luther breathed deeply, taking in the night air. He could tell a storm was approaching — one of those typical North Carolina rampages of heavy wind and rain, which caused flash flooding and downed power lines. He remembered the television had shown the usual warnings scrolled across the bottom of the screen, indicating a thunderstorm watch was in effect.

Traffic was fairly light Luther noticed as he turned onto U.S. 70 east toward Durham. As he eased down the highway, he sang along with Marvin Gaye's "Sexual Healing" which played on *Soul 104*. Cradled in his right hand and between his legs was the cold bottle of beer and on the seat next to him, a bag of barbecue pork skins, already opened and emanating a delightful aroma.

Switching his left hand to the wheel, Luther grabbed a handful of skins and crunched them tastefully, chasing them with a ten-second gulp from the bottle.

"Ahh! No need to milk this baby," Luther said to himself, tapping the second bottle next to him. "I've got his twin brother right here."

With the first bottle almost empty, Luther began feeling the dizzying effects produced by drinking on an almost-empty stomach. It felt good, though. A set of flashing lights ahead caught his attention as he downed the last of bottle number one.

The car was on the westbound side of the highway and the red lights flickered quickly like those foreign jobs did. He crunched another handful of skins and twisted off the top of the twin as he passed the car, seeing that it was a Mercedes.

The entire area around the car seemed desolate to Luther. Traffic was almost non-existent in the dark stretch between the new 540 loop and the outer limits of Durham County. The wrecker jumped as Luther downshifted to slow at the crossing of the median, which was about a quarter mile east of the car. After turning around, Luther put the bottle to his mouth again, taking a fifteen-second refreshing gulp that burned his throat and produced a long and loud belch echoing in the dark night.

Luther pulled the wrecker in front of the Mercedes and

saw no one inside.

"Must've gotten that ride," Luther mumbled. "Didn't want to stick around for the greasy nigga tow-truck driver to come. Naw, wouldn't want to mix with the po' folks of the world."

Metal grated as he shifted the gears and moved backwards toward the car's front end; with a bump harder than usual, the wrecker was in place. Leaving the motor running, Luther turned on the rotating amber lights on the truck's roof, opened the door and jumped down to the pavement, still crunching on some pork skins. Hands covered with crumbs, he wiped them lazily on his pants as he walked toward the car. Luther pulled on the handle of the driver's door, and the interior light shone brightly. With the exception of a black leather bag lying in the back seat, the car was empty.

As he stretched his head into the car in search of the key, Luther enjoyed the refreshing smell of the leather seats. There was no key in the ignition and he remembered the white man said it would be under the floor mat. Luther inched his hand under the carpeted mat feeling for the key. His fingers found the jagged edge. He pulled his hand from under the mat and painfully bumped his wounded knuckle on the seat frame. Luther winced in agony, "Fuck me in the ass!" he shouted.

He tried to shake the piercing pain from his sore hand and held it with the other, examining the bandage. Blood seeped from the gauze, dripping to the floor.

"Goddammit! Fucking German pieces of shit!" Luther shouted as he pounded both his fists together on the steering wheel.

Gingerly, he reached his left hand into his back pocket in search of the greasy towel he kept there. Instead, he found his gloves and recalled he should have been wearing them again.

Shoulda been wearing your gloves, Luther.

He inserted the key and turned the engine over. The

motor quietly hummed and music accompanied by a female voice poured from the speakers, "Don't be stupid," the woman sang. "You know I love ya."

It sounded like country music to Luther, and he turned down the volume on the CD player. Luther was puzzled at the Mercedes' quick start, thinking of the nature of his call.

She just said it quit running, and told me to call a tow truck, the white man had said.

Maybe it was the transmission, Luther reasoned and pulled the gearshift into "Neutral" and turned off the motor. His hand still throbbing in pain, Luther stepped from the car and spied the black bag in the back seat.

I wonder what's inside the goody bag?

He walked around to the passenger side, opened the door and took a seat, his head a little lighter from the beer and his throbbing hand. Not really noticing that his hand continued to bleed, Luther pulled on a zipper, and a whiff of perfume wafted from the opening. Inside the bag he found an assortment of clothes: spandex tights, a towel, hairbrush, make-up kit, tennis shoes, socks, and a pair of panties.

The clothes and towel were moist, evidently wet with sweet perspiration from the female driver. So were the panties, and Luther brought them to his face, feeling the silky softness against his stubbled cheek. He took a deep breath with his nose in the crotch, trying to get a hint of musky aroma lingering from her "treasure box." His mind drifted into an arousing remembrance of deeds in the past.

Luther Rivers was driving home late that night in 1987 after an evening playing pool with the boys. As he drove along, he noticed the faint flashing of red lights along the shoulder. As he grew closer, he saw a lone car parked with its hood raised. Standing under the hood trying to decipher what problem existed was his victim. Although the darkness prevented a true look, Luther could see by the tight skirt and long legs that she was ready for some action. His headlights illuminated her for a split second and blood rushed through his veins and inside his pants. He knew a monster had awakened.

After he passed by the girl's car, Luther trained an eye in his rear view mirror, watching for a companion with the long-legged beauty. She was blonde with her hair pulled back.

Not for long, Luther thought. He would pull down her hair and rub it all over his face; Luther closed his eyes in the fantasy. Not seeing anyone else, Luther turned his truck around along the median and returned to help his "damsel in distress."

Just being a helpful hand for a lady in need, Luther mused.

It was so easy, Luther remembered. She was young and impressionable, and better yet, she was naive to the dangers of the world. The blonde was probably 19 or 20, with shapely legs that jutted perfectly from the short skirt and would fit nicely around his waist. Luther looked and dressed like a mechanic and since he was working at a Jiffy Lube at the time, he smelled like a mechanic.

When he walked to her car, Luther remembered seeing the smile of relief that someone bothered to stop and help. And he also remembered her face later—when she cried, begging him to let her go and to stop what he was doing. Luther nodded and a smile emerged on his face.

"No, it looks like you're not going any further with this baby. Not tonight at least," he recalled telling her after giving a once-over glance under the hood.

She didn't have a cell phone. Hell, no one had one then, Luther reflected, unless you were rich.

It was so easy, he thought, as she mulled over in her mind whether to accept the ride to the nearest telephone from the stranger who had stopped to help. When he saw the answer in her eyes, his lust grew stronger. They never made it to a phone. *She* didn't at least.

Luther turned off at the next exit but bypassed the Amoco station at the corner, provoking a tone of fear from her lips as he put his hand under her skirt. After a few slaps and the displaying of his trusty fishing knife, she relented to pleading for mercy.

Along a deserted unpaved road, Luther had his way with the young woman and despite her cries of fear and pain, he knew she had liked it.

They all did. They all liked to be taken—taken in a way that scares the hell out of them but makes them sopping wet between their legs. Of all the women with whom Luther had been involved, they all liked being taken. Women liked to be fucked forcefully and fantasized they were being raped by some dirty stranger or the cable man who visited when their husbands were gone. They liked to be fucked hard. That was what he did to Carolyn Glenn—his *victim*.

He remembered fucking Carolyn hard from behind and every which way he could before he blew his load degradingly in her face. Just like he saw in the porno movies. She panted and groaned and although she begged him to stop, he knew she was just "playing her role" as the submissive bitch who loved to get fucked hard.

Luther felt generous that night and decided he would return the favor to sweet Carolyn. He'd never gone down on anyone. One taste and he knew what the white boys were talking about. She tasted delightful and she moaned, grabbing his head, pulling his face and tongue deep inside her. That was when she did it.

She clubbed him. The bitch played along while he gave her some undeserved pleasure and she hit him. She smashed a rock over his head while he was going down on her. That was how she thanked him for making her feel especially good. That was the way she thanked him for his generosity.

The fucking bitch.

The blow to his head was what had allowed Carolyn Glenn to escape and what had convicted Luther as well. It took seven stitches to close and seven years of his life in a prison cell.

The fucking bitch.

Luther's mind returned to the back of the Mercedes. Thinking about the blow to his head, he ran his fingers under the cap atop his head and traced along the scar's surface. A souvenir? Or a painful memory?

Thank God, they didn't know about his other *victim.*

He still clutched the woman's panties and he sniffed them once again—feeling their moistness. The erection remained in his pants, and Luther pondered whipping it out and blowing his load in those sweet panties.

"No, Luther," he said aloud. " *That* would be sick." He laughed at his joke.

Luther returned the contents to the bag and wondered about the woman who belonged to the car. If she was working out, she probably wasn't doing it for the husband. Most likely, he wasn't giving proper attention to her sexual needs. She was getting some on the side, with some young stud at the gym perhaps. That was where she was and it was the reason the car was running fine. It was her alibi.

Fucking slut.

With the bag packed as neatly as Luther could remember, he rummaged through the front of the car finding some compact discs. Frank Sinatra, Shania Twain, Alan Jackson, and along with about ten others, Luther's favorite, Marvin Gaye.

At least she has one good CD. Better yet...had. Luther put the disc cases in his jacket pocket and continued his search under the front seats. They would bring some beer money at the pawnshop.

In the glove box he found a cellular phone and quickly he dialed his number at home. Luther's wife, Trenesa, was six months pregnant and would be worrying he'd gone to play pool instead of coming home like he'd promised. Just a quick call to tell her he had a pick-up and would be late. When he ended the call, Luther thought about it and realized his number would show up on the woman's phone bill. People might get suspicious, he thought. Decisively, he dismissed the idea, knowing rich white folks don't check their phone bills. They just pay them.

With nothing else to take from the car, Luther returned the phone to the glove box. Leaving the phone behind was odd for a woman who was either broken down or stepping out on her husband. She would need the phone later, he thought. Like before, his thoughts quickly dissipated, and Luther hooked up the Mercedes.

In minutes he was driving through the night en route to the storage yard at Capital City Towing, unaware that inside the Mercedes was a cargo that would change his life forever.

CHAPTER

3

FOREVER AND A DAY. It seemed to have been longer than six months since it happened. Six months — almost to the day — since he lay on the floor exhausted from a tremendous battle with a serial killer.

Six months and a couple of days since his friend and partner, Lloyd Sheridan, was critically injured by the same killer.

Six months and a few weeks since four women were lured into a web of ominous death by a charismatic killer.

Six months since his daughter Elizabeth brushed perilously close to the grasp of a monster. At the same time, her friend had been sucked into a psychotic fantasy of torture and death.

Six months since a killer terrorized Hager almost to the point of insanity — sacrificing his own peculiar insight into the criminal mind.

All of them were victims—victims of the man the media dubbed, "The Strangler."

Forever and a day.

But "The Strangler" no longer existed. Clark Hager achieved ending the killer's spree of death. Hager had pumped numerous 9mm rounds from his partner's Beretta into "The Strangler", ending his life and a duration of pain and suffering that had touched many people.

Hager remembered returning to his office a month after the battle. Standing in the lobby, he had gazed across the room taking notice of the holes in the walls. The room had smelled musty and desolate. He'd counted ten holes on the two opposite walls, signifying the position of the two combatants during battle. To his right were six more—about head high on the wall near the door.

Those were meant for me.

He shuddered when he replayed the battle in his mind.

The room was empty and seemed to have lost its previous warmth. All that remained were the walls tattered with bullet holes and the carpet—clean in spots untouched by feet or once covered by furniture.

Hager followed a trail from the hall entrance along the floor to his left until his eyes found the stains. Two stains—red from blood—and one larger than the other, plotted the location where he and "The Strangler" ultimately fell, culminating a gun battle where more than twenty shots were fired in a matter of seconds.

Hager had stared at the smaller stain created by his own blood. He remembered facing his opponent—rapid-firing the pistol until the slide locked back empty. Fearful in retrospect as the event replayed itself as it had over and over again in his dreams, Hager felt proud he'd not only survived, but he'd also defeated "The Strangler."

It was his first gunfight in a long career, as well as the first time he'd ever been shot. The ones who experienced it before were right. It hurts like hell, but you only really feel it afterwards. The shot to his shoulder burned like acid, and he still felt lingering effects of the wound from time to time. But he survived. Hager had won.

Despite the sense of pride and accomplishment Hager felt in winning, a feeling of fear lingered in his recollections and nightmares of the ordeal. The Monday-morning-quarterback in him second-guessed his entire movements, causing him to fear he'd done something wrong.

Tactically, what he did wasn't the soundest approach to a gunfight, but he'd won, had he not? Plus, he'd killed someone. Even someone who, more than most, deserved to be killed, Tom Moffitt was a human being, and Hager was traumatized like any normal person would be after such a violent struggle.

But why, after six months had Hager chosen to recall his tortuous ordeal with "The Strangler?" What was so important about July 15, 1997?

Other than it was like any other day with the air thickened by North Carolina humidity and temperatures in the 90's, July 15 was Missy Campbell's birthday. Missy was Elizabeth's college friend — "The Strangler's" fourth victim. Missy would have been twenty-one that day. A life ended so early.

What had caused Hager to remember Missy's birthday was the reason he, Vanessa, Lloyd, and Elizabeth were on the road to Hickory. The Campbells had invited Hager and Elizabeth to be a part of a blissful occasion in remembering their daughter's birthday instead of a gloomy ceremony on the anniversary of her death.

Lloyd and Elizabeth were seated in the back seat of Hager's Ford Crown Victoria. Lloyd had awakened from the coma the same night Hager killed Tom Moffitt. Still on convalescent leave from the bureau, Lloyd had improved greatly in his recovery from the terrific beating he'd suffered. The blows to his head had caused some memory loss, but Lloyd seemed to be as normal as ever — if Lloyd could ever have been called "normal."

A scar traced the side of Lloyd's head along his brow

from the hairline across his temple and almost to his ear. Serving as a subtle reminder of the past, it proved to be more a character line than anything else — something Lloyd could tell stories about.

Lloyd was massaging the discolored mark with his finger as he gazed out the car's windows. Was he remembering the beating, and rubbing the scar served as a "play" button turning on the tape recorder of memory?

From what Lloyd had told Hager and everyone else, he didn't remember anything about his encounter on the interstate with "The Strangler." Hager wasn't convinced because Lloyd seemed to fall into spells of daydreaming during Hager's frequent visits over the past six months. And he would finger the scar like he was doing then — with the same inanimate look on his face. When asked, Lloyd would only respond in true Lloyd fashion that he was thinking about having sex with his wife.

Lloyd was ready to go back to work. The bureau had almost insisted he retire, but Lloyd was too stubborn to listen to them, Hager, or his wife Martha who begged for Lloyd to end his career. Hager knew how his partner felt about the inevitability of retirement. As good as the word sounded in language with thoughts of sleeping late, playing golf and traveling around the country, 'retirement' had only one definition: 'useless.'

Coming to terms with longevity didn't affect only Lloyd, but soon after Hager returned to work, Assistant Director Bob Maxwell informed him they were grooming a replacement when Lloyd ultimately retired. Hager took it as an affront.

A former FBI agent who came to the SBI after ten years of trying to escape a mounting caseload in the New York field office, Matt Huston was currently working in Charlotte, waiting for the call to come up to the big leagues. With his experience in the FBI, the 32-year old Huston was sure to have been qualified for a position in the unit, but what offended Hager mostly: he wasn't consulted before the decision was made. The director had made it on his own, and Hager knew what that meant. Huston wasn't only Lloyd's replacement, but he would be Hager's eventual successor as Special Agent-in-Charge of the Investigative Support Unit. And Hager would be responsible for mentoring this youthful agent with an accounting degree from UVA.

At least he wasn't a lawyer.

Lloyd continued to stare out the window in silence. Elizabeth was casually flipping through the pages of *Cosmopolitan* and Vanessa was dozing in the seat next to Hager.

"God, she is beautiful," Hager said to himself.

Hager felt he was the luckiest man alive to have found Vanessa Roman. Momentarily taking his eyes from the road, Hager started at her beautiful chestnut brown hair, her face with its sensuous lips, and her breasts; down her left arm ending at her hand, and brilliantly sparkling on her finger, a diamond ring.

Hager and Vanessa were engaged in May with the wedding planned for Christmas. He proposed to her while paddling a rowboat on a small pond at the Scenic Overlook Bed and Breakfast in Pilot Mountain. Hager remembered rowing the boat to the center of the pond. They floated, taking in the bright sunny day.

Hager had planned to propose sometime during their weekend stay. He'd thought about asking her to be his wife during the dinner he'd arranged Saturday evening at the acclaimed Colmant House, but he felt romantic as they glided atop the water in the warm breeze. With the ring in hand, Hager balanced himself in the teetering boat, looked deeply into Vanessa's brown eyes. He told her he loved her and popped the question. What happened next served as a hilarious reminder of a wonderful day, intended to be perfect in every way, but as luck would have it, resulted in disaster.

When Vanessa said,"Yes" to Hager's proposal, he

reached for a kiss and the boat swayed, spilling both of them into the cool mountain water. Instead of trying to climb back into the boat, they both chose to swim about fifty yards to shore where the laughter began.

Kissing and laughing, cold and wet, lying on the grassy bank, the two of them finally sloshed their way back to the room and into the hot water of the Jacuzzi tub. In the warm confines of the bubble bath, they consummated their engagement. A smile emerged on Hager's face in recollection of the entire weekend.

Elizabeth continued to read from the magazine and now she was giving Lloyd a sex quiz. Hager shook his head listening to his twenty year old daughter talk sex with his crude partner. He didn't want to listen.

Elizabeth was out of school for the summer. She'd found a job as an intern for a law firm in Raleigh — Harrison, Wheeler, and Ross — an upscale firm that handled everything from traffic cases to corporate litigation. She'd been working there since June and seemed to like it. Still intent on becoming an FBI agent, Elizabeth was trying to acquire some experience in the field before she pursued a law degree. With a law degree she could apply to the bureau without having any prior law enforcement experience.

Vanessa stirred awake when Elizabeth laughed at Lloyd's response to a question in the sex survey. She yawned and smiled at Hager, leaned over and planted a soft kiss on his cheek, resting her head on his shoulder. Life seemed to be getting back to normal for Hager.

"But would it last?" he asked himself, taking the exit from the freeway.

CHAPTER

4

HAGER PUSHED OPEN the door to the new Investigative Support office. In March 1997, the unit was moved from its home on Old Garner Road, down the street to the recently opened SBI lab facility on Tryon Road.

Since the Investigative Support Unit worked so frequently with the laboratory, the director thought it best to move Hager and his crew to the new building and away from the bureau's headquarters. Located on the fifth floor, ISU shared the floor with the Intelligence Section. A reward for a job well done, Hager was told by Assistant Director Bob Maxwell.

The agent strode toward the desk of Judy Carroll, the unit secretary. Judy was on the phone and waved for Hager to stop. She cupped a hand over the phone.

"Clark, two messages. First, Bob Maxwell wants you to call him right away, and Rich Miller from the *News and*

Observer called again."

Hager rolled his eyes at the latter message and continued to his office. Miller was the reporter who wrote a weeklong series on "The Strangler" murders for the Raleigh paper. The media, always friendly toward Hager, again cast the agent as the brave hero who risked his life for the people.

Written in a daily journal format, the writer described how Hager and his partner put it all together after the murder in Ahoskie. The series was up for a Pulitzer and there was talk—reminiscent of Jerry Bledsoe's *Bitter Blood* series of the mid-1980's—about a book and possibly, a movie.

Miller had contacted Hager with an offer to co-author a book detailing the case from the beginning to its suspenseful conclusion. Miller told Hager that literary agents would be foaming at the mouth, promising at least a six-figure advance from one of the major publishing houses.

More than a movie, the book seemed more interesting. With a book, length was generally not a factor in non-fiction and Hager could use actual photographs; being co-author he could make sure the *true* story was told.

Hager had been ducking Miller's calls recently. He'd called at least once a day the past week, but the agent had more pressing matters on his plate—a murder profile.

The small western city of Brevard was the last place where Hager thought he would receive a profiling request. Hager had visited the pristine city situated on the North Carolina-Tennessee border some years ago when he was a field agent in the Western District.

As with the majority of his profile requests, Hager was tasked to examine crime scene photos and provide a personality sketch of the Un-Sub, or unknown subject.

An elderly woman was the victim of an alleged home invasion. The victim was found nude with multiple stab wounds, which the autopsy revealed as the cause of death. Interestingly, the medical examiner determined she had been sexually assaulted after her death. Hager spent the better part of three days thumbing through reports, a victim profile, and poring over crime scene and autopsy photos.

The lab report indicated although the woman was sexually assaulted, it was likely done with an object rather than a human organ. A crime scene photo revealed a glass bottle was found in a trashcan near the body location.

Hager supposed the sexual assault was committed to cover up the actual motive for the murder and make it look like a sex crime. Due to the number and deep thrusts of the stab wounds, Hager theorized the killing was committed in a homicidal rage that pointed to someone emotionally close to the woman—like a male relative who may have lived with her.

When Hager called the detectives in Brevard, he informed them of his conclusions. The detectives told Hager the victim's grandson had a history of mental illness; coincidentally, he was the one who found the body. The investigators had suspected the grandson from the beginning but had only briefly questioned the man without obtaining any incriminating statements. He also appeared to have an airtight alibi. The Brevard detectives needed information to put pressure on their suspect, and they hoped the SBI profiler could provide that information.

Hager suggested a unique interrogational strategy, which the agent believed would elicit a confession from the killer. The detectives, along with the assistance of an SBI agent, strategically displayed crime scene photographs at eye level in the room where the interview took place. In addition, the detectives scattered some of the victim's personal effects around the interview room. The clincher was a blown-up picture of the victim and grandson together directly facing the killer as he sat in a chair.

From what the investigators told Hager, the grandson couldn't look at the picture and turned his body away to avoid her glaring eyes. Finally, after he couldn't take it anymore, he confessed. But what surprised Hager, he confessed not only to the murder of his grandmother, but to killing a teenager ten years prior when he was only 13 years old. The victim, a child who lived in the killer's neighborhood, had been reported missing but had never been located.

Hager picked up the phone and touched the speed dial button for Bob Maxwell's office.

"Bob? It's Clark. Judy gave me a message to call you."

"Yes, Clark. The director got a call from the Brevard chief-of-police this morning. The chief wanted to express his appreciation for your help in their murder case last week. I haven't read your final report. I guess it was a success?"

Hager briefly summarized the case and what he'd contributed. "The profile fit the grandson, and the cops there thought it was him all the time. All I did was confirm that and suggest a way to conduct the interview. We got lucky with this kid. He would've probably killed someone else."

"Uh-huh. I heard about the boy he killed some years ago. You did good work, Clark. The director's sending a letter out this week along with a press release."

Hager rolled his eyes. "Bob, I made my contribution, that's right. But the detectives in Brevard along with Speer from the Asheville office deserve more credit than I. All I did was make a suggestion. They got the confession."

"Confessions," Maxwell corrected. "And it probably wouldn't have happened if you hadn't made the suggestion. Oh, Clark don't worry about those guys. They're getting their rewards. The director just likes to publicize it when you and ISU do something great. It's good for business."

Hager shrugged his shoulders. "Politics, you mean. It looks good on Taylor's record when it comes election time."

Artemis Taylor, Director of the SBI, had his sights set on the Governor's race in 2000. Although he hadn't officially announced his candidacy for the Republican nomination, it wasn't hard to figure out. Taylor had been more *visible* over the last two or three months, replacing Bob Maxwell as the usual mouthpiece for the SBI. It was the beginning of a campaign.

Maxwell sounded surprised. "Election time? Clark, I don't know what you're talking about," he said with obviously gritted teeth.

Maxwell ended the conversation and Hager hung up the phone. "Politicians...you can't live with 'em...can't live without 'em."

"Women problems, Clark?" Judy asked, standing at the open door.

Startled, Hager jumped in his seat. "Pardon?"

"You said, 'can't live with 'em...can't live without 'em.' I assume you're talking about women."

"Not women. Although the same goes for them, too." Judy's glare turned icy. "No, not you, Judy. Just some of them. And I was talking about politicians, not women." Her arms were crossed and she still wore a cool look on her face.

"Well, it's almost five and I thought if you didn't mind, I was going to leave a little early. I'm throwing a baby shower for Nina tonight and everyone's supposed to get there around six-thirty."

"No problem. It's almost Grandma time, huh? You gonna feel weird being called that?"

"It won't be Grandma. I want my grandchildren to call me 'Nana'."

Hager laughed.

"What's so funny, Clark? It won't be too long before Elizabeth gets married and gives you grandchildren."

"She's only twenty. Plus, she's not even dating anyone. I don't think I have to worry about that for a while, yet. I'm not old enough to be called Grandpa."

He tried to stop his mouth from moving, but the words came out anyway.

Judy slapped his shoulder hard.

Hager saw her steely look again. He tried to cover him-self. "Ow! I didn't mean—"

"I know what you meant. Boy, first the women shot and now this. You're on my list, Clark Hager," she said with a smile on her face.

CHAPTER

5

HAGER ARRIVED HOME at the usual time—around 6 o'clock. The summer sun still burned a sweltering heat that produced beads of perspiration from the simple task of getting out of the car to check the day's mail. North Carolina heat and humidity were sometimes unbearable, so hot it seemed to drain all the energy from a person. Once inside, the refreshing relief of a cold Ice House beer and the air-conditioning quickly revived Hager.

Roscoe scampered down the stairs and joined Hager in the kitchen. The English Bulldog wagged his nub of a tail, seemingly in veneration for his master. Unconditional love.

"Well, ol' boy. It looks like it's just the two of us tonight. What do you say we order a pizza and vege out on the couch watching some baseball, huh?"

Roscoe looked as if he understood what Hager had said. His eyes remained fixed and he cocked his head to the side in his own "doggy" acknowledgment. "What'll it be, buddy? Domino's or Papa John's?" Hager opened a drawer and pulled out a telephone book. With the bottle in one hand, he flipped through the Yellow Pages until he found the listings for "Pizza."

"Papa John's it'll be," Hager said, reaching for the phone.

Before his hand could grab the receiver, the phone rang.

"Clark?" a male voice asked.

"Yeah, this is Clark. Who's this?" Hager asked, not recognizing the voice.

"Clark, it's Phil Craven. I'm sorry to bother you at home but—"

"Oh...Phil. Don't worry about it, Phil. What's up?"

Phil sounded worried.

"Well, I just got back into town from Atlanta this afternoon and I can't find Cynthia. She knew I was coming in today and...I don't know. I tried calling the house and her cell phone the past few days before I came home and I never got an answer."

"Do you think she might have gone to the beach for the week? I remember she used to go there a lot during the summers when Kelly was alive."

Phil Craven and Hager were roommates, fraternity brothers, and the best of friends throughout college. Phil's wife, Cynthia, and Hager's late wife, Kelly, were very close at Carolina as well. In fact, Cynthia introduced Kelly to Hager one night at a fraternity party.

The Cravens had remained fairly close friends over the years prior to Kelly's illness and were of enormous help to Hager after her death almost six years ago. Phil was a regional vice-president for sales at Bayer Industries in Research Triangle Park and without having any children to rear, Cynthia played the role of the perfect country club wife. But after the initial period following Kelly's death, Phil and Cynthia came around less frequently. And before the ordeal with "The Strangler", Hager had not heard from

Phil in almost a year. His wife Cynthia was another story.

No more than three months ago, Hager saw Cynthia Craven at a restaurant in Durham. Under normal circumstances, Hager thought it would have been the usual lunch group with Cynthia's *friends* from the nearby Treyburn Country Club. But Cynthia wasn't with the country club wives who made a daily routine of playing tennis at the club, eating a light lunch afterwards, and topping off the afternoon with a few glasses of wine.

Cynthia was sitting at an out-of-the way table with a man. And her companion wasn't her husband. Instead, the man was considerably younger — maybe thirty to her forty-five years — and appeared to be in great physical shape. From the intimate look in both their eyes, this was no casual meeting.

Hager remembered feeling a little uncomfortable, and he did his best not to be seen as it would only lead to something that wasn't his business. Also knowing his good old friend Phil had indulged in a few indiscretions of his own, Hager felt it was only fair for her to play the game, too. Hager had an idea where Cynthia might be. But telling Phil would be the last thing he would do.

"No," Phil said. "We sold the beach house two summers ago. After Hurricane Fran, the insurance premiums were too high to keep it. Besides, we still have the house at Lake Jordan. She would've gone there if she wanted to get away."

"Did you try the lake, Phil?"

"Yeah. The boat's still in the same place and the house looks the same as it did when we were there two weeks ago. I checked with the next-door neighbors, too. They haven't seen her."

Hager pictured Cynthia and the man together, she gaping and batting her eyes. Hager took a drink from the bottle.

Don't say anything.

"Well, Phil...I don't know what to say. She's probably just gone out of town for a few days. What about her lady friends from the club? Could she have hitched a ride with them to the beach or something?"

"She only hangs around with one or two of the club bitches any more—Laurie Briggs and Catherine Molderson. Laurie left five messages over the past three days. I called her back and she hasn't seen Cynthia. I couldn't get hold of Catherine."

"She's probably with her...with Catherine. They're just out picking out their new fall wardrobes. I wouldn't worry too much, Phil. You know how women can be sometimes when they're shopping."

Hager hung up the phone with the nagging feeling that his friend Phil wasn't convinced of Cynthia's whereabouts. He seemed convinced, however, that his wife may have been busying herself in his absence. Hager presumed that a needed void in Cynthia's life was being filled.

Hager finished his beer and placed the pizza order. He picked up his mail from the counter, grabbed another beer from the refrigerator, and strode easily into the living room. Seated on the couch with the television tuned to *Sportscenter*, he flipped through the envelopes, separating junk mail from bills.

One letter was from *Cooking Light* magazine. Hager figured the letter was a solicitation for a subscription renewal. He discovered it was an invitation to compete in a national cooking contest sponsored by the magazine. First prize was a 7-day vacation in Hawaii, $5,000 cash, an entire set of expensive gourmet cookware, and an appearance not only in the magazine, but the winner would be a guest on the *Emeril Live* show.

The regional qualifying round was to be held at the Marriott in Downtown Charlotte during the first week of August. Qualifiers would then travel to Phoenix, Arizona for the national competition in September. The contest consisted of preparing a five-course meal. Ideas flashed through Hager's head.

What would I cook? Something like Beef Wellington or rack

of lamb. Quail or rabbit? Or maybe that Seafood Portofino I always wanted to try.

Hager's mouth began to water just thinking about the delicious food he could prepare. Decisively, he told himself he'd do it. He would enter the contest. And if he won, there wasn't a better time to go to Hawaii — the perfect place for a honeymoon.

He folded the papers and returned them to the envelope. The rest were bills. Nothing of major importance.

Hager flipped through the channels, stopping at program on A&E. Dan Rather's face filled the screen, then the camera pulled back and the graphic *Eye of the Beholder* appeared over his right shoulder.

The topic of the show was to show how three different people, who were witnesses to a crime, told three different versions of the event, thus illustrating how a person's different qualities, age, race, sex, and background, can determine their perception and how a person relates that observation.

Hager remembered conducting a similar study at a seminar he was teaching at the SBI Academy. Hager was impressed with the program's content. When it was over, he switched to baseball, falling asleep on the couch while the Cubs shutout the Reds at Wrigley Field. The telephone awakened him around ten o'clock, and he wondered if it was Phil Craven again.

Instead, Elizabeth's voice was on the other end of the line. She sounded nervous, but excited at the same time. "Hi, Daddy, what's happening? Did I wake you?"

"Well—"

"I'm sorry. I didn't realize it was that late. Can you forgive me?"

"Elizabeth, I was just on the couch watching the ball game. Don't worry about it. Did you need anything special or is this just a social call?"

"Well...it's about tomorrow night. You know, I was supposed to come over for the cookout with you and Vanessa and Lloyd and Martha."

"Yeah, don't tell me you can't make it. We're celebrating Lloyd coming back to work."

"Oh, it's not that I can't make it...it's...uh...I was wondering if I could bring a date?"

"A date?" Hager asked in a tone only a father of a daughter can produce. "I thought you weren't dating anyone, Elizabeth. Who's this *date*?"

"It's...I mean he's not just a date, Daddy. I've been seeing him for some time. I just haven't mentioned him to you yet."

This didn't sound good. Usually when Elizabeth failed to *mention* her boyfriends, it meant that her father would not approve of them.

"Hmm...and how long is some time, pumpkin?" Hager asked using her age-old pet name.

"Oh...it's been a while. A couple of months. Since April or so." She still sounded nervous.

"Well, are you gonna tell me his name or what?"

"I want it to be a surprise, Daddy. He's very nervous about the whole thing. You know, meeting you for the first time and all. I don't want you to get a bad impression of him before you meet him. That's all."

Oh, shit. It's definitely bad when she doesn't even want to tell me his name.

"What?" Hager shouted. "You don't want me to get a bad impression of him? How about you, Elizabeth? Why shouldn't I get a bad impression of you for hiding this...this guy, please tell me it's a guy—"

"Yes, he's a guy, Daddy. Damn, I think you've gone off the deep end. Of course he's a guy. What else would he be? Forget I asked that question."

"Why all the mystery, honey? What's so bad about this guy that you have to keep it from me for so long? Since April? I thought we trusted each other. What is he...a lawyer or something?"

Elizabeth didn't respond. Hager heard her sigh in the

phone and knew the answer.

"He *is* a lawyer isn't he?"

"Daddy, wait! I didn't say anything about Owen—"

"Oh, it's Owen, huh? Well, now we're getting somewhere, aren't we? C'mon, spill it."

Elizabeth's whining could be heard through the phone. She knew better than to play a psychological game of cat and mouse with her old man. "All right. His name is Owen and I'm not saying any more. You'll just have to wait until tomorrow. Why did I even call you? I should've just brought him with me. I wouldn't have had to face all the third degree from you."

"Because you love me and respect my opinion. That's why."

Elizabeth hung up the phone after agreeing that she did love and respect her father's opinion. Hager now worried about what all fathers worry about. Another man was taking the spotlight of his daughter away from him.

CHAPTER

6

ANOTHER STIFLING DAY of heat bore down on Raleigh. Jess Kemp, owner and operator of Capital City Towing, pulled off his glasses and wiped his forehead as he stepped from the curb in front of the main office. He took a deep breath of the thick, steamy air and noticed a hint of rotten-ness to it. Jess wrinkled his nose in a familiar "smells like shit" gesture.

He'd kept a half-dozen or more dogs on his lot to keep away trespassers and maybe he was down wind of a recent "call of nature." He shook his head in disgust and, unbelievably, inhaled another deep gulp of air to confirm his suspicions. "No," Jess said to himself. "That's not shit I smell. That's something dead out there."

Maybe, Jess thought, one of the dogs had either died or killed something and it lay rotting under the burning sun in his yard. Whatever it was, it had to go. And who better to take care of it than his trusty "colored" driver, Luther Rivers? Jess looked at his watch and saw that it was almost three. Soon, Luther would be strolling into work at his usual "Three o'clock—CPT." CPT standing for "Colored People Time" which, for Luther, usually meant around 3:30.

Jess pulled off his cap and ran his fingers through his sweaty gray hair, realizing that despite Luther Rivers being "colored" and a convicted felon, he was as reliable a driver as he ever had. He was better than some of his redneck mechanics who would spit in his drink sooner than look at him.

Jess turned around to open the office door when a cloud of dust indicated Luther's arrival. The tow truck pulled to a stop directly in front of the office, and Luther hopped out the door, holding a brown paper bag.

As a reward for his hard work and reliability, Jess allowed his only black employee to take his oldest tow truck home. Luther and his wife had only one car and she needed their car to drive to her job, so in order for Luther to get to work, he needed transportation. Jess looked at his watch— 3:00 P.M. on the dot. He smiled, thinking his watch must have stopped.

"How's it goin' there, Mr. Kemp?" Luther asked, slamming the wrecker door closed.

"Luther." Jess nodded. "Fine, son, everything's fine."

"Sure is a hot one today," Luther said, his forehead beaded with sweat and shiny in the sunlight.

"Yes, it is. Say, Luther, you smell something funny from the yard out there?"

Luther took a deep breath and shook his head.

"Naw, sir. It just smells like air to me, Mr. Kemp. Why, you smell something?"

Jess made a face—the same "smells like shit" face from before. "Jesus Christ, Luther, can't you smell it? It smells like something died out there. Go on out there and see what the hell is dead and get rid of it, ya hear. And another thing, that Mercedes you picked up the other night. It's still out in the yard. When's that man supposed to come and get it?"

Luther looked confused and his eyes searched the yard where the silver Mercedes was parked. "I don't know, Mr. Kemp. The man said he'd be around to pick it up when he got back into town. I guess he ain't got back into town yet. I can call him if you want...to see when he's gonna pick it up."

Jess thought about a mounting storage bill for the broken down Mercedes. Mercedes-Benz meant money and Jess envisioned dollar signs from just the five dollars per day fee. Even though he ran a repair shop, Jess knew he wouldn't dare touch any car not *Made in America.*

"Well...if you want to. You're right. He probably hadn't gotten back yet. What was wrong with that Kraut piece of shit anyway?" Jess asked.

"I don't know. The man didn't say. His wife just told him she broke down, that's all."

"Well, just see about that stink, Luther, 'fore it gets too dark to see what's around here."

Luther put the bag that held his dinner in a mini refrigerator and stuck his head inside to cool off for a second. After closing the door, he stretched his arm along the wall to turn on the radio to *Soul 104.* Snapping his fingers and humming to Diana Ross, he grabbed a shovel and headed for the yard in the direction of the smell, now evident to Luther's nose. Luther raised his head, and his nostrils flared like an animal in search of the odor. He walked in the direction of the Mercedes where it became much stronger.

Luther stopped at the rear of the car. He looked around for something dead on the ground. Some flies buzzed around the trunk of the Mercedes, but he didn't see anything around it or even under it. But he was sure the smell was coming from that general area. He walked away in search of a carcass, but found nothing.

"Maybe it was a skunk," Luther said. "Or maybe you just shit your britches, Jess Kemp, and you don't want anyone to know it."

Luther returned to the Mercedes and remembered Jess' request to call the owner to see if he was going to pick up the car soon. He opened the door and burning heat poured from inside. Luther sat down in the passenger seat, opening the glove box. The interior of the car smelled worse than outside and Luther held his breath while he fumbled through the console. Papers dropped onto the floor, and Luther located a North Carolina inspection certificate with the name of Russell Phillip Craven.

Luther blew out his breath as he jumped from the car and closed the door. "Whew! Something sure did die out here, but I don't know what the fuck it is. But whatever it is, it sure is ripe."

HAGER LEFT the office early. His guests were to arrive at seven o'clock, and he wanted to stop at the grocery store and pick up the steaks he'd ordered for the celebratory dinner. Six thick New York strips trimmed to perfection were waiting for him. All he had to do was put them in his favorite marinade and throw them on the grill. Taking care of the steaks was all Vanessa had asked Hager to do as she told him she would do the rest. Hager's exuberance over cooking had affected Vanessa similarly, and Hager assumed she wanted to impress the group with a fine complement to steaks on the grill. "It's a surprise!" she'd said.

When Hager pulled down his driveway, he spotted Vanessa's BMW parked in the open garage. To his left in the front yard, he caught a glimpse of long tanned legs protruding from a pair of white shorts. Hustling toward Hager's car was his old pal, Roscoe. Vanessa was apparently letting his English bulldog get some badly needed exercise. Hager looked up and watched the intended Mrs. Clark Hager gracefully walk in his direction, a glass of wine in her hand—no shoes, hair pulled into a ponytail and wearing a red top with spaghetti straps. She smiled radiantly. Hager was speechless.

"Did you get the steaks, Hager?" Vanessa asked.

Carrying a paper grocery sack, Hager stepped from his Crown Victoria. Roscoe was at his feet, snorting. Hager could feel the dog's nose poking at his slacks. He put down the bag, crouched and scratched Roscoe's head. "What's up, buddy?" Roscoe's attention went directly to the bag.

Vanessa stopped a few feet away. "Well?"

"Oh, yeah. Cid really came through this time. New York strips. Take a look at these beauties." He picked up the bag and opened it for her to see.

"Not bad, not too bad, but I think you've forgotten something." She had a serious look on her face.

Hager wrinkled his brow. "Forgotten something? What?"

She pouted those beautiful lips of hers. "You didn't say 'hello' to me and scratch my head."

Hager laughed, took two steps and wrapped his free arm around her waist and pulled her to him. "Oh," he moaned and tickled her neck with his tongue. "Please forgive me." Hager dropped the bag and scratched Vanessa behind her ears, then pulled her into a long passionate kiss.

They were interrupted by the dog's growls as he tore into the bag. Quickly, Hager picked up the bag after a small tug-of-war match with Roscoe.

"Well, since I provided the meat for tonight, what's your contribution? What's the big surprise?" Hager asked.

Vanessa smiled devilishly. "You'll see."

LUTHER RETURNED the phone to its cradle after leaving a message for Mr. Craven to pick up his car. He'd found the phone number in the telephone book after verifying the name and address he compared to the inspection certificate. Still curious about the foul odor in the lot, Luther ventured out again in search of the stench. Again, his nose led him directly to the Mercedes. Flies still buzzed around the trunk of the car. Luther pulled out a towel from his pocket and wiped the sweat from his face. Remembering what Jess had said about the odor smelling like something dead, Luther suddenly was overwhelmed with an eerie feeling.

Dead...flies. This God-awful smell. Oh, shit.

Slowly, Luther walked around the car. He looked inside. Everything was okay. Just the bag of women's clothes in the back seat and nothing in the front.

But what about the trunk? Luther heard himself ask.

Luther shook his head, knowing he shouldn't be doing what he was getting ready to do. He reached in his pocket for the key. He pulled it out and stared at it—knowing it meant trouble. Standing at the rear of the car, he inserted the key. Slowly, like he was diffusing a bomb, he turned his hand to the right until he heard the familiar *thump* of the lock disengaging. Sweat trickled down his face, back, and chest; his breaths were deep and controlled. His heart pounded.

The trunk lid sprang open as if someone had pushed it from the inside. A swarm of flies, along with a wave of sickening stench, exploded from the interior. Luther shrieked and jumped backward as the trunk lid bounced at its apex. Luther crept forward until he saw what he desperately feared he would see.

Inside the trunk was the body of a nude woman, swollen beyond all Luther's comprehension. Only by the long hair and breasts could the form inside be considered "female." Her face was malformed—eyes wide open in a state of horror no movie could ever match. Her skin was split open like it had exploded from within, but there was no blood. Luther's stomach was churning. The flies still buzzed around his head.

Trouble, Luther. Get the hell outa' here.

Luther quickly closed the trunk lid and backed away

from the Mercedes. He wiped his hands on his pants, trying to erase all memory of this gruesome sight. Luther regarded the consequence of his discovery. He whispered,
"A fuckin' dead body in the trunk of a car *I* picked up.
They gonna think I did this. White woman dead. Picked
up on the road. Just like the last time. Fuck this!"

Luther ran to the wrecker in a desperate panic.

CHAPTER

7

THE SUN was sinking slowly toward the horizon as Hager relaxed uneasily in a patio chair on his deck. At 6:30 P.M., they still had about two more hours of daylight to enjoy. Two more hours of heat thick with humidity to endure as well. Hager looked at his watch for the second time in less than a minute. Elizabeth was late.

"Does it move faster when you look at it a lot, Clark?" Lloyd asked, sitting in a chair opposite Hager. "What time she say she'd be here?"

"I told her around six, but you know how she is. Six is seven...seven-thirty."

Lloyd stuffed three fingers full of potato chips in his mouth. "What are you worried about then? Quit looking at that goddamned watch of yours. She'll be here when she gets here."

"I guess," Hager proclaimed and took a long swig of beer.

"Hey, Clark, did I tell you how I been fuckin' with those telemarketers over the last few months? Man, they'd been drivin' me nuts before, but I've got a system that fucks with 'em real bad. You ever get calls from those people?"

Hager shrugged his shoulders. "Once in a while. I just listen to their pitch and then tell 'em 'I'm not interested.' I figure they've got a job to do. The least I can do is let them try."

"How boring." Lloyd shook his head. "Man, those assholes don't know when to quit. You gotta let me fuck with one of 'em if they call tonight. I've got this one line I've been saving. All right?"

Hager laughed at the vision of Lloyd on the phone saying something totally absurd to some unsuspecting telemarketer. "Sure, Lloyd. Whatever you want. It's your night."

The sliding glass door squeaked and Hager looked to see Vanessa and Martha coming out to the deck. Vanessa walked over to Hager and wrapped her arms around his neck from behind, kissing him on the cheek. Hager smelled her soft perfume, Kashmir—her usual stuff—but always a favorite.

"Everything's ready. All we need now is Liz. I wonder what's keeping her?" Vanessa said.

Hager groaned. "I'll bet she doesn't want to bring her new boyfriend to meet me. She must've changed her mind."

"Nonsense, Clark. She's wanted to introduce you to him for some time now. This was her best chance because she thinks you won't act like a jerk in front of Lloyd and Martha."

"Did she tell you that? A jerk?" Hager was steaming. "And just how did you know about this...this Owen?"

Vanessa blushed like she'd revealed a great secret. "Oh...well, I've known for some time, Clark. You know she and I are very close. We were discussing the wedding plans and she told me."

Hager's eyes grew wider and his face turned red.

Vanessa seemed to sense that Hager was about to blow his top and changed the subject before he could speak. "Oh, Martha, tell us about what you heard at lunch the other day."

Martha looked up, obviously not paying a bit of attention to the conversation. She looked to Vanessa for support. "I'm sorry, Vanessa. What did you say?"

"You know, Martha, what you were telling me inside about that fitness center?"

The light turned on in Martha's eyes. "Oh, yeah. Clark, I heard there's this fitness center in Durham where male trainers do more than training, if you know what I mean."

Hager was about to respond with an "Oh really?" when he heard a car door slam at the front of the house and he jumped from his chair.

When he opened the door, his daughter was walking up the porch steps beside some yuppie-looking guy. Hager looked in the driveway and saw a black Volvo sports sedan. A lawyer, Owen looked to be around twenty-eight, maybe older, depending on how long he'd been a member of the bar. Clean shaven and not much taller than Elizabeth — Hager guessed around 5'9" — he was wearing a pair of kacky shorts, a white golf shirt, and brown leather sandals.

Elizabeth was radiant, as usual. She wore a sundress, the hem a little shorter than Hager liked, sandals, and carried a bottle of wine in each hand. Hager did a double take.

Wine? She's only twenty! She's not old enough to buy wine!

Hager's blood pressure started to rise.

"Hi, Daddy!" Elizabeth began. Owen smiled and Hager gave her quick hug. She kissed him on the cheek and made the introductions. "This is Owen Harrison."

Owen offered his hand and Hager took it, squeezing firmer than usual. "It's good to meet you, Mr. Hager," the lawyer said. "I've heard a lot of good things about you from my dad. He says he never wants to face you in court."

"Oh, Harrison. That's right, I'd forgotten Malcolm Harrison had another son. And a lawyer, too?" Malcolm Harrison was the head of the law firm where Elizabeth worked.

"Yes, sir. I've been out of law school for three years. I worked as an Assistant DA in Forsyth County before joining up with my dad. I'm trying to get into corporate work. This criminal stuff just isn't for me."

Hager looked Owen directly in the eye, trying to get a feel for him. He looked down at his clothes and something didn't seem right. He seemed out of place for whatever reason. Maybe it was Owen's simple anxiety about meeting "the father."

Elizabeth beamed as she stood by Owen's side. It was obvious she was smitten with this man. Hager stared at the bottles in her hands with a look of disapproval. Elizabeth blushed and handed them to Owen.

"Oh, Daddy. Owen brought this wine for dinner. They're from a winery in Winston-Salem."

Owen handed Hager the bottles. "Liz said you liked wine and my mom always taught me to never come to a party empty-handed. 'It's rude,' she'd say."

Hager looked at the label. *WestBend Vineyard* 1994. "Very nice. Thanks, but you know *Elizabeth's* only twenty?"

Elizabeth noticed the correction of her name and the cut. Her face turned red. Owen was about to respond when Vanessa walked up from behind. "Hey, chick," she said to Elizabeth and then to Owen, "Hi, Owen, it's good to see you again."

Elizabeth grabbed Owen's hand and led him away and out to the deck. Vanessa apparently noticed Elizabeth's anger in her sudden departure. "What did you say to her, Clark?" she asked in a demanding tone.

Hager took a step back, holding up the wine bottles in defense. "You see these? They brought wine. Elizabeth's only twenty and *he* brought wine." Hager could feel himself getting warm.

Vanessa shook her head in disgust. "What did you say? You insulted him, didn't you?"

Again, Hager retreated. "No, I didn't insult him. I just asked him if he knew Elizabeth was only twenty. That's all."

Vanessa sighed and shook her head again. She took a step toward him and whispered coolly. "Clark, don't be an asshole, okay? This is important to Liz. Owen is a real nice guy. He just wants to make an impression and she needs your approval if you haven't noticed."

Elizabeth and Owen were chatting with Lloyd and Martha. Hager felt bad for the shot he took at Owen, but he realized he was acting as only a protective father should. Consciously, he saw that the man appeared to be clean cut and nice, but subconsciously, he knew that he was a man. And Hager felt a strange residue of grime after talking to Owen.

Most lawyers were slimy people anyway, but the agent sensed a different dirt in Owen. They hadn't been at the house more than five minutes, and Vanessa had already chewed his ass once and she still seemed pissed.

Lloyd curiously eyed Hager when he came out to the deck with a platter containing the marinated steaks. Lloyd looked up from petting Roscoe and gestured toward Vanessa and smiled. Hager shrugged his shoulders. Vanessa told Martha about Owen's gift and Hager heard her apologize to Owen for Hager's behavior. Lloyd joined Hager at the grill.

"Hey, those steaks look good. Where'd you get 'em?"

"Over at the Winn-Dixie. Cid, the butcher, always hooks me up. Gives me primo cuts."

"What's the deal with Liz's boyfriend? Does he think he's Jesus or something with those sandals?"

Hager looked at Owen's feet and chuckled. He didn't like the sound of boyfriend.

"I don't know if it's boyfriend, Lloyd. He seems all right,

I guess. Just a little squirrelly."

Lloyd took a sip from his glass of iced tea. "Liz and Vanessa don't seem too happy with you, partner. What'd you say?"

Hager shook his head in embarrassment. "Oh, something stupid. I guess I came on a little strong and said something I shouldn't have."

Lloyd grinned. "Tell me and I'll say it, too."

"No way, man. You don't want to get in Vanessa's doghouse, too. I wouldn't wish that on my worst enemy."

Lloyd laughed. "You're probably right. Drink another beer. Maybe it'll make you behave yourself."

The three couples ate dinner inside where it was cool. Vanessa had prepared a medley of fresh vegetables sautéed in olive oil and placed on a bed of linguine. Freshly baked bread with real butter completed the meal. The steaks were tender enough to melt in their mouths. Hager's marinade once again flavored the meat to perfection.

Dinner wasn't without its tension, however. Always aware of other people and sensitive to their eating habits, Hager about choked when Owen asked for steak sauce. To Hager, it was the ultimate insult to a chef to cover up the taste of his dish.

Vanessa was well aware of her fiancé's reaction, and she met Hager's eyes with a "don't you dare say anything" look. Hager told Owen he didn't have any steak sauce and restrained himself in not telling him to shove the steak up his ass if he didn't like the way it tasted.

Elizabeth piped in, smiling in a vengeful sort of way. She, too, was well aware of her dad's irritation. "Oh, yes we do, Daddy. I know where it is." She rose from her chair with a big grin on her face.

Hager looked to Vanessa for help. She continued to stare him down unsupportively. Lloyd and Martha just ate without looking up, not wanting to take sides. Hager felt helpless.

What soon became worse was that Hager witnessed his

own daughter, the biggest fan of his steaks—one whom he would never think to commit such an act so offensive—take the bottle of A-1 and pour it all over her steak, her eyes locked in an "up yours" message with a grin bordering on a spiteful smile. "Take that," her eyes said silently. It was all Hager could do to control his outrage.

Thankfully, Owen was oblivious to the entire episode. Elizabeth's counter to her father's earlier attempt at belittling her date cut like a dagger in comparison. Why Hager tried to compete in games of spite with women, he'd never know. Instead, he chose to eat his meal quietly thinking this was *some* party to celebrate Lloyd's return to work.

With tail between his legs, Hager silently walked into the kitchen and just as he opened the refrigerator door, the telephone rang.

"Clark? It's Phil Craven."

"Phil, how's it going? Have you heard from Cynthia, yet?"

"Sorry to bother you again at home, but I've got a favor to ask you."

"Okay. What's the favor?"

"I still haven't heard from Cynthia and when I got home from work a few minutes ago, there was a message on my phone from some towing company. Sounded like some black guy and he wanted to know when I was going to pick up my Mercedes."

"Hmm, that's strange. Was she having trouble with the car?"

"She shouldn't. It's practically brand new. A '96 E-420. No, there's something wrong. She would've never called a tow truck while I was out of town. She's too scared of people, you know. She would've left the car and called one of her friends if something like that happened."

"And none of them have heard from her?"

"None of them. I got a hold of her other friend Catherine, and she hasn't seen hide nor tail of her. I'm worried, Clark. I've got this weird feeling."

It was time for Hager to spill the beans about seeing Cynthia with another man. "Phil, have you checked her closet to see if any of her clothes are missing. Her toothbrush, make-up. You know, personal items she wouldn't go without for more than a day."

"Yes, I checked the bathroom and everything's still there. I can't tell about her clothes because she has so many."

Here goes. "Look, Phil—"

"Clark, will you go with me down to this tow company? The car's there; maybe we can shed some light on this mystery from the car."

"I don't know, Phil. My daughter's here and..." Hager quickly realized this could be his convenient excuse to leave all the tension. "Well, I guess if you really need me. All right. Lloyd's here, too. We'll both come along."

"Thanks, Clark. I really appreciate this."

CHAPTER

8

CAPITAL CITY TOWING was on the east side of Raleigh, not far from downtown and just off New Bern Avenue. On the way over, Hager explained Phil's request to Lloyd and also told him about his old friend's suspicion that his wife was missing. Hager also told Lloyd about seeing Cynthia with the other man a couple of months ago.

The agents arrived at the business about 9:30 P.M. Phil Craven's Lincoln Navigator was parked parallel to the curb, just outside the gate. Hager's headlights shined brightly on Craven as he stepped from the truck. His face looked worn and his clothes disheveled like he hadn't been to sleep recently.

With his hands buried in his pants pockets, Phil walked nervously toward them. Hager and Lloyd got out. The air was still thick with heat in the moonless night. Dew had already begun to settle on the surfaces of Hager's Explorer.

"You find out anything?" Hager asked Phil.

"No, I just pulled up before you did."

"Well, let's go see."

The three men entered the compound through an open gate. Hager found this to be odd due to the fact that most towing companies are fairly secured facilities, usually patrolled by guard dogs. In fact, two large signs flanked the entrance to the lot warning intruders of attack dogs. Hager stopped abruptly just inside the gate.

"Maybe we should call before walking into something we might regret. I'm not sure I want to be any dog's dinner. Do you, Lloyd?" Hager said, pointing at one of the signs.

"There's gotta be a public entrance to this place. An office or something." Lloyd responded.

Phil stood silently, his head moving back and forth in a nervous twitch like he was looking for something to jump out at them. Both Hager and Lloyd followed Phil's eyes. Hager noticed a wooden door to his right up a small set of stairs. To the right of the door was a sign.

OFFICE

Floodlights illuminated the entrance, but the rest of the business, including the car lot, was covered in darkness. Lloyd hurried up the stairs as Hager stood guard against a rear attack by the dogs. The office door was open and Lloyd entered and immediately returned to the landing.

"The office is dark, Clark. There's no one here." Lloyd said.

"I don't see a wrecker around. Maybe they're out on a call. We'll wait a few minutes." Hager said.

Phil's eyes scanned the lot in search of his car. The bright lights just ahead of them made the lot appear much darker. "Did y'all bring a flashlight with you?" Phil asked.

Hager remembered the flashlight in his Explorer. "Yeah, I have one in the truck. I'll go get it."

When Hager returned with the flashlight, Phil was standing at the edge of the lot facing the mass of cars. Hager flicked the light on and aimed its beam into the rows of colored metal. Several dogs barked, loud angry howls in warning of imminent danger. To Hager, the barking sounded confined to the rear of the lot. Maybe there was a pen where the dogs were kept during daytime hours only to be released for their watch after closing.

Hager walked closer and shined his light at the rear of the lot, nothing answering his question, other than the continuous barking. A very familiar odor was present, although Hager didn't consciously acknowledge it.

"What time does this place close?" Hager asked. "I bet they don't let those dogs loose until after closing."

Lloyd shrugged his shoulders. "Since the office door was unlocked, I guess they're still open unless someone just forgot to lock up. I think I saw a sign out front that had the business hours." Lloyd stepped down the stairs and walked out of the gate. He returned seconds later. "They don't close until midnight, Clark. I'd bet you were right about those dogs."

"Let's just find my car and forget about those dogs, can't we?" Phil snapped.

"Phil, we can't just walk around here like we own the place," Hager explained. "First of all—"

"All I want to do is find her car. That's it. We don't have to do anything with it. I'm not going to take it away without paying for its release. I just want to see the car. Maybe it can tell me something."

Phil's voice reeked with desperation. He was truly worried about his wife. Poor guy.

Sensing Phil's inner torture, Hager directed the beam of light into the rows of cars. "C'mon, Phil." Hager said, handing Phil the light. "Find the car."

"I'll stay here and wait for the driver," Lloyd said.

For the first time, Hager was consciously aware of the pungent odor of decaying flesh. Whether it was a dead animal or not, Hager didn't like all the coincidences and he stopped, allowing his old friend to walk ahead.

Wife missing, car towed, smell of death and the final coincidence, however subtle...Phil Craven's nervous behavior.

Phil's stopped, and suddenly darted in between a row of cars. "Here it is! Clark, I found it!"

The flashlight's beam knifed through the night sky as Phil ran toward the Mercedes. Suddenly, he stopped. "Clark, do you smell that? It smells like something died out here. You think one of those dogs killed something?"

Hager walked hurriedly toward the beam of light. Phil directed the blinding beam at Hager's face. Yellow and white spots filled his vision.

"Phil!"

"Hey, the key's still in the trunk," Phil said.

Hager was still partially blinded from the light, but he knew what Phil was going to do. He was going to open that trunk and find...

"Phil, get away from the car! Don't touch it!" Hager ordered.

Hager arrived where Phil was standing and the stench was stronger. He snatched the flashlight away from Phil and pointed it at the trunk. Flies covered the lid.

"What the hell is wrong with you, Hager?" Phil snorted.

"Look, Phil, wait a second." Hager was panting. Sweat rolled down his back. He turned to where Lloyd was standing. "Lloyd, come out here!"

Phil had an angry, confused look on his face. In his eyes, he had the look of fear.

Fear of what Hager feared.

The fear of death.

"Phil, I didn't want you to touch the car because..." Hager looked to see if Lloyd was getting nearer. "Look, Phil. Look at the trunk. The flies. And the smell. You smelled it before. What did you say? Something must've died out here. Right? Think about it, Phil."

Phil's face remained solemn, unwavering.

"Phil, Cynthia's missing. She's not with her friends. The car. Phil, the smell, the—"

"No!" Phil screamed. "You can't be thinking..." he bent over and buried his face in his hands. "Nooooo!" He stood upright and took a step toward the car. "I have to see."

Hager jumped in front of him, wrapping his arms around his torso. Phil was larger and it took all the strength and leverage Hager could muster to fend off his old friend. Lloyd's arrival was perfect timing as he pulled Phil away. Phil stood motionless with tears welling in his eyes.

"How will we know if we don't..." Phil's voice trailed off.

"Believe me, Phil. If it's what I think. You don't want to see." Hager said.

Hager walked around the car, using the flashlight to illuminate the interior. There was nothing in the car but a dark bag on the back seat. He returned to the rear. The key was still in the lock. Some of the flies had scattered, but about a hundred or so remained resting on the lid. The pungent odor still lingered.

Hager had an idea. "Lloyd, take Phil back to the office to see if you can contact someone from the business. There has to be an after-hours number. I bet they're probably on the City's wrecker rotation list. Call the PD if you can't find a number inside."

Lloyd understood what Hager wanted to do. As soon as Phil left, he would open the trunk to confirm what he already knew. A dead body was inside. Who it was, Hager wasn't sure, but his best bet would be Cynthia Craven.

CHAPTER

9

LUTHER'S EYES FLASHED back and forth from the rear view mirror to the dark road ahead. Desperation had been driving him for the last two hours or so — desperation with a beer chaser. On an empty stomach the beer he'd guzzled at the Cue 'N Brew on Peace Street had gone straight to his head. The beer swirled in his head, making him dizzy. His eyes were barely open as he steered an unknown course of futility.

After leaving the garage, he didn't know where to go. He couldn't go home; they would look there first. He couldn't go to his mama's house. They would look there, too. Luther needed to find a place where he could think about what he was going to do. He needed to feel something — something other than the knots of doom tightening in his stomach.

Luther knew he was going back to prison, returning to

the place he swore he would never see again—a place where he'd promised his mama would never have to visit him again. Luther heard his mama's voice.

The Lord knows you's innocent, Luther. You go talk to the man. You tell 'em what happened.

Despite knowing the fact that he didn't kill that white woman, he knew it didn't matter. He was a black man and if a black man was anywhere close to a crime, he was guilty. In this case, he was more than simply *close* to this crime. He was right in the middle of it. With his record, and with all the other evidence pointing at him, the police would be fools for *not* suspecting him.

"They'd surely convict me on what they call 'circumspective' evidence or something like that."

The headlights coming toward him were piercingly bright. Luther rubbed his eyes, trying to keep the truck between the yellow lines. Something made him check his rear-view mirror. Luther's eyes froze, staring at the flashing blue lights. Panic overwhelmed him. His heart pounded and his fists clenched the wheel.

"I won't go down this easy," Luther mumbled as his foot slammed the accelerator to the floor.

THE FIRST PATROL CAR arrived several minutes after Hager had opened the trunk, finding the decomposing body of Cynthia Craven. The second followed soon thereafter, and minutes later, a sergeant and crime lab techs arrived in succession.

After identifying himself, Hager told the first officer what he'd found and showed the curious officer the macabre sight. As in most death cases, the smell was the hardest to handle—and this one stunk to high heaven. It took one look with his nose covered to convince the patrolman. Quickly, they both retreated to fresher air where the questions started.

Who? What? When?

The patrol sergeant joined the group and Hager summarized what he knew from his friend—from Cynthia's disappearance, the call from the towing company—reciting approximate times—to where they were at the time. The officer nodded and wrote down names—Hager's, Lloyd's, Phil's, and lastly under the heading <u>Victim</u>:

Cynthia Craven

Another officer stood guard at the gate, preventing any unauthorized persons from entering the crime scene. Camera flashes brightened the night sky as lab techs snapped photos. Radios squawked through the summer air. Phil sat sullenly in his Navigator while Lloyd watched him from the gate.

The sergeant stood resting an arm on his potbelly, a toothpick in his mouth. He told Hager, "I called the watch commander and the captain said that he'd like for you to stick around—at least until the detective gets here." The sergeant's name badge read, *England.*

"No problem." Hager asked the sergeant, "Who's the detective en route?"

"Captain said McLendon was on call. Two detectives and a sergeant from Crimes Against Persons usually come out to homicides."

"Is Keith Moreland still sergeant back there?"

England nodded. "Yeah, I'm not sure who the other detective will be."

"McLendon? Don't think I know him."

England rolled his eyes and made a face like he'd smelled a bad fart. "You're not missing anything. He worked for me a couple years ago—out here on the street. Not the brightest star in the sky, if you know what I mean. Hell, they call him "Brick" because he's no smarter than one. Plus, he's got a serious attitude problem."

Hager was about to ask England about McLendon's so-called attitude problem when a pair of headlights belonging to a big Ford pick-up silhouetted them. The patrol officer guarding the entrance stopped the truck just short of the driveway. The officer spoke to the man briefly, then he yelled to the sergeant, "Hey, Sarge, he says he's the owner of this place!"

Hager told the sergeant, "My partner called him. His name's Jess Kemp."

England nodded. "What's his name?" he yelled to the officer.

"Kemp."

"Let him in," England ordered.

Jess Kemp pulled into the lot amidst the police vehicles. He got out of his truck, sleepy-eyed and scratching his head. Hager and Sergeant England walked over to Kemp. Hager identified himself and explained what they had found in the trunk of the Mercedes.

Kemp shook his head. "Damned nigger. I thought something was strange about that smell."

"Wait, Mr. Kemp. Who are you talking about?" Hager asked.

"Luther Rivers, my night shift driver. He's supposed to be working 'til midnight. He hasn't come back, yet? I figured he was out on a call when you got here."

Hager looked at his watch — *10:07*. "No, he hasn't been here. Do you have a way to contact him in the wrecker?"

"We have a CB radio." Kemp turned around and sat in his truck, the door open. He picked up a microphone, "Luther, you there? Luther? Come in, Luther. Answer the radio, Luther!" He tossed the microphone onto the seat. "He's not answering. Damn, Luther!"

"Mr. Kemp?" Hager asked. "What does Luther have to do with this?"

Kemp took off his hat and wiped his face with a handkerchief. "Luther picked up that Mercedes the other night. I asked him when the man was going to pick it up and he said he would call him. I thought I smelled something awful this afternoon...thought it was a dead dog or something."

"Do you know where Luther picked up the car?" Hager

asked.

Kemp's eyes closed in thought. "I think it was on the highway somewhere." He started toward the office door. "We keep the tickets inside."

Hager and England followed Kemp into the tiny office. The owner shuffled through papers on a greasy clipboard. Hager smelled motor oil, grease, and the smell of rubber — repair shop smells. In addition to running a wrecker service, Capital City Towing also did minor repairs — brakes, tire repair, oil changes and the like. He looked through a glass door and saw the repair shop area. Curious, he pushed the door open and stepped in.

The smells were very familiar to the agent and brought back fond memories. As a child and through college, Hager worked in the service stations his father had owned. He'd functioned as a gas attendant, tire repairer, and oil changer in his teen-age years. He knew his way around a repair 'bay' or 'pits' as they were called.

Darkness didn't allow Hager to see much of the shop but by the silhouettes of toolboxes, hydraulic lifts, and hoses suspended from the ceiling, he envisioned it looking very much like where he'd worked. Hager realized he'd gotten caught up in reminiscing, turned around, bumping into a seemingly immovable object. The pain centered in his leg, about thigh level. Grimacing, he looked at what he'd collided with and recognized it as a brake drum/rotor lathe.

He touched the machine and his hand came back filthy from a greasy, gritty substance. Immediately, he recognized the metal shavings mixed with axel grease consistent with what would come from a used rotor. Not wanting to wipe his hands on his pants, Hager felt around and found a cloth towel, wiped his hands as clean as they could, and returned to the door.

"Here it is," Kemp said. "July fourteenth. A Mercedes on Seventy between Raleigh and Durham. He wrote down the name, Craven. And here's a phone number."

Kemp handed the ticket to Hager. The phone number

written on it was Phil Craven's, but it was written in black ink—the other information in blue. It was likely the number was written later, and that would be consistent with what had occurred up to this point. Phil had received the phone call from Luther Rivers today.

Kemp shook his head and wiped his sweaty face again. "Shoulda known that boy was trouble. They all are—coloreds, blacks, now African-Americans—you can take 'em out of the jungle—"

"...but you can't take the jungle out of the nigger," a raspy voice from behind said.

Hager turned around to see a black man in a golf shirt and slacks, carrying a notebook. A gun was strapped to his side, a badge clipped on his belt.

"Is that the way it goes?" the black man asked smiling.

Sergeant England spoke up, "Agent Hager, meet Detective McLendon."

Detective R.D. (Brick) McLendon was about thirty-five, dark-skinned, clean-shaven, about five-nine, with a stocky build. His hair was cut close with no discernible style. He nodded in recognition. "SBI, right? They called you already?"

"No, I found the body."

McLendon's eyes had a look of surprise.

"It's a long story," Hager said. "Why don't we go outside and I'll bring you up to date."

They walked out, leaving England and Jess Kemp in the office.

"Who's the cracker?" McLendon asked.

"What?" Hager asked not believing what he'd said. "Cracker?"

"Yeah, cracker! Oh, I guess since he called me 'nigger', it's still not proper to call him 'cracker'?"

"Look, man. He wasn't talking about you. He was talking about his driver. And regardless of his word choice, you should be more professional than that." Hager pointed his finger at him. "You're the one wearing a badge."

"Whatever, Hager. I know my job so tell me why you're here."

Lloyd and Phil walked over and another car pulled onto the lot. Hager glanced at the blue Ford Taurus and recognized Keith Moreland behind the wheel. Hager made the introductions to McLendon and explained how they came to discover Cynthia Craven's body. Moreland walked over and then, another car pulled in the drive — another Taurus — this one silver.

"Must be the second detective," Hager said to himself.

Hager waited to proceed until the entire investigative gang was present so he wouldn't have to repeat himself again. Moreland walked up. The other detective got out of his car. It was Larry Phillips. Hager had worked with Phillips before and he was glad to see him, especially since the agent and McLendon hadn't gotten off to a very warm and loving start. They all said their 'hellos' and waited patiently for the profiler to speak.

The circle of cops and a somber Phil Craven looked more like a football huddle than a briefing — and for that moment, Hager was quarterback. But it wouldn't last long.

CHAPTER

10

FRIDAYS USUALLY MEANT going out for breakfast. Instead of getting bagels to go, which was the customary practice Monday thru Thursday, the two agents would go to a café where they filled themselves with a big breakfast. This morning they were on the way to a place called Big Daddy's.

Hager and Lloyd had spent a late night at the Raleigh PD headquarters, trying to get a grip on what had happened to Cynthia Craven. Plus, it was Lloyd's first day back and they wanted to celebrate. Judy was supposed to meet them at the restaurant. Maxwell said he'd be there, too.

Hager drove and they pulled to a stop at a traffic light. Hager's car was in the right lane several cars back, and when the light turned green, traffic was slow to start.

"What the hell's taking so long?" Lloyd growled.

Curious of the delay, Hager glanced over the other cars. Standing at the corner, a haggard looking man held a sign,

Hungry Please Help.

A car had evidently stopped to donate to the poor man's cause, and he sauntered over to the passenger side door with his hand out and a smile on his face. The car's window rolled down and a thin arm passed some paper money to the outstretched paw of Mr. Homeless.

Hager shook his head and looked beyond the bum's head to the large golden arches of a McDonald's Restaurant sign. In spite of having served "billions and billions," the long-time wonder chain was hiring, hence the sign *Help Wanted* on the billboard below.

"Look at that, Lloyd. McDonald's needs help and that fucker stands right under the sign begging for money!"

Lloyd nodded and groaned.

Hager continued to rant, "And what's worse is these dumb-assed people give that bastard money *knowing* he's just too lazy to work." Lloyd shook his head this time. "You believe that shit?"

Hager pulled forward, staring at the bearded man with the worn clothes. A horn blew behind him. Hager checked the mirror and a woman waved her hands across the steering wheel, somehow to shoosh traffic forward.

The man eased his way along the line of cars with a swagger bearing confidence that more bleeding hearts would add to his already inflated take for the morning. A horn blew again—this time ahead of the Crown Vic.

Smiling and nodding a pitiful thanks, the man stopped at every window, craning his neck to see the occupants—to size them up.

A woman ahead of Hager reached across the passenger seat. Hager growled, anticipating another 'good Samaritan' becoming a victim to this con artist's fraud. Instead, her hand popped down on the manual door locks in an blatant signal for the stranger to keep away.

"Good girl," Hager said and coasted the car forward.

Seeing two adult males occupying the black sedan, the man looked ahead for more likely *contributors* to his cause.

Using the automatic control, Hager rolled down the passenger side window.

"What the hell are you doing, Clark?" Lloyd asked.

The man kept his focus behind the agent's car. Hager stopped and hit the horn. "Hey, man!" he yelled to the bum.

Surprised, the man strutted over to Lloyd's window, put one arm on the door and leaned into the window. Another horn blared behind them. The bum looked backward and yelled, "Hold your horses! Can't you see I'm conducting business here?"

Down in the window opening again, the man smiled with his rotten teeth, the odor of cheap wine emanated from his breath. Taking from the old adage, the man said in an articulate manner, "Can you spare some change for a hungry soul, Brother?"

Hager answered, "No, what I can-*not* spare is sympathy for a no-good son of a—"

"Fuckin' cops," the man turned and walked away."

"No-good son of a bitch! That's what you are! Get a fuckin' job, you lazy asshole!" Hager shouted.

Lloyd laughed. Horns sounded again and cars began to pull around, giving the state car's occupants dirty looks as they passed. Road rage was brewing.

Lloyd continued to laugh and Hager joined him. He was still miffed at the sight, but the agent chuckled just the same at what he'd said. Hager pulled forward and across the intersection.

"I've always wanted to tell one of those assholes off. Until now, I never had the right frame of mind to do it. I guess that 'help wanted' sign set me off," Hager explained.

"Guy's just trying to make a living is all, Clark. What's the problem?" Lloyd asked, intentionally adding fuel to the fire.

"That fucker's able to work like the rest of us. I don't buy into that shit: 'I'm homeless, and down on my luck. Please help me,'" Hager whined mockingly. "Fuck that son of a bitch! He's a lazy bastard and it burns my ass to see people giving money to him when he should be out here earning it!"

Lloyd grinned, knowing he'd achieved getting Clark Hager on a soapbox. "Looks like he's making a better living begging than he would working at Mickey-D's. I'd say he's *earning* it. It's probably hotter than forty hells out there already—"

Hager's face turned red. "Lloyd are you telling me—"

Lloyd burst out laughing.

"Fuck you, Lloyd. Fuck you!" Hager chuckled.

At eight-thirty, Hager pulled the car into the lot of Big Daddy's Restaurant, a diner with upscale qualities. Not upscale in a 'fine dining' way, but upscale in comparison to other diners.

It had fully upholstered booths, clean tables, and a staff of forty something women who happened to love both Hager and Lloyd. Best of all, the food was good and affordable on a state employee's salary.

Dixie, the head hostess, waitress, and head whatever else, greeted the hungry agents with a denture-filled smile and a drawl that would make Jesse Helms cover his ears.

"Well, look what the cat dragged in," she said, chewing on a piece of gum. "If it ain't our two famous crime fighters."

She hurried around the counter and gave Lloyd a big hug and kissed his cheek, leaving a red impression Hager would consider telling him about before he went home to his wife.

"Lloyd, it's so good to see you out and about again. When are you coming back to work?"

Lloyd blushed for what Hager thought was the first time. Dixie stepped away, but held Lloyd's arms, giving him the once over.

"Hey, good-lookin'," Lloyd said. "Today's my first day back."

"Well, that's pretty quick," she said. Then she glared alluringly at him. "You must be a fast healer, huh? Quick recovery?"

Lloyd fell right into her rhythm. Pumping his eyebrows, he whispered toward her ear, "Strong as a mule and hung like one, too."

This time, she blushed. Then she giggled in a flirting way like all women seem to do.

"Hey, what about me?" Hager asked.

"What about you?" Lloyd snapped.

Hager looked at Dixie who smiled saying, "Clark, we just saw you last week. It's been a long time since Lloyd's been here. We just want to make him feel welcome again."

Another waitress named Barbara walked up and gave Hager a hug. "There ya go, Clarky. Feel better?"

Barbara was short, round and soft, her perfume strong and cheap.

"Oh, yeah, much better. Thanks, Barbara."

Dixie seated them at a large table and both of them ordered coffee while they waited for the remainder of the party to show. Judy came in first. A minute later Bob Maxwell followed her with a thirtyish well-dressed lawyer type at his heels. The three of them sat down.

Maxwell made the introductions. "Clark, Lloyd...and Judy, too. I want y'all to meet Matt Huston. He's one of our new field agents in Charlotte, now. But soon, he'll be joining ISU. Matt? Clark Hager, Lloyd Sheridan, and Judy Carroll."

Huston smiled and shook hands with all of them. Hager knew all about Matt Huston—UVA grad with an accounting degree, former FBI, soon-to-be partner. Now he finally laid eyes on his eventual successor.

Lloyd shuffled a couple of quarters—a prior tip—from the middle of the table to the edge. "Hey, Clark. I bet your *friend* in front of McDonald's would turn his nose up at this chump change. I told you he's making more with his hand out."

Hager's face turned a shade redder than usual.

"Oh, I saw that poor man on the way over here," Judy

said. "I was going to give him a dollar, but I remembered hearing somewhere that people with jobs stand on the corners and collect money. And they make hundreds of dollars a day. Can you believe that?"

"I believe it." Lloyd said.

Hager shook his head. "Let's not talk about it. I don't want to go off again."

Judy wrinkled her brow.

"Yeah, Clark cussed out a street person panhandling on the corner on the way over here," Lloyd said without thinking.

Maxwell looked grimly at Hager. "What's this about, Clark? You cussed out a homeless person?"

Hager glared at Lloyd. "*No*, Bob...I didn't cuss him out. I simply stated my opinion to him that included some choice language. That's all."

"Well put," Huston said and raised his glass of water. Hager nodded in concurrence.

Dixie saved Hager by showing up at the table. Everyone ordered and Maxwell told her to put it on one check — he was paying. Hager almost spit out his coffee.

The remainder of breakfast was spent chatting across the table. Matt Huston, despite his good looks, FBI-issued navy suit, and his predestination for replacing Lloyd first, then Hager in ISU, seemed to be a nice guy.

Damn him!

Hager brought Maxwell up to speed on the Craven case and told him he and Lloyd would be helping Raleigh PD in the investigation. Hager failed to mention that he knew the victim's husband — aka "Suspect #1" personally — a mere oversight on his part. The meal ended with Maxwell asking everyone to chip-in for the tip.

So much for Maxwell, the big spender!

CHAPTER

11

THE TWO AGENTS walked into Raleigh PD's Persons Crimes' office. They were told McLendon was out, but instead they met with Larry Phillips. Phillips sat at his desk while the two agents took chairs. Phillips shuffled through some papers. Radios squelched, telephones rang, and voices covered the room.

"So, Larry, what have you got so far? Any word from the wrecker driver?" Hager asked.

Phillips sighed. "No word, yet. We asked the owner to call us if he heard from Rivers or got word about the wrecker. We also put out a BOL for the wrecker. You ought to see this guy Rivers' record. Shit, if he ain't our man, I don't know who is."

"Record?" Hager asked.

"Yeah, we ran his criminal history late last night after you left. He just got out of Caledonia Prison eight months ago for guess what?"

Hager looked puzzled. "It's not murder, is it?"

"Almost. First Degree Rape, Kidnapping. White woman, too. Back in eighty-seven—did seven years for it."

"Hmm. What's McLendon think?"

"You know how *they all* stick together. He doesn't want to go and accuse one of the *brothers* of anything unless he has to. He's something else, Clark."

"Well," Hager stammered, hesitating to disagree with Phillips. "I don't necessarily think we should rush into anything. Let's put it all together first, then make the right charges on the right guy, okay?"

"You don't know Brick. First of all, he's as dumb as a stump, and last, he's a racist—bigger than any member of the Klan."

"A racist?" Hager asked.

"Yeah, you've seen 'em before—the blacks with the Malcolm X attitude. Better yet, he's a racist, but his wife is white," Phillips stated like it meant something.

Hager was dumbfounded. "His wife is white? What's that got to do with anything? Don't you find it odd that a black racist—who apparently doesn't like white people, right—has a white wife?"

Phillips leaned forward in his chair and whispered, "It's the ultimate payback to the white man, Clark. Black man, white woman. A trophy, that's all. You should see her—he must be into farm animals." He sat upright again. "Trust me, he doesn't like white people, and that means you."

Hager remembered how defensive and confrontational McLendon was at their meeting. Could Larry Phillips be right?

Phillips eyes locked behind Hager's head. Both agents turned to see the black detective walk into the office. Hager stood and Phillips picked up his telephone. McLendon took off his jacket and placed it on a hanger, then hung it on a rack behind his desk. He suspiciously eyed the agent as Hager approached, like Hager was

69

about to attack him.

"Hey, McLendon. Lloyd and I just stopped by to see what you'd like for us to do this morning."

Hager looked on the detective's desk. There was a picture of McLendon and a heavy-set white woman embracing. Some books were on a shelf behind the desk: a Malcolm X biography, Muslim teachings, and the *Koran*, works by Louis Farakhan and Reverend Al Sharpton. From the sight of the detective's reference library, Hager was starting to see what Phillips was talking about.

"Hadn't done anything, yet, Hager. And you can call me Brick. That's what most people call me."

"All right, Brick. And please call me Clark."

"We're gonna need to talk to your friend Phil again about his wife and his whereabouts the past week."

"Okay, I'm sure he'll do whatever he can to cooperate. I know you're just trying to cover all the bases here. No problem with that, but I don't think Phil's your man. He was out of town all last week. He's a VP for Bayer in RTP."

McLendon looked coldly into Hager's eyes. "And you know that for sure?"

"Well, no," Hager stammered. "But I've known Phil Craven for years and I saw him. He was there when we found her. He looked truly grieved."

Hager didn't know why he'd found himself defending his long-time friend when, in fact, he didn't know what Phil was capable of doing.

Quickly, Cynthia's face flashed in his mind. Her face smiling with another man seated closely to her. What if Phil found out about Cynthia's affair?

Could he have come home and found them in the sack and simply gone berserk and killed her? Maybe he killed both of them.

His phone call to Hager could have been his first step in covering his tracks—his old buddy Clark, who just happens to be the state's leading expert in criminal profiling.

Should I tell him about Cynthia's probable affair?

Hager looked to Lloyd for support and his partner gave him a concerned face. Suddenly, Hager remembered Luther Rivers. "Oh, Phillips told us about Rivers' record. Just from his history, he should be a priority."

McLendon shook his head and smiled. "SBI. You think we've never investigated a crime before? I know about Rivers' sheet. I called his wife last night. Said she hasn't heard from him since yesterday afternoon. Didn't seem too worried about it, though. She might be covering for him. I'll go over and talk to her—see how he'd been acting the last couple of days. What do you think? I'm some fuckin' cherry or something?"

Hager started feeling it in the pit of his stomach. A feeling he'd not experienced in a long time—the sense that *he* was wrong and McLendon was right.

What am I doing?

"It's not that, Brick. I just don't want you to forget about Rivers is all."

McLendon chuckled. "Forget about Rivers? How could I? Shit, he's possibly the last person to see our vic alive. I'm not forgetting a thing, including checking out the husband. Look, Rivers is on the run, for whatever reason. But all the same, he's not available for questioning right now. Until then, I have to...like you said, 'cover my bases' and your friend Phil Craven happens to be base number one. Rivers will be number two, and whoever else will be number three."

This was Hager's moment. Like it or not, the agent was compelled to put everything on the table when working a murder case. No stone unturned—no one ignored. Check and eliminate.

"I'd better tell you this before I forget about it" Hager began. "I'm saying this knowing it will swing the eye of suspicion more towards Phil, but it's something we have to deal with."

McLendon remained silent, waiting for Hager's revelation. Lloyd crossed his arms, already aware of what his partner was going to say.

"A few months ago, I saw Cynthia Craven at a restaurant having lunch with another man. It wasn't your ordinary lunch, you know? They were both pretty cozy."

McLendon nodded and pursed his lips in thought. "You're right. It does add a little more to your friend's motivation. Any idea who the boyfriend is?"

Hager shook his head. "No. From the way he looked, all pumped up, I'd bet he was her personal trainer," he said using his fingers as quotation marks. "A younger guy—probably late twenties or so. The bag we found in the back of her car was full of workout clothes like she'd been to the gym—probably the same day she was killed. It might be a good place to start narrowing down the time of death window. I think I can recognize the guy if I see him again. Plus, from the looks of her body, I'm not too sure the M.E. is going to be able to give an accurate time of death."

"The cell phone," Lloyd interjected.

"Oh yeah," Hager continued. "I almost forgot. The cell phone found underneath the seat. Phil said it looked like hers, but he wasn't sure—the battery was dead. As soon as we can get another battery, we should be able to find out. Everything we got from the car has gone to our lab for prints and trace evidence."

The detective wrinkled his brow. "Your boy Phil know what gym she went to?"

"He said it was some place over in Durham, close to the country club. He'd have to check at home to get the name."

"Why'd she go all the way over to Durham just to work out?" McLendon asked.

"You know the country club life? All the ladies getting together for tennis and drinks after lunch. Both Phil and Cynthia were into *the club* big time. My guess is that she really went over there for another reason. And she was having lunch with him."

Lloyd nodded. McLendon smiled, his teeth brilliant against his dark face. "It looks like we've got base number three, huh, Clark? We need to call your friend."

CHAPTER

12

CIGAR SMOKE DRIFTED from behind the chair. Classical music was playing softly. The old man turned around to face the desk. He regarded his nervous subordinate. "You saw it on the news this morning?" the old man asked. "How can you be sure it's Lyle's girl?"

"I've seen her at the club before. She was one of Lyle's regulars." Lou Yates said.

Yates sat anxiously in the leather chair. He wore a white golf shirt and black jogging pants, tennis shoes. The shirt had an embroidered logo on the left breast: *Royal Fitness Center.*

"Cynthia was a good lookin' woman, too. What a lucky fucker," Yates said.

The old man puffed on his cigar again. Simon Legard was about seventy, but looked fifty. The years of lifting weights and maintaining a high level of fitness had worn well on his frame. Still muscular for his age—his skin fit loosely around his joints indicating he'd been a lot larger in previous years. In fact, Simon was a U.S. amateur body building champion back in the 1960's. Legard owned the Royal Fitness Centers—a chain of large, well-equipped places where people paid thousands of dollars a year to keep themselves in shape. All centers—six of them to be exact—thrived on the phrase Legard coined, 'We give our customers the royal treatment.'

Based in Atlanta, Legard had taken over a recently bankrupt Gold's Gym in 1994 in the Atlanta suburb of Buckhead and started what had been a dream. In addition to the Atlanta location, he had stores in Miami, Nashville, Charlotte, and Richmond. The newest Royal center in Durham, which opened its doors in May 1996, was his biggest risk to date.

The Raleigh/Durham area wasn't exactly Atlanta or Miami. Legard needed large metropolitan areas where there were many affluent people to support the expensive membership fees. The large cities were also places where Royal Fitness could get lost in the shuffle of other similar operations.

But his son-in-law Lou Yates had convinced him there would be enough of a market to sustain the luxury facility and also keep Royal's other membership *features* from becoming common knowledge.

"Well, she's dead now. Do you think Lyle had something to do with it?" Legard asked.

Yates shook his head, worried. "No idea, Simon, but either way, if someone—the cops that is—finds out she came here...there're bound to be questions. With questions from the cops, that means somebody might slip up. I know we don't need to be in the public eye, not with what our big business is. Someone's likely to get wind of what else's going on here, you know?"

Legard nodded slowly, pondering a decision. He looked at his son-in-law grimly. "Bring Lyle to me. I want to talk to him—personally!"

Yates held his head down. Slowly his eyes met Legard's eyes, which were steely blue and dagger-like when he needed to be intimidating.

"There's another problem, Simon." Yates said, wiping the sweat from his upper lip. "I think Lyle and the woman had something going on besides business. One of the girls told me he'd asked her if she had ever fallen in love with one of her clients."

Legard sighed and covered his face with his hands, his elbows resting on the desk. "Fuckin' whores," he said softly.

Simon glared at him with those fiery eyes and leaned across the desk. "This is definitely a problem!" he shouted angrily. "Why didn't you do something about it before now, Lou?"

Lou retreated back in his chair. "I only found out about it a couple of weeks ago. I didn't think it was that much of a problem...until now."

"Yeah, *now* it's a problem! Lou, when a prostitute falls in love with his client, it's a problem! For business and for other reasons! Love has no place in this business, you know that!" Legard screamed, spit flailing from his mouth. "I told you, find Lyle—now!"

CHAPTER

13

COLIN LYLE HUNG UP the phone frustrated. For two days he'd called Cynthia—with no response. Just Monday night, after a dinner and evening of passion, she'd said she loved him. To show her love, Cynthia had surprised him with a key to *their* new townhouse. Wanting him out of the apartment where he was living then, she had insisted he move in during the coming weekend. She'd said it was too close to the gym, and plus, she wanted the two of them to have a place of their own when she left her old man.

She hadn't shown up at the gym on her regular work-out day—Wednesday, and with it being Friday, Colin thought he would call her to see if she were going. He looked at the clock on his living room wall—*11:15*.

Their usual workout began at eleven forty-five with some weights. After an hour of pumping iron, they would go out for lunch, and then to his place for the aerobic portion of her training, ending with a hot shower and deep body massage. By not answering the phone, he figured she was probably on her way and Colin knew that since she'd missed their Wednesday appointment, she would be especially horny—even more than normal. He wondered why she'd missed Wednesday and assumed her husband had come back into town, preventing her from coming—no pun intended.

The *News & Observer* lay on the coffee table in front of him. "Body Shaping" was on ESPN2. Colin picked up the paper, turning over to the bottom flap, and spotted an unbelievable photograph. It was Cynthia. Colin read the headline.

RALEIGH WOMAN FOUND DEAD IN CAR

Not believing his eyes, Colin stared at the photograph, then returned to the headline, switching back and forth. A wave of emotions swept over him.

"It can't be. It just can't be," he said with tears rolling down his face. His stomach ached, his hands trembled as he placed the paper down on the table.

He buried his face in his hands. He didn't want to know. It wasn't true. The woman in the picture was someone else—another Cynthia Craven of Raleigh. No, it wasn't true.

Colin picked up the paper again and started reading.

Late Thursday evening, police discovered the body of a Raleigh woman in the trunk of her car. The woman was identified as Cynthia Craven, 44. The victim's car was found in the storage lot of Capital City Towing on Trawick Drive in Raleigh by SBI Agent Clark Hager.

Police would not speculate how Craven had been killed nor did they release any details regarding any possible suspects. A police spokesperson said that although the cause of death had not been determined, they were handling the death as a homicide. Police would also not say to what extent Agent Hager was involved, and attempts to reach him through the SBI were unsuccessful. The body was taken to Chapel Hill for an autopsy.

Colin still couldn't believe what he'd read. He picked up his key ring and found the newest one—the key to the townhouse. It was warm in his fingers, and it reminded him of Cynthia. "This can't be happening," he said to himself.

Instead of the overwhelming grief he'd experienced minutes before, an eerie coolness invaded his body—the cold chill of dread. His heart pounded, his palms wet with sweat.

He mumbled to himself, "She wasn't around Wednesday. I haven't talked to her since Monday night." He bit his nails. "I may have been the last one to see her alive—other than her killer. Killer? Who would've killed Cynthia?"

Nervously, he paced the room, still gnawing on his fingers. Suddenly, he stopped at the answer.

"Her husband! He must've found out about us! I've gotta get out of here!"

STANDING AT HIS DESK Hager picked up the phone and pushed the speed dial number for the M.E.'s office in Chapel Hill. Lloyd walked in and made a gesture that simulated eating, telling his partner he was ready for lunch. Hager returned the signal with his index finger asking him to wait a minute. Lloyd took a seat on the corner of a desk. The ringing stopped, replaced with a breathy female voice. Hager knew it was Bertha.

The agent exchanged greetings with the M.E.'s office friendly receptionist and asked to speak to the pathologist who did the autopsy on Cynthia Craven. She transferred him to Dr. Clemmons.

"Dr. Clemmons? Clark Hager, SBI. I was calling about Cynthia Craven. You did her this morning."

The doctor paused. "Yes, Craven. The one who was stuffed in the trunk." He sighed. "What a mess. It's hard to believe what ninety degree heat will do to a body in a closed area. Whew!"

Hager recalled the ghastly sight and how could he forget the smell. "Yeah, I remember. Look, Doctor, I was calling to get the preliminary results of the autopsy."

"Oh, it was tough to get her out of that trunk. We had to—"

"Yeah, I saw the body," Hager interrupted the doctor's lurid description of how the body must have been peeled carefully from the trunk of the car, careful not to rip off any limbs. It wasn't a pretty picture. "What about the autopsy?"

"Right. Anyway, once we got her on the table, it was pretty basic. A single stab wound to her mid-thorax, right rear. Whoever did this knew exactly what he was doing. Destroyed her right kidney, severed her spinal cord and tore up a bunch of other organs with one twist of the knife. It was done with a big knife—sharp, too. The puncture cut clean, like a razor. Could be one of the large military knives, or the hunting or fishing types based on the width of the blade. The wound was deep—around five inches. It didn't take long for her to bleed to death."

"My guess would be a military-style knife since he only stabbed her once. That smells of military training. Single thrust, deep and with a twist for good measure. It was definitely someone who knew how to kill quickly. What direction was the twist?"

"Clockwise, from right to left," Clemmons answered. "This killer was right-handed. My guess is that he sneaked up behind her, left arm around the mouth or throat, right hand with the knife. We took good photos of the wound trajectory. I figured you might be able to get an idea of how tall the assailant was."

"Good. Did you find anything else? Any sign of sexual assault?"

"Uh," the doctor grunted like he wasn't sure. Lloyd's stomach growled loudly. Hager looked at his partner who was rubbing his belly.

The doctor continued, "There was a bite mark on the left side of her chest. We took measurements and photos of that. There were also some dead leaves in her hair. Her body was too decomposed to make a definite conclusion of sexual assault from examining the vagina, but we did find some fluid evidence in her pubic hair and we did the usual swabbing inside her vagina and mouth just in case there was semen present. And now for the kicker—your killer left a present inside her."

Hager shook his head, not totally believing what Clemmons had just said. "Say what? Inside her?"

"Yep."

"What, and are you talking about where I think you're talking about?"

"You got it. He left a key," the doctor said like he'd found a key inside a dead woman's vagina everyday.

Hager resisted the urge to laugh. It certainly wasn't funny, but the puns created by this new discovery could be classic. Lloyd would have a field day with it.

"Well, what kind of key is it?" Hager asked, his mind preparing for the quip: *Here goes.*

Dr. Clemmons paused as well. Hager didn't know if the good doctor was pondering a witty retort; it would be perfect timing for one, and in comedy, timing is everything.

Clemmons cleared his throat and Hager detected a slight chuckle, but the doctor evidently thought more of retaining his sense of professionalism than to make a joke at the expense of a murder victim.

"I don't have any idea, Clark. It looks an ordinary house key to me. We bagged it. I figured you'd want it separate from the rest of the other evidence."

Hager was right. Clemmons was a smart guy—and a helluva forensic pathologist. "Thanks. What about time of death? Can you make a guess?"

Clemmons groaned again. Or was it Lloyd's stomach? "Hmm, the heat in that trunk really did a number on our ability to give a time of death. I checked her stomach content and there was still food present—looked like spaghetti was her last meal."

Hager grimaced at the vision he'd created.

The doctor continued, "We'd have to see when she ate last. But my best guess would be that she was dead for a couple of days. Killed probably early this week, maybe Monday or Tuesday at the latest."

"Some of the forensics people collected the maggots from her body," Hager offered. "We'll see what an ento-mologist can do with a time frame."

"Good, but that's the best I can do until we find out about when she ate last."

"Okay. Raleigh PD is handling the majority of the case. I'm just helping out, but I'll see if I can get the rape kit and photos sent to our lab. I'll let Bertha know who'll pick it up or where to send it. Thanks a lot, Doctor Clemmons." Hager said and ended the call.

Hager sat bewildered. A key? It had to be something symbolic—a message from the killer, representing a rea-son for her death. Or could the key be the solution to the puzzle instead of a symbolic manifestation of the killer's motivation?

In addition, the key's location was extremely important in analyzing the correlation. It could have some mythical meaning, representing some pagan ritual or more simpli-fied, the use of the key could be the product of the killer's own fantasy—unknown to anyone but him. He shook his head, "This case is getting more interesting."

Confusion was all over Lloyd's face. "How so? What did the doc say?"

Hager told him about the key and the rest. Lloyd smirked. "So, the key's the key to this whole crazy case!" He chuckled at Lloyd's attempt at alliteration.

Hager laughed. "I don't know what it means."

The agent also considered the proximate time of death. If Cynthia Craven was killed early this week, then Phil couldn't have done it. Phil had told him during the first phone conversation that he'd just gotten back into town.

"We're gonna need that key from the M.E.'s office," Hager said. "Who knows what it fits or where, but rest assured we'll try it in every lock we come across."

"Let me get this straight. We might be looking for an ex-military guy who's right handed and also has a key fetish?"

"Yeah, that about covers it for now. We'll just have to wait and see until we get a look at what the lab turns out. We need to go over to Chapel Hill and get that key."

"Let's do it later. I'm starving. What are your plans for lunch?"

"I'm meeting Vanessa at China Garden. She said she wants to talk about what happened with Elizabeth and Owen last night. You wanna join us?"

Lloyd laughed, "I'll pass on that one, partner. Don't want to get involved in any marital squabbles."

"It's not a marital squabble, Lloyd," Hager said. "How could it be? We're not even married, yet."

His partner rolled his eyes. "That's like saying it's not pre-marital sex if you don't plan on getting married. Besides, we had Chinese last night for dinner and you know me when it comes to the buffet. I always get my money's worth. I'll go over to Chapel Hill and get the key and hit the drive-through. Later," he said and walked out the door.

CHAPTER
14

VANESSA SAT ACROSS the table from Hager. As he'd done so many times before, Hager watched her lips as she put the fork in her mouth. His knees became weak. Only when she slurped down a noodle of *Lo Mein* did Hager come out of the spell.

The shapely Chinese hostess with the tight black slacks and crop top revealing her belly did a lot to tear Hager's attention away.

She was stunning. Not as pretty as Vanessa, but beautiful in an exotic way. What mostly attracted Hager to the hostess was not her beauty, but the fact she stood at the cash register piling stacks of cash into a bank deposit bag.

At least that's what I'd tell Vanessa if she asked what I was looking at.

Vanessa had already asked about Cynthia's death and Hager had given her the eleven o'clock news version—

thirty seconds of highlights and not much details. He'd been forgiven for leaving the party—only after he'd called and told her what they had discovered—but the matter of Hager's remark to Elizabeth's new boyfriend was still an issue that needed to be settled in Vanessa's mind.

"So, you're still going to act like a stubborn mule when it comes to Owen?" she asked.

Hager shifted his eyes from the girl to Vanessa and caught himself in her hypnotic brown eyes.

I am certainly blessed.

"Stubborn mule? Vanessa, I act this way around all of Elizabeth's boyfriends. What do you want me to do—be his buddy? I'm her father, for Chrissake."

She shook her head in a way only a woman could—a way that made a man suddenly regret what just came out of his mouth. Her fork clinked on the plate.

"Yes, you're her father and as a father, you should be more supportive of your daughter. At any rate, what's so bad about Owen? He's cute and from what Liz says, he treats her good. Don't you want that for Liz?"

Cute?

Hager made a face. "Of course, I do. But being cute doesn't make him the perfect guy for Elizabeth." He chuckled at the vision of Owen wearing those geeky sandals and how they didn't seem to match the intrinsic nature of the young lawyer. "You think he's cute?"

"Yes, I do. Why are you laughing?"

Still chuckling, he stuffed a shrimp with some rice in his mouth. "Well, I've seen better looking guys, not that I look. But there's something else—I don't know what it is, but something doesn't seem right about him. You ever get a feeling that someone isn't sincere when they say something? You know, like they're playing a role. That's the impression I got from Owen. He doesn't seem genuine— slimy is the feeling I get."

"You're just mad at him for putting steak sauce on your precious marinated steaks."

"Yeah, I could've shot him for that—and Elizabeth! She played right along, getting the A-1 and bringing it to him." Hager continued in a mocking voice, "Here you are, Owen. Do you need anything else?" Real voice now, "Can you believe that?"

Vanessa laughed, picked up her fork and resumed eating. "You're such a little baby sometimes, Clark," she said in a kidding sort of way. "It's not like she's going to marry him or anything. He's just a boyfriend right now. Please, for her sake, just keep your comments to yourself and support her. She *is* the only daughter you have."

Hager didn't respond as he spooned out some Chinese mustard and put it on his plate. Egg roll in hand, he dipped it in the yellow goo and took a bite.

Chinese mustard isn't the typical mustard. It's more like the Brylcream catch phrase where "a little dab'll do ya." It has a way of hitting a person from the blind side, starting in the sinuses just above the nose with a raw burning sensation that explodes fully into the face and eyes.

The only natural reaction is a quick lunge for the nearest water glass. In this case, Hager always bit off more than he could chew. Hager guessed he'd built up a tolerance to the cheapest cure for a stuffy nose. He was wrong.

Sinuses screaming for relief, Hager quickly downed his half-empty glass of ice water and reached for Vanessa's. With an evil grin on her face, she pulled hers to her chest— a bargaining chip. Now for the negotiations.

"Uh-uh, sweetie," she said shaking her head. "Promise me you'll try to be nice to Owen."

Hager's eyes were about to burst. He fanned his face, trying to put out the fire from the mustard. Like a terrorist, she waited for his answer. Unable to talk, Hager nodded in surrender. Grin still planted on her face she offered the glass, only to pull it back, just out of his reach. "Ah-ah. Promise?"

Hager moaned and nodded again. With a toothy smile, she pushed it forward to Hager's gracious hand. Smoke should have come from his throat and ears as he doused the flames caused by the dangerous substance. He sniffled loudly and wiped his nose with a napkin. "You should've been in politics as ruthless as you are."

"Maybe I should've. It seems to work on you."

The burning sensation subsiding, Hager's eyes quickly glimpsed the attractive hostess as she headed for the front door. Under her arm, the bank bag seemingly bulged at the seams.

This place must do some business.

By herself, bag in plain view, the woman strolled out the door like she was walking her dog—not carrying the mother load of cash. Hager recalled there was a BB&T in the same shopping center. It was a robbery waiting to happen—no, not waiting—asking.

She'd better be Bruce Lee in a woman's body.

From his seat and over Vanessa's shoulder, Hager could see the woman walking quickly toward the bank. He shifted his attention back to Vanessa and her beautiful eyes.

"Are you all right?" she asked pushing her plate to the side, indicating she was finished.

"Yeah, it's all better now." He looked behind her again. She turned and followed his stare.

"Is something going on at the door, Clark? Whatever it is, it certainly has your attention."

He returned to Vanessa's curious look and began to explain. In his peripheral vision he saw the hostess, who had walked in between two cars, had suddenly disappeared. Like a flash, she reappeared, her arms flailing. A man came into the frame, his arms wrapped around the frantic woman.

Robbery!

Hager's chest thumped. Overwhelmed with energy, Hager jumped from the booth like a cat and out the door, his hand reflexively reaching for his pistol.

The woman was down. The man—black, wearing a gray tank top and denim shorts—was hovering over her, yanking the bag from her death grip. She kicked and Hager heard her shrieking pleas for help. Cars continued to pass, oblivious to the crime in progress. The robber stood erect. Like a shot and bag in tow, he took off running east through the parking lot toward the road.

Hager jumped from the curb in the direction of the downed woman. He was at a full sprint. Decisions—decisions. Go for the bad guy or attend to the victim? A quick glance revealed the woman had gotten to her feet, screaming something in Chinese.

With the woman okay, Hager pursued the fleeing felon. Still sprinting, he tracked the man as he darted across the pavement. Hopefully, someone called the police.

With sweat dropping in cool streaks down his back, Hager focused on his prey who was outdistancing his pursuer. This part of the parking lot was empty, therefore easy to make an escape. Across the street was a strip shopping center under construction and behind it, a wooded area bordering a housing development. The thief was headed right for the woods.

He crossed the street. Hager's lungs were on fire—his legs screaming for him to stop running. As he watched the man leave his line of sight behind the building, Hager slowed his pace. No way he'd catch him. He holstered his pistol and jogged to the corner of the building, gasping for air.

Without breaching the corner, he quietly listened for any movement. He heard nothing. Slowly, he crossed over the corner and to the rear of the building where a large ditch prevented anyone from further passage.

He has to be back here. There's nowhere else to go.

Slowly and as quietly as he could while trying to catch his breath, Hager crept along the surface of brick. He reached a corner and knelt down to look around it. A quick glance was all it took to see a BFI dumpster adjacent to a door.

Sensing the robber was hiding somewhere in or near

the dumpster, Hager pulled his Beretta and held it at waist level. He heard a rumbling noise coming from the dumpster. Should he issue a challenge? Or just force the issue? *What the hell.*

"Police officer! You're under arrest!" he shouted. "Come out from behind the dumpster! Now! With your hands up!"

Hager waited and wondered if he'd scared the shit out of all the rats in the trash instead of the criminal. Then, he heard a muffled 'shit' and some grunting as a pair of dark hands rose above the top of the blue trash can.

"I give up, man! Don't shoot, don't shoot!" the man said in a desperate voice.

He was inside the dumpster.

"Climb out of the dumpster—slowly! And keep your hands where I can see them," Hager shouted.

With the ease of a gymnast, the man pulled himself to the top of the dumpster and sat with his legs still hiding inside. His dark skin glistened with sweat. Hager had the Beretta's sights pointed at the center of the man's chest. It was the same guy—black male, gray tank top with denim shorts. The sweating also gave him away.

"Come down, and lie flat on your stomach—do it slowly!"

In the immortal words of the musical group Kansas, this was the *Point of No Return* for this criminal. He could surrender and risk probably going to jail or he could lure the arresting officer into relaxing and then suddenly take off running again, continuing in flight. The eyes would give him away. If they shifted, looking for an escape route, Hager had better get on his horse.

But, apparently like his pursuer, this felon was in no shape to run any longer and he slowly scaled down the metal and plopped down on the asphalt, hands in front of him.

Hager would have to holster his weapon in order to handcuff the crook, which would leave him vulnerable. He remembered his survival training.

Strong commands followed by speed cuffing.

Like he'd done it every day of his life, Hager reverted back to his training, ordering the man's hands behind him. Slowly, his pistol still out, he approached his prone suspect. Quickly holstering and removing the cuffs, Hager cuffed the first wrist, then the second. It was over.

Hager did a quick search of the man, not finding the bank bag. Sweat rolled down his back, face, and arms.

"Where's the bag?" Hager asked.

"Don't know what you talking 'bout, man! I was just looking for cans is all!" the man answered.

Hager had the urge to slap him—especially since this mutt attacked a young woman and caused him to run at full speed in ninety-degree heat with a full stomach and a suit on—it came with the heat of the job.

Hager could hear sirens quickly approaching. No one knew where he was and they, the police that is, would probably be searching for him. Satisfied the man wasn't armed, he helped him to his feet and walked around to the front of the building as police cruisers arrived on the scene.

Hager kept one hand on the man while he fished for his badge. The first officer took custody of the prisoner and put him in the back of the patrol car.

Hager had caught his breath. "I think the bank bag's in the dumpster. I didn't see him drop it anywhere," he told the officer. "I'll walk back around if you'll watch him."

The officer nodded and Hager, realizing how hot it was, removed his jacket, loosened the tie and unbuttoned his collar. He returned to the dumpster and before he lumbered into the dirty trash container, he checked on the ground nearby.

Finding nothing but scattered empty beer and wine bottles, the agent pulled himself into the dumpster. It reeked of sour milk, piss, and some other sickening odor reminiscent of a person's daily bathroom break. As luck would have it, the bag wasn't on top of the trash, which was about halfway to the top of the receptacle.

Goddammit! I should've slapped that fucker for just making me get into this trashcan!

Hager shook his head, knowing he had to jump into the mess. He landed on an uneven surface of cans, boxes, and other trash.

The smell hadn't changed. Breath held, Hager fished around, moving bottles and assorted disposals until he came to the ultimate in trash gruesomeness: a dirty diaper. Not the kind that's filled with pee, but the black baby shit that makes parents wonder from what planet their beautiful child came. *Get me out of here!*

He kicked the shitty diaper out of the way and moved some other trash around. He picked up a seemingly empty 12-pack carton of Bud Light; it felt heavy. Hager looked inside. Bingo! One bank bag for one scumbag.

Looking for cans, my ass!

After he counted the money, which turned out to be $9,640.00, Hager turned over the evidence to the investigating officer and bid *adieu* to the mugger, who still refused to divulge his name. Hager, being a smart ass, called him "John" for John Doe.

A Raleigh PD sergeant gave Hager a ride back to the restaurant. Vanessa was waiting in her car, air condition probably on full blast. Hager had to wonder what had gone through Vanessa's mind when he jumped from the seat and later learned that her fiancé was chasing a dangerous criminal, or can collector.

Vanessa opened the car door with a smile on her face. She didn't look worried.

"Well," she said. "Did you get him?"

Hager spread his arms and stood still. "What, no 'are you okay, honey?' just 'did you get him?' Is that all you care about?"

Vanessa's eyes glanced downward, and then returned to Hager's. "It looks like you're okay from where I'm standing. I want to know if jumping from the table was worth the effort. Did you get him or what?"

Hager smiled, half trying not to, but still smiled nonetheless. "Well, let's just say that in order to catch a rabbit, you don't necessarily have to be fast, but smart. Does that answer your question?"

"Wabbits?" she said in her best Elmer Fudd impression. "Is that what you were chasing?"

"Wascally wabbits. Shh! Be very, very quiet," Hager slurred as Vanessa closed in for a loving embrace.

It didn't take her long to detect where Hager had been playing recently. "Damn, Hager! What did you step in out there?" she asked pushing him away.

Hager smiled proudly, knowing he'd paid her back for her thoughtlessness. He then grimaced in remembrance of the smell. "Oh yeah. Had a little treasure hunt in a dipsy dumpster. But I recovered the bank bag."

"You're my hero," she said in a loving but sarcastic tone. "I'll give you your prize for a job well-done *after* you've had a shower."

Hager pumped his eyebrows. "Care to join me?"

Vanessa held her nose. She shook her head and said in a nasal tone, "I said *after* you shower." She puckered her lips and blew him a kiss. "I'll see you later."

"I love you, too."

CHAPTER
15

WHEN HAGER RETURNED to his office, a message from Phil Craven awaited him. Lloyd called to him from his office as he walked by the door. Noticing his partner's change of clothes, Lloyd looked at his watch and said, "Uh, Clark, you changed clothes. What, you and Vanessa couldn't wait 'til later to rip each other's clothes off?"

Hager smiled. "Boy, Lloyd, I can't get anything by you. You ought to be a detective or something."

"Serious? That's what happened? Must've been some conversation during lunch. I see, the passion of arguing overwhelmed you both and y'all just had to get in a quickie."

It was always sex with Lloyd. He and Freud would have been good friends.

"Nice story. I wish it were true," Hager said and went on to tell his partner of how he caught the robbery suspect.

Lloyd grinned and shook his head. "You think of that bullshit during the drive over? Pretty good, Clark. Chasing a robbery suspect down, climbing in a dirty dumpster," he said nodding his head. "Yeah, believable story. You should really write fiction. I like my version better."

"You would, but mine's the truth unfortunately."

Lloyd nodded again. "Judy tell you Phil Craven called?"

"Yeah, you speak to him?"

"No, I was out at the time. I had my own muggers to chase down."

"I asked you to come with us. Didn't I?"

Lloyd made a face. "I don't do threesomes with another guy. Only women."

"You're a sick fucker, Lloyd," Hager said laughing. "Did you get the key?"

Lloyd held up a clear plastic bag with a silver key inside. "Right here."

He walked into Lloyd's office and took hold of the bag.

"Looks like a normal house key to me," Hager declared. "What do you think?"

"I think it's the key to her chastity belt."

Hager laughed and walked across the hall to his office. He sat down and called Phil. The number he'd left was different than his home phone.

"I need to talk to you, right away," Phil told Hager. His voice had an urgent tone.

"What's up, Phil?"

"Can we meet somewhere?"

"I'm at the office. You can come here."

"No, not there —"

"What's the matter, Phil? Why can't you come here?" Hager asked, thinking maybe Phil was experiencing the first episodes of grief over his wife's death.

"The black detective called me. He said he needs to talk to me about something he found out today."

Hager automatically thought McLendon wanted to confront Phil with the information he'd given the detective that morning about Cynthia's alleged affair. Brick was moving too fast on Phil.

Should I tell him and risk jeopardizing the importance of his reaction during interrogation?

"Phil, McLendon just needs to be sure of his information in order to clear you as a suspect. It's all pretty normal, you know. The husband is always a suspect in the death of his wife. I told you to expect this."

Phil sighed. He was under severe stress. "I think he wants to talk to me about my trip to Atlanta."

Hager thought carefully. Phil was still a suspect in this case and if he was starting to confess something, he needed to make sure he was paying attention to everything Phil was going to say. "What about your trip to Atlanta?"

"Not over the phone, Clark. We have to meet. Do you know a place called Jillian's? It's near the university just off Hillsborough Street."

Hager recognized the name. Elizabeth had told him she'd been there just that summer. She'd said it was the coolest place: a sports bar, restaurant, video games, beach volleyball, Ping-Pong, and a dance club aptly called "The Love Shack". Hager also remembered he didn't like the fact that his daughter would be frequenting a place named after the infamous B-52's song.

The agent had to ask himself, *Why there?*

"Wait a sec, Phil. I just can't take off from here and meet you at a bar." Hager could, but he wanted to get more information from his friend so he could be prepared for what Phil had to tell him. "What's the problem with your trip to Atlanta?"

Phil breathed deeply—severe stress kicking in high gear. "Remember I told you I got back into town Wednesday afternoon?"

Uh-oh. "Yeah, I remember."

Now for the bomb, courtesy of Phil. "I didn't. I came back early—Monday afternoon. I think that's what he wants to talk about. I lied."

"Phil—"

"I'm not saying any more. I'll tell you when you get here," Phil said and disconnected.

SIMON LEGARD picked up the phone and puffed his cigar. Lou was on the line.

"Any word from Lyle, yet?" Legard asked his son-in-law.

"No, he didn't come into the gym today. I sent Brenda over to his apartment. She couldn't get anyone to the door. His car wasn't there so I guess he's out. He may already know about the woman's death. Hell, he may have killed her. Shit, I don't know, Simon. What are we gonna do? The cops will certainly be coming around soon, asking questions and all."

Legard took a long draw from the cigar and blew out a stream of smoke. He smacked his lips together, tasting the flavor of the tobacco.

"I've been thinking about that, Lou. We don't need some whore spilling his guts to the cops about our operation. Prostitution is only a misdemeanor in North Carolina, but distribution of steroids is a felony. Plus, it's bad for business for cops to be around. The people we deal with are very influential, if you know what I mean. They certainly don't want the whole world to know what they and their wives are doing. I run a discreet operation. This could blow up in our—no, my face if we don't get a handle on it." He sucked on the Cuban again, this time holding in the smoke, savoring the taste.

Simon continued, "We need to find Lyle. Talk to him, convince him to leave town for a while—maybe permanently. Give him some cash if he needs it. And, if all else fails, take Al and Dennis with you. They can be very convincing, if you know what I mean."

Al and Dennis were two thugs who collected the debts

for Legard. They were big, ugly, and very violent.

"Yeah, I know what you mean. Simon. We can't hurt Colin, can we? It wouldn't be right."

Legard leaned forward on the desk and gritted his teeth. He didn't need all this stress. "Lou, you know you could go to jail right along with all of us? We need Lyle silenced. Either he takes a permanent vacation or we punch his ticket for him. Understand?"

"I guess."

"Just take Al and Dennis with you. I'll fill them in. They'll know what to do," Legard ordered and hung up the phone.

Legard sat back, taking a draw off the cigar and lamenting his current predicament. Lou was being too squeamish about resorting to violence with Lyle, and the longer a problem like this lingered, the more likely it would bite him in the ass.

"Quick and easy," Legard whispered, picking up the telephone. He punched the numbers. "Don't worry about a thing, Lou. Al and Dennis will take care of this themselves."

CHAPTER

16

BRICK MCLENDON ANSWERED his phone on the first ring. His voice was still raspy, but slower. Hager guessed the detective talked slower in the latter part of the day.

"I just got a call from Phil Craven," Hager informed McLendon. "He said you wanted to talk to him again about something you found out today. You're not confronting him about his wife's affair, are you?"

"No, I did some checking on your boy Phil Craven. You know, I tried to check out his story and something doesn't jive and I want to ask him about it. You gotta problem with me doing my job?" Brick didn't sound happy.

"No, I don't. What's this something that doesn't jive?"

"I'm not so sure I should tell you, Hager. Being his friend and all, you might spoil it for me and ask him about it yourself." McLendon sounded like he was gloating and insinuated Hager couldn't be trusted.

"I thought we were working this case together. Why all the secrecy, Brick? Just because he's my friend doesn't prevent me from doing my job. If I thought he'd killed his wife, I would've told you."

"I'm not so sure about what you think, Mr. SBI man. But he's still a suspect until I clear him from the list—then and only then. But you're gonna find out soon enough so I'll tell you. In your boy Phil's statement, he told us he was out of town from Wednesday July ninth 'til Wednesday afternoon, the sixteenth—the same day he called you saying she was missing, right?"

Hager realized McLendon had found out Phil had lied.

"Right. That's when he called. Is that not the truth?"

"Nope. During my background check, I happened to check with a source who does fraud work for one of the credit card companies. I asked him to fax over Craven's credit card statements for the month so far. Did you know your boy Phil has seven Visa and Master Cards?"

"No, I didn't. What does having seven credit cards have to do with his story?"

Brick cleared his throat. "Well, one of those Visa Platinum cards was used to purchase a hotel room at the Sheraton in Research Triangle Monday afternoon. Paid for two nights. I called the hotel and had them fax over the guest register—folio is what they call it. Don't you find that interesting?"

Time to spill the beans.

"Actually—"

"Your boy ain't so squeaky clean now, is he Hager?" McLendon *was* gloating. "I think this little fib of his just put him up to suspect *numero uno*. Plus, I just got off the phone with your boy's insurance company. Seems he may have been planning for something like this to happen to his old lady. He's the proud beneficiary of a three million dollar life insurance policy—just recently upped. That, Mr. SBI man, looks like we have motive."

Hager could feel his blood pressure rising. This cocky

detective had made a discovery a rookie could have made, and he was shoving it in Clark Hager's face.

"Look, Brick. I don't know what it means, but I'll tell you what. One lie and a hefty insurance policy isn't enough for a warrant which means you haven't got shit!"

Why was Hager defending Phil so strongly? Maybe he was too close to this case.

"No, but I'll tell *you* what. These little pieces of the puzzle keep adding up and it puts me that much closer to nailing his white bread ass to the ground. You hear me?"

Hager was about to explode. He stood and paced the floor, extending the reach of the phone cord. If the two of them had been standing face-to-face instead of on the phone, there would have been blows exchanged. So much for interdepartmental cooperation.

"Well, I guess you won't be with us to hear the explanation from Mr. Whitebread!"

"What the hell does that mean?"

"It means that like I told you, he called me. He wants to meet and explain. He knows you found out about him coming back early."

"How did he find out?"

"How the hell should I know, but I'll let you know what he says. Later!"

"You knew about it the whole time? And now you're telling me?"

"Yeah, at least I called you when I found out. That's better than you," Hager said and slammed down the phone. Before the receiver crashed, he heard McLendon's voice asking, "Where?"

JILLIAN'S BILLIARD CAFE was actually on West Street a couple of blocks from Hillsborough Street. It was a little after five when Hager and Lloyd entered the place. They entered through the restaurant, which centered a large bar on one side, about twenty pool tables on the other, and on the far side of the bar, and fortunately away from the dining tables, a cigar bar—the new trend in social circles. This was some place, indeed. Upstairs, there had to be a hundred video games for the overgrown children, big screen TVs, and a beach volleyball setup. It looked like the adult version of Chuck-E-Cheese's.

Seated at the far end of the bar, Phil looked up when he saw his friend and partner emerge. Phil picked up his beer and met them about mid-bar.

"Let's sit over there," Phil said, pointing at the tables.

He leaned over the bar to get the bartender's attention and pointed to the tables. Lloyd and Hager sat, and then Phil joined them. An attractive young waitress approached. Phil ordered another beer, Hager asked for water, and Lloyd wanted iced tea. She left with a cute smile and promised to return in a few minutes.

Phil looked tired. His clothes, a pair of Levi's and a golf shirt, looked like they didn't fit his large frame correctly. Hager couldn't tell if they were too small or too big. They looked like someone else's clothes. His eyes were glassy from the beer, baggy from obvious stress and lack of sleep. Hager knew what he was going through. A man doesn't lose his wife and look like he'd just stepped from a shower after a three-hour nap.

Phil began, "I made the funeral arrangements today. I never knew there was so much to do. She wanted to be cremated. The service will be Tuesday afternoon at one."

Both agents nodded in support. After a moment of silence, Phil started the explanation with an apology—as sincere as Hager had ever heard—for his indiscretion. He told Hager basically what McLendon had said—not in the same terms, but all the same, he covered it. The early return, the Sheraton, the credit card—he explained it all and apologized again.

Knowing Phil like he did, Hager said, "I assume you weren't alone in the hotel room."

Phil's eyes brightened from either the beer or excitement this woman gave him. He then bowed his head. Guilt has a way of getting to a person at a late stage of the game.

"You're right. I wasn't."

Phil gulped his beer, his eyes drifting to the increasing number of patrons arriving after quitting time. Bob Seger's *Night Moves* played at a respectable level.

Above the bar only a few televisions were turned on. A black and white rerun of *The Andy Griffith Show*, a local news program, and a sports channel—probably ESPN—covering a BMX event. Happy hour certainly wasn't prime time for TV.

Phil continued his gaze around the place. He pulled out a pack of Winston cigarettes and stuck one in his mouth. He lit the end and puffed nervously. Lloyd glanced at Hager, then back to Phil, impatient for him to continue.

"I didn't kill Cynthia," he said flatly, eyes still wandering.

"I didn't say you did, Phil," Hager answered.

"I know you didn't say it, but I know it's coming. I just figured I'd go ahead and say it now."

"Phil?" Hager asked, trying to be easy. "Was it a woman you were with?"

Phil blew smoke out of his nose and flicked ashes into the ashtray. "Yes, it was a woman and I know you're going to ask who she is. It seems very simple." He sighed. "But it's not. Not like you think."

Hager felt like a psychologist probing a time-bomb patient, waiting for him to explode. He would carefully get to the bottom of what he needed to know, but it had to be done with kid gloves.

Phil was severely stressed, had been drinking—and from his speech, drinking a lot—and he'd just lost his wife. From his behavior, Hager wouldn't have been surprised if Phil was suicidal. Now he had to deal with being a suspect in his wife's murder. First things first—find out about the woman, and then ask about the insurance policy. He and

Lloyd had already agreed not to mention the discovery of the key.

"Tell us about it, Phil. Who is she?"

"That's the problem. I don't really know who she is. We met on the plane from Atlanta. She had a layover for a couple of hours so we had a few drinks at the airport bar and then..." he pumped his eyebrows and a quick smile emerged on his face. He straightened his face. "One thing led to another and we ended up at the Sheraton."

"That's giving the word *layover* a new meaning," Lloyd said.

The brief smile crept to Phil's face again.

"For two days?" Hager asked. "How long was her layover?"

"Oh, it was only supposed to be for four hours, but...well, you know?"

"Did you even get her name? I would've at least gotten her phone number if you all went at it for two days."

Phil put the bottle to his mouth and downed the rest of his beer. "Yeah, but you know how these things are, Clark. She's married. I'm married. There are no strings. It was just a chance meeting and we hit it off."

"What did she say her name was?"

"Yvette."

"Yvette? That's all?"

Phil nodded and puffed on the Winston. "She said she didn't like last names. Too personal."

"Where's she from? Did you ask?"

"She said she was from Maryland. I don't know what city. I'm assuming somewhere in the Washington area since the plane's next stop was DC."

"She give you a phone number?"

"No. I gave her my cell phone number in case she ever came back into town."

Hager shook his head. "You know, Phil, this doesn't help you much. What the hell were you thinking?"

Phil shrugged his shoulders and suddenly got very serious. He leaned over the table and said with clenched teeth. "What, you think I should've remembered to get this woman's name, address, and phone number just in case my wife gets killed while I'm away, so I'll have an alibi? Come on, Clark. Be real!"

Hager retreated in his chair. He knew Phil was right. "No, I didn't mean it that way. You know you need someone to verify your whereabouts and activities. This little surprise doesn't make it any easier to clear you from the suspect list, Phil. And speaking of surprises, McLendon said he'd checked with your insurance company."

Phil's eyes suddenly grew wide.

Hager continued, "The life insurance policy on Cynthia was just recently increased?"

Phil shook his head and lowered his eyes. A guilty man does that when he's defeated. "Damn. I'd forgotten all about that. Look, Clark, it was all Cynthia's idea. Her friend Catherine Molderson sells insurance and she needed some extra points to earn this trip they planned on taking after Christmas so Cynthia increased the benefits on *both* of our policies. It's not like that." He looked at both agents and shook his head, smiling—all in apparent disbelief.

Lloyd looked unconvinced. Hager tried to keep a poker face.

"You've got to be fucking kidding me," Phil said. "You believe I would be that stupid to increase her insurance policy, kill her and then have the perfect alibi and *not* get her name so it will make it more difficult to clear my name?"

Phil was displaying another guilty sign, rationalizing how dumb it would have been to kill his wife. For someone whom Hager thought was innocent—not "innocent," but rather "not guilty," Phil was acting more and more like a guilty man. Hager was worried and he needed to back off, create some distance between himself and his old friend. As he'd thought before, he *was* too close to Phil to be objective.

Phil rose from the chair and signaled the waitress. "This

is fucking ridiculous. You're actually interrogating me. I thought you were going to help, Clark. You sit there and question me like I was a suspect. I'm leaving."

Lloyd took a drink from his glass and shot a serious glance at Phil. "You are a suspect."

Phil turned quickly toward Lloyd. "What the fuck—"

Hager stood and jerked Phil's arm, turning him around so they were face-to-face. "He's right, Phil. You are a suspect. But neither of us thinks you killed Cynthia. That's why we're here. We're trying to help you so we can concentrate on finding who did this to her. Damnit! I'm sticking my neck out defending you, and you come up with all these bullshit surprises when you should've come clean from the very beginning. Put yourself in our shoes. What would you think?"

Phil pulled away. Hager glanced around the bar; people were curiously watching the show. Lloyd remained seated, calmly drinking his tea. The waitress arrived with the check. Behind her stood a man who looked like he was the manager, wearing a concerned look on his face. Phil gave the girl a twenty and she walked away with a smile after her question about needing change was answered. "Thank you," she said in her infinitely cute way.

The manager remained. "Everything okay here, fellas?" he asked.

Phil spoke up, "Yes, Joey, everything's fine. Just a slight disagreement. No problem. I'm leaving."

Joey smiled and said, "Good, Phil. Have a good one and be careful driving home." He turned and walked away.

When Joey was far enough away, Hager remembered Phil had been drinking, and from the glassiness of his eyes, drinking too much to drive. "I'll drive you home, Phil."

The look in his eyes was again one of disbelief. "I didn't say I was going home, Clark. No thanks."

"I think I'd better take you on home, buddy. You shouldn't be driving."

Phil snickered. "What're you gonna do—arrest me?"

Hager didn't respond. Without blinking once, he looked Phil dead in the eye and let the look on his face answer Phil's question.

Phil sighed and shook his head. "You guys are price-less."

CHAPTER
17

HAGER DROVE Phil's truck while Lloyd followed. During the drive Hager told Phil they needed a blood and hair sample from him. In his current mood, Phil's reaction wasn't pleasant, but the agent explained it was necessary to eliminate him from the suspect list.

After dropping Phil at his house, Hager joined Lloyd in the car. It was nine P.M. and darkness had fallen. This day had lasted thirteen hours and both agents were feeling the effects of fatigue. Hager stared into the street-lighted darkness, mulling over the evening's sudden turn of events.

Lloyd looked over at Hager. "What's our next move? Find this woman?"

Hager shook his head and took a tired breath. "No, let's leave McLendon on Phil. I'll fill him in on what happened Monday and he can find the woman." He shook his head again. "We need to find this lover of Cynthia's. First thing

Monday, we check out the Royal Fitness Center. Maybe someone there knew Cynthia and maybe her boyfriend will be there. I think I can recognize him if I see him again."

"What about her friend Catherine? You think she might be any help?" Lloyd asked, spitting into a cup.

"We're gonna have to talk to her anyway to confirm Phil's story about the life insurance. While we're at it, I'll mention the boyfriend."

Lloyd nodded. "Can't wait for Monday."

Hager chuckled softly. "Yeah, me, too. I just wish that wrecker driver would turn up. He could fill in a lot of blanks for us. And with his record, I'm not too sure he didn't do this to her."

"My bet's either on the boyfriend or Phil," Lloyd said and spit again. "But like you, I have a gut feeling it ain't Phil, but it's hard to ignore some of the coincidences. Sure looks fishy to me."

Hager shook his head. "No. Phil didn't do it. I talked to Dr. Clemmons in the M.E.'s office. One stab wound—in and jerk." He held up his hand and twisted his wrist. "Just like that. No, it was too quick to be the husband. Husbands would kill in a rage and there would be holes all in her. No, this guy has killed before, maybe in the military. That's why I think Rivers is the one."

"He could've had someone do it for him. A pro. Phil's got a lot of money, Clark. You never know. Arrange for a trip out of town while the deed is done. It happens all the time."

"And come back early—*before* it was done? That wouldn't have been too bright of him to do that."

"Nobody said he was that bright, Clark. Listen to yourself—you sound like *him* with the rationalizing. And how do you know he came back *before* she was killed? You forget to tell me something on the autopsy report?"

"No, the time of death's still not definite. McLendon's working on a time line, going over her recent credit card activity. Her cell phone bill will probably narrow it down a lot. But from what I saw in the trunk, I'd put her death no later than Monday afternoon. And that's when Phil came back from Atlanta."

Hager sighed and rubbed his weary eyes. "That's why I need to separate myself from Phil's end of this case. I can't look at it objectively. I'm too busy trying to defend him, rather than finding out the truth. You're right though. Phil does have money...no, it's not him."

Lloyd smiled at Hager's loyalty to his friend. They arrived at the parking lot and Lloyd parked next to his Caprice. Both agents got out of the car and Lloyd said, "I have to agree with you, partner. Not because I like you or anything, but because my gut tells me different. We just need to look at it from all angles."

Hager nodded this time. "Yeah, and that's why it's so important we find Rivers and the boyfriend. I'll see you Monday."

The house was dark except for a few lights. Hager pulled down his driveway and pushed the button on the garage door opener. As the doors slowly rose, Hager saw Vanessa's BMW parked inside. A smile emerged on his drained face, along with a warm sense of security that goes with knowing someone is home waiting for you. It was a good feeling. Thinking of Vanessa, Hager forgot all about being tired.

After being greeted by Roscoe at the entry door, he let the dog out for a bathroom break. He found his beautiful fiancé curled up on the couch with the TV on, a magazine in her lap, glass of wine in her hand. She didn't get up so Hager leaned over and planted a long kiss on her lips. The smell of her perfume was mouth-watering.

"Hey, baby," he said, standing in front of her. "Did you eat yet?"

She smiled and shook her head. "No, I thought I'd wait

for you. Did you?"

"No. We took Phil home from Jillian's and then I came straight home. I'm starving." Hager tugged on his tie and loosened the knot. "Where do you want to go?"

Vanessa set the glass on the table and stood. She was wearing a gray sleeveless top, a pair of jeans, no shoes. Fingering the ends of his tie, she gently rubbed the soft silk.

Their eyes met—hers a little glassy and his red from fatigue. Her tongue slithered over her lips and she jerked the tie, bringing him closer. Food wasn't on her mind. Hager's heart was pounding. She smiled devilishly and licked her lips again.

"Where do I want to go?" she whispered and batted those sexy brown eyes. "I think you know."

With the warmest sensation a man could ever feel, Hager smiled at his soon-to-be-wife and pulled her close. Heat radiated from her body. She was so soft and beautiful.

Hager still trembled just before making love to her. Hot sensations flashed through his body and a feeling of all-consuming passion seemed to fuse them both together as one being. Their kiss sent his brain into an oblivion incomparable to what any drug could manage. He was that much in love with her. It was incredible.

The progression from clothed to unclothed was not the panicked haste of teenagers, but the sensually deliberate peeling away of an outer skin—an indulgence of lovers savoring each and every moment.

Both their climaxes were profoundly strong—an explosion of ecstasy symbolic of their genuine love for each other. And as they nuzzled on the floor, their bodies beaded with silky sweat from the heat, panting from the exertion, Vanessa paid Hager the ultimate compliment.

"I love you, Clark," she whispered.

The smile returned to his face. "I love you, too, Vanessa."

The telephone rang on their way up the stairs. Without

a stitch of clothing, Hager clutched a cool bottle of Chardonnay with two glasses and hesitated at the top step. The phone had rung its fourth and final time before call answering picked up. Hager heard water running in the bathroom. Vanessa was drawing their compulsory after-good-sex bubble bath.

If Hager hadn't been tired from the draining passion of making love to her, he knew lying in warm bubbly water with Vanessa in his arms, both of them drinking wine, would put him fast asleep.

"Did you get the phone?" she asked walking into the bedroom. She was still nude.

Hager was fumbling with the wine bottle opener. His hands were still trembling. "These damned things," he said, pulling the cork free with a soft pop. "Why do they have to be so tight? Damn!"

"You didn't answer the phone?"

Hager poured wine into the glasses. "No," he said, shaking his head. "I had my hands full with this. Plus, I couldn't get to the phone in time anyway. I'll check the messages in the morning."

In lieu of eating anything substantial, they opted for a dinner of cheese and crackers, leftover from the previous night's party. The Havarti and sharp cheddar cheeses would go so well with the wine.

Under the light of a single candle, they soaked in the warm water with David Sanborn's mesmerizing sax filling the air. They fed each other, drank the bottle of wine and licked each other's toes while laughing and talking about the future.

Their talk of plans made him think of their honeymoon. Hager mentioned the cooking contest and the prize for winning. Hawaii would certainly be a great place to go.

Sleepy and depleted from the effects of the warm water, they left the bath, their fingers shriveled and pruny. The bed was cool and smelled of clean sheets — another benefit of having a woman around. She washed the sheets regularly and always made the bed. Sleep came quickly to both lovers.

CHAPTER

18

VANESSA SAT DOWN next to Hager on the bed. Her weight stirred his sleep and she raked her fingers through his hair.

"Time to get up, sleepy-head," she said softly.

Hager groaned and turned over, away from her.

"Clark, it's nearly ten. You need to get up or you'll be groggy all day. I made coffee."

He turned over, her face coming into view — murky at first, but slowly coming into focus. From the look of her, she'd already showered and dressed like she had to go somewhere. Hager smiled. He was wide-awake now.

"You're already dressed? Where you off to so early?"

She grinned like she had something in store for her fiancé. "I'm not going anywhere. But *we* are. Come on and get up. I need you to go somewhere with me," she ordered and tugged on his arm.

"Now? You need to go now? Where are we going?" he said sitting upright, feet touching the floor. "What's the big hurry?"

"It's a surprise. There's no real big hurry, but I want to go see it today—this afternoon."

Hager threw her a quizzical look. "It? What's this 'it'?"

"You'll see. I told you; it's a surprise." She picked up a coffee cup and handed it to him. "Here, get a shower and get dressed. I want to leave in about an hour."

"You're awful bossy today," he said with a joking smile.

"Just trying on my wifely privileges. One of them being your boss."

Hager rolled his eyes and groaned. "Boss? Yeah, right," Hager laughed. "I remember now. Yeah, once you say, 'I do', I become your slave. Is that right?"

Her head turned for one of those womanly looks that could kill. As quick as it came, the look evaporated and she smiled. "You weren't complaining last night, big boy. Were you? I'll make you my love slave in no time."

"That'll be the only slave I'll be," Hager said under his breath.

"What was that, honey?" she asked with a bit of sarcasm.

"Nothing." Hager turned quickly into the bathroom.

He barely heard Vanessa's voice over the falling water of the shower. "Did you say something, Vanessa?" he asked peaking his head from behind the door.

She was making up the bed. She nodded and said, "Yes, I said you have a message on your phone. It's probably that call from last night."

"Oh, you didn't get it for me?"

She smirked. "No, you haven't given me the code."

Hager laughed. "Ah, it's probably that woman who won't leave me alone. I get those calls all the time. Crazy women."

Vanessa suddenly got very serious, at least she looked that way. She straightened her head and looked directly into Hager's eyes. She shook her head and in a disbeliving tone she said, "Not."

Hager turned and stepped into the shower. Twenty-five minutes later he descended the stairs, dressed in a pair of khaki shorts, white golf shirt, and Docksiders. He found Vanessa in the kitchen. She was sitting at the table reading the *News & Observer* and drinking a cup of coffee. Hager refilled his cup and noticed that her eyes were glued to the pages in serious concentration. He walked over to her.

"What's so interesting in the paper?" he asked, placing a kiss on the top of her head. Her hair smelled like peaches.

She looked up and smiled. "Nothing, really. Just a story about a woman who was attacked in her car last night. It happened over at Crabtree Valley Mall."

"Hmm. What does it say?"

"This woman had been at the mall and she went out to her car and drove away and a man was in the back seat. He held a knife on her, but she was able to get away at a traffic light."

Hager read over her shoulder.

CITY WOMAN VICTIM OF CARJACKING

"Does it say anything else?" he asked.

"Nothing other than she wasn't injured and the guy drove away in the car. She was lucky. Damn, why don't these women lock their doors?"

Hager smiled seeing the opportunity to bash the fairer sex. "Probably because they know they'll be coming out with all these bags and won't be able to get to their keys."

Vanessa gave him a poisonous look. "Yeah, but what would you do without us?"

"I can think of a few things," Hager said under his breath as he walked over to the refrigerator.

"What was that, Hager? You say something?"

He opened the door to the fridge and looked inside. "Nothing." He blushed. "Did you have breakfast?"

"Yeah, go ahead, change the subject. I know what you said." She folded the paper and sipped her coffee. "While you were still unconscious upstairs, I ate the last bagel."

"The last one? How dare you eat my last bagel."

"Hey, you snooze—you lose."

He closed the icebox, walked over and wrapped his arms around her and gave her a tongue-tickled kiss on her neck. "But you know I was dreaming of you, baby."

He felt her shiver from the kiss. She smelled so good; he could stay at her neck all day.

"Are you ready, yet?" she asked.

"Yep. Give me one more minute. I need to check that message. Elizabeth may have called."

He picked up the phone and punched in the code to access the voice mail.

"Okay, I'll go brush this coffee off my teeth," Vanessa said and left the room.

There was one message. A man's gruff voice came on, his southern accent evident.

Yeah, Agent Hager? Uh, this is Jess Kemp from Capital City Towing. You told me to call ya when I heard any news about Luther or my wrecker. Well, I got this letter in the mail today from the Highway Patrol in Raleigh. Says a motor vehicle registered to Capital City Towing was impounded in Rocky Mount, North Carolina on July nineteen. Let's see, uh, that was yesterday. It doesn't say anything about Luther. I thought you'd wanna know about it.

Kemp ended the message giving his phone number.

"Damn!" the agent whispered. Hager quickly pushed the button to hang up, then dialed Kemp's number. No one answered and Hager disconnected without leaving a message. He stood at the counter by the phone, tapping a pen on the counter top.

If the wrecker was impounded by SHP, then an arrest must've been made. If it broke down somewhere, a trooper would only put a sticker on it unless it was blocking traffic. Rocky Mount?

As Hager picked up the phone again, Vanessa walked back into the room. She smiled and gestured a look of impatience. He dialed information, asked for the number for the Nash County jail, jotted it down and pushed the button again.

"Nash County jail?" Vanessa asked. "What's going on, Clark?"

Hager dialed the numbers, "The Craven case. They found the wrecker in Rocky Mount."

Vanessa gave him an understanding nod.

A woman answered the phone, "Booking desk, Sergeant Lucas speaking."

"Yes, Sergeant, this is Clark Hager, SBI. I'm calling to see if you have someone in custody there."

"What's the name?" the sergeant asked.

"Luther Rivers. Should've been brought in last night sometime." He heard a keyboard being stroked.

"Rivers? Nope. No Luther Rivers here. You sure of the name?"

"Pretty sure. Like I said, he should've been brought it last night by the Highway Patrol. A black male."

He heard more clicking from the keyboard.

"Let's see," the sergeant said. "I'm looking at the blue sheets from last night." Papers were shuffling and she whispered names. "No, still no Rivers. You say he was a black male?"

"Yeah, black male, late thirties, early forties," Hager said trying to remember Rivers' birth date.

"Well, we gotta John Doe black male. Brought in last night by a trooper. What I heard, they had to fight him all the way to the jail. Beat him up pretty bad, too. This might be your man."

"What are the charges?"

"Uh," she paused, shuffling more papers. "Let's see, here it is. Yeah, John Doe. DWI, assault on a government officer, resist, obstruct, and delay. He's gotta bond of five thousand but can't get out until someone comes up with an ID. That sound like who you're looking for?"

"Pretty much. Does it have the trooper's name anywhere?"

"No, they don't have any details on the blue sheets. Just the charges, court date, and the bond, but you can call over to the magistrate's office and find out. So, this John Doe's real name is Luther Rivers?"

"I'm not positive it's him, but I think it is. Can you call me if someone comes up there with an ID or bonds him out? I don't want him leaving the jail until I've had a chance to talk to him." He gave the sergeant his name again and pager number and hung up the phone.

The day began hot and hazy with the humidity thick and soupy. While he drove, Vanessa gave Hager directions, still not revealing their destination or purpose. "It's a surprise" still came from her lips.

Hager called Lloyd and McLendon from his cell phone and relayed the news about the wrecker's recovery and the phone call to the Nash County jail.

With Rivers probably being the John Doe in Rocky Mount, Hager felt relieved that another piece of the puzzle would soon come together and this case would soon be behind him. Monday's agenda would be comprised of confirming Rivers' identity, conducting an interview, and going to Royal Fitness Center to locate Cynthia's boyfriend. Hager suggested McLendon focus on Phil Craven and the time line for Cynthia's death.

Hager turned off Cary Parkway; a few right turns and a left turn later, a housing development under construction emerged. The sign at the corner read: *Ashton Lakes*.

Vanessa directed him down the paved road sprinkled with clods of tire-impressioned mud tracks. Most of the houses were still under construction; some were finished — spacious multi-level brick homes with "For Sale" signs posted in yards covered with straw.

The remainder of the development was filled with empty lots tattered with surveyor's stakes marking property lines. After making a left into what appeared to be a cul-de-sac, Vanessa ordered him to stop directly in front of a large empty lot with a sign reading: *SOLD.*

Seemingly larger than normal lots — maybe two acres — the span of land reached to what Hager guessed was Ashton Lake with lots adjacent to both sides. It was a beautiful scene. Hager looked over at the smiling Vanessa.

"Well?" she asked. "What do you think?" She looked like a kid at Christmas.

Not really knowing why they were here, Hager was at a loss for words. He shrugged his shoulders. "Well, it looks like a nice piece of property. You're not thinking of getting into the real estate business, are you?"

Vanessa rolled her eyes and sighed. "Oh, Clark. No, silly. You see the sign?" she asked pointing. "It says 'Sold' right? Sold to me." She was beaming.

Hager was shocked. They were supposed to be getting married in December and she had bought a plot of land in July.

Why would she want a lot? Lots were for building houses. Why would she want to build a house when she would be living with me?

The realization slapped his face. "Oh," he said, cognizant that Vanessa intended on the two of them building a house and living in it after they were married.

She continued. "I figured that if the builder gets started on it now, it should be ready for us to move in after we're married. I just closed the deal yesterday." She pulled some papers from her purse. They looked like blue prints. "They have several floor plans available or we can have it custom made." She was so excited. "Here, look."

It wasn't anger that fueled the adrenaline flowing through his body. It was the fear of an argument. Vanessa had clandestinely purchased an expensive piece of property with the full intention of their building a house and living happily ever after, thus leaving Hager's only tangible connection to his late wife Kelly.

How dare she!

"Clark?"

He took the papers with a reluctance similar to taking a

bottle of poison. "Honey, why did you do this without asking me?" he asked. "I thought we were going to live in my house after we got married."

The look again. A venomous glare with razor sharp edges appeared on her face. It disappeared again. "Clark, that's *your* house. I want us to live in a house that's *ours*."

"It will be ours as soon as you move in. Hell, the damned thing's practically new—only seven years old. Kelly and I had it built special."

The look flashed to her face again, her eyes dagger-like. Then her eyes filled with water—she was hurt. She snatched the blue prints from Hager's grasp and folded them back into her purse.

"Yeah, that's right," she proclaimed coolly. "You and *Kelly* had it built special." The air suddenly grew very cold inside the car and it wasn't from the air conditioner.

A penetrating feeling of guilt is like having an autopsy performed. The pathologist removes all organs and cleans out the body completely, then stitches it back up. Hager was now on the table with a Y-cut to his chest.

Kelly.

Old wounds never do heal and Hager had just opened up a monumental wound in his life and Vanessa's. Six months had passed since the most recent correlation of Kelly and Vanessa. Hager thought he was over it.

The thought of severing his only palpable link to Kelly had jerked him up by his collar. It hadn't even entered his mind—typical of a man—that Vanessa wouldn't want to live in his and Kelly's house. Why did women attach such emotions to materialistic things like houses and cars? Hager shook his head, not yet realizing his own hypocrisy. "Women and their emotional bonds," he said to himself.

Vanessa was mad, hurt, and crying. "Take me back to my car."

"It has nothing to do with Kelly, Vanessa. It just doesn't make sense to build a new house when we've already got a perfectly good one." Obviously, Hager's own revelation hadn't swayed his decision to move.

She sniffled and Hager thought she'd growled. "Oh, *we* don't already have a house! You do! I don't want to talk about this any more. Just drive me back to my car."

"No. Look, Vanessa. I thought you'd gotten past all this Kelly business. It's time to move forward. It's not me I worry about, honey. It's Elizabeth. That house is the last living memory she has of her mother. I don't want to give it up just because you can't get past this competition with Kelly's memory."

There's an old saying about fish never getting caught unless they open their mouths. Clark Hager, after hearing his own voice, wished he'd applied the lesson behind that saying. The look on her face sent chills up Hager's spine. His eyes must have been deceiving him because he would swear her head turned completely around á la *The Exorcist*.

Oh, shit.

Vanessa remained silent. She was no longer crying; her eyes were wet but the tears had not affected her mascara. A blazingly hot shaft of light flashed from her eyes. Never before had Hager witnessed such a spectacle. He was scared to death. Still, she said nothing—her gaze lasering a hole in his face with those once brown eyes. When he began to speak, she looked away, her head down, ignoring any pleas for forgiveness.

"Vanessa," he said, touching her shoulder. She flinched away as if she were disgusted by his touch. "Vanessa, look, I'm sorry. I shouldn't have said that. I'm trying to consider how Elizabeth's going to react to this. Don't you understand?"

She looked forward, staring out the windshield. "Yeah, I understand. I wasn't going to tell you this before because I wanted to see how you'd react—to see if you were really over Kelly. This house was going to be ours—the beginning of our life together but I had to know for sure. It's not Liz who's the problem. It's you, Clark. You don't want to leave that house because you don't want to give Kelly up. She's dead, Clark. Damnit! She's gone and I'm here. Look at me! I'm here! I'm the one you supposedly love—not her!" She started crying again.

"That's not true. I told you; it's not about me. It's Elizabeth; you have to understand—"

Vanessa sighed. "Oh, Clark, just be quiet. Can't you see? I've already talked to Liz and showed her the lot. She's ecstatic. She didn't even mention her mother. She was just glad for us. You're the problem. You don't want to let go. I can't deal with this. Please take me back."

Hager sat silent, looking at the beautiful lot thinking about how in the world he'd managed to screw this up.

He was angry, too. Again, Vanessa had gone behind his back—to his own daughter for Chrissake and arranged this *test* of hers. That's what it was—a test to get his reaction.

Damn her!

That was the way this relationship was going to be? A series of conspiracies fathomed by his intended wife and his daughter to trick him into playing their little female games. The two of them against him, alone to wage a psychological war against two women. Talk about a battle of attrition.

Instead of blowing his top and escalating the argument into a full-blown event, Hager slammed the shifter into drive and screeched away.

When Hager was truly angry, especially at a loved one, instead of yelling and screaming, he usually remained silent, alone with his thoughts, his temper smoldering until his anger erupted into a momentous tirade.

He drove the Explorer with a purpose, ignoring the speed limit. His turns were abrupt, as were his stops and starts. The duration of the drive to Hager's house was achieved in total silence, both of them stewing for a later battle. Pulling into the driveway, the journey came to an end.

Eye of the Beholder

Vanessa hurried from the truck, her jaw tightened with fury; she threw her purse inside her car, started the engine and jerked the car into reverse with a screech of the tires. With a sickening feeling in the pit of his stomach, Hager watched the BMW roll speedily up the driveway and onto the street. He stood at the garage door wondering why he was such an ass.

CHAPTER

19

THE REST OF SATURDAY consisted of an Ice House bottle connected to Hager, one side to his hand, the other to his mouth. Twenty-four hours and as many beers later, the telephone rang. Hager hadn't slept. He'd passed out for a few hours, sometime between seven and eight that Sunday morning. Reclining in the same chair, a bottle cradled between his thighs, others scattered on the living room floor, Hager awakened to the ringing sound. *Vanessa.*

He lumbered from the chair, suffering a major head rush that smashed directly into his gut with thundering force. Trying to work up some moisture in his mouth, he parted his lips, but his tongue stuck, dry and thick as a wad of cotton. The stench of beer and vomit permeated the room.

On the floor was evidence of a drunken trip to the bathroom never achieved. Since he'd not eaten breakfast the day before and his only intake during the previous twenty-four hours was the golden brew from Plank Road, most of the agent's cookies were liquid in form. The rest came up in the form of dry heaves.

By the time he reached the phone, it had stopped ringing. He picked it up nonetheless and heard the static dial tone, indicating a message was waiting. Dizzy from the walk over to the phone, Hager braced himself and tipped the bottle to his mouth, killing the last soldier. Still drunk, he ambled over to his recliner and fell into it fast asleep.

Wild, vivid dreams of falling haunted Hager's sleep. Combined with a vision of being torn in half, his mind flashed from darkness to light in strobe light fashion. A pounding noise filled his ears, then ringing, and more pounding. A doorbell sounded, then more pounding and ringing in a symphony of noises.

Hager's eyes opened ever so slightly, peering at the tiny clock on his VCR, the green image blinking in time with the beat of his heart. The room was dark, the pounding, ringing, and doorbell sounds now in a deafening performance.

In a haze Hager rolled from the chair. The pounding continued in both his head and at the door. He didn't want to stand erect, knowing the inevitable surge of blood from his head. Hager covered his ears and staggered bent over to the front door.

Hager slid back the curtain to see his partner standing on the porch, cell phone in hand and a grim look on his face. He ratcheted the lock and pulled open the door. Lloyd, looking genuinely pissed, pushed a button on the phone, closed the flap and shook his head.

"Where the fuck have you been?" Lloyd demanded stepping inside. "I've been calling and knocking for almost a half-hour. My knuckles couldn't take much more of this pounding."

Still dazed and probably still legally drunk, Hager swayed upright, holding his gut with one hand, squeezing his temples with the other. All he could muster in lieu of words was a long, painful groan.

Lloyd took a deep curious breath, looked around, and then sniffed at his partner. It didn't take a recovering alcoholic long to figure out Hager's problem.

"What the hell happened, Clark? We've been trying to get a hold of you since Saturday night."

Hager groaned again. He turned and headed for the kitchen and a glass of water. Upon turning, he collided with the wall and he felt his arm wrenched by Lloyd's helpful hand. They made it to the kitchen. Lloyd turned on the overhead light, blinding his partner.

"What time is it?" Hager asked with semi-closed eyes.

"It's nine-thirty," Lloyd said as he turned on a light in the living room and from his reaction, he'd noticed the pile of bottles. "Jesus Christ! I've never seen you like this before, partner. What the hell happened with you and Vanessa?"

Hager braced his elbows against the kitchen counter and rested his swollen head in his hands. He looked up. "How did you know about me and Vanessa?"

"Liz called and said she'd been trying to get in touch with you. She said you and Vanessa had a big fight and she wanted to see how you were."

"How the hell did —" Hager answered his own question. Of course, the two co-conspirators would be in touch with each other. In all probability, Elizabeth was calling to chew his ass for the way he'd treated Vanessa.

"How the hell did what, Clark?"

"Nothing. I know how Elizabeth knew. Vanessa."

Lloyd kicked a bottle on the floor and it clanked into another. He looked down at his feet, seeing the yellow puddle of puke. He shook his head and smiled.

"I see you paid your respects to the porcelain gods. Shit, couldn't you even make it to the bathroom?"

He made a sickened face and held his nose. Lloyd walked over to the phone and picked it up. "I'd better call Martha and have her come over. We need to get this place cleaned up."

Hager moaned, "Oh, I think my head's going to explode!"

"You need to get your ass in the shower and then back to bed. You aren't gonna be worth a shit tomorrow without some sleep."

"Tomorrow's Sunday, Lloyd. What are you talking about?"

"Hey, babe!" Lloyd said softly into the phone. "Hold on a sec, Martha." He looked at Hager with surprise. "It's Sunday night, partner. Now get on upstairs." He returned to the phone. "Yeah, he's all right. Put on a drunk is all. Can you come over and help clean up this mess?"

Hager turned and walked slowly upstairs.

Sunday?

"Damn!" Hager mumbled. "Hager, what the hell have you done?"

CHAPTER
20

SIMON LEGARD rested in his easy chair while watching the world television premiere of the blockbuster thriller *Seven*. Brad Pitt and Morgan Freeman were staring at a corpse on a bed. Written in red on the wall behind the bed was the word: *Lust*.

A babbling man sitting in a chair was talking to one of the cops declaring, "He made me do it...he made me do it." Legard thought how fitting this prostitute had died such a cruel death. Legard reflected on the irony of his current situation with one of his own prostitutes. How one of them had gone out of control and possibly killed his *client*.

The phone rang just as the movie broke for commercial. It was Al.

"Yes, Mr. Legard, I just wanted you to know that we found our friend Lyle and everything's taken care of."

"Taken care of?" Legard asked lighting a cigar.

"Yes, Mr. Lyle has decided to take a well-deserved vacation, if you get the gist."

"I trust you left no traces?"

Al chuckled. "You know my work better than anyone, Mr. Legard. What do you think?" Al disconnected.

Legard puffed on his cigar and smiled just as the movie returned. He glanced at the clock—*10:45*—picked up the phone and dialed. Lou answered after three rings.

"This is Simon. I wanted to let you know the problem with Mr. Lyle has resolved itself. Keep to the plan as we discussed. You understand?"

"What happened to Colin? Did he leave town?" Lou asked.

"Let's just say that he took a well-deserved vacation and leave it at that. Just stick to what we discussed earlier if the cops come around," Legard ordered and hung up the phone.

MORNING CAME QUICKLY and Hager awakened without the headache from the previous day, but his mouth was dry, his throat raw. He was hungry, too. Rolling over the bed, he caught the faint aroma of Vanessa's perfume from the pillows. He inhaled deeply to savor her scent and smiled, but the smile quickly evaporated.

Almost like the past two days had been a dream—a terrible dream—Hager stepped into the shower wondering why he still felt a lump of guilt in his gut. As the hot water poured down, steam rising and clinging to the mirror, the agent realized that the argument with Vanessa wasn't a nightmare.

The two of them had quarreled before—minor disagreements and jealous over reactions mostly. This spat was more than a simple dispute; it was a full-blown crisis with potentially catastrophic consequences. In all the years he'd known Vanessa Roman, he'd never seen her so angry, and she'd never abandoned a fight. As he toweled himself dry, he knew she wasn't only incensed, but she was deeply hurt, crushed.

Hager shook his head stubbornly, his evil side telling himself that he was right for his objections and for feeling tricked with this "surprise" of hers, knowing he would be forced to make a choice. His good side communicated to Hager via his chest and stomach with the aching hollow pains of guilt.

But Agent Hager didn't have the time or energy to concentrate on a personal issue that would eventually work its way out. There was a murder case to solve—a killer to catch.

Judy was in her usual place when Hager arrived at the office. She smiled but her eyes cut deep into him in a way that Hager perceived to be hostile. Did she know or was he paranoid?

He continued walking back to his office, not returning her "Good Morning" greeting. As he passed Lloyd's door, his partner cleared his throat and folded the newspaper he was reading. Hager didn't stop; instead, he proceeded to his office, took off his coat and unbuttoned his collar, loosening the tie. He was sweating.

Lloyd's silhouette appeared in the doorway, a cup of coffee in one hand and a paper bag atop another cup in the other. He'd obviously been to the bagel shop. Hager shifted some folders filled with paper, trying to look busy.

"How're you feeling this morning, partner?" Lloyd asked.

"Better. Is that for me?" he asked gesturing to the bag.

Lloyd nodded and stepped forward, placing the bag and cup on the desk. "I figured I'd start where we left off six months ago."

The agents had alternated getting bagels each morning. He pulled off the cup lid. "I'm glad you went. I completely forgot about it on the way over. Thanks."

"You're welcome. Everything okay?"

Hager nodded. "Uh-huh. Great."

Lloyd crossed his arms and leaned against the doorframe. "Sure doesn't look like it. You seem out of it, if you ask me."

Hager pursed his lips and shook his head. "No, I'm fine. I probably just need some coffee to wake up." Hager leaned back in his chair and stretched.

They both remained silent for a minute until Lloyd cleared his throat. Sensing his partner's disquieting behavior, he figured Hager wanted to get something off his chest. Hager opened a folder and began flipping through its contents.

"You talk to Vanessa?" Lloyd asked.

"No." His eyes were still on the papers.

"You want to talk about it?"

"About what?"

"About what happened."

"No."

"Why?"

"Because."

"'Cause why?"

"Bec—" Hager looked up at his partner. His arms were still crossed. The scar on his forehead was bulging in the overhead light. "Lloyd, it's no big deal. We just had an argument. That's all. Whatever happened will work itself out. Now quit asking me about it. We need to get going to Rocky Mount."

Lloyd sighed. "Suit yourself." He turned and took a step into the hall and stopped. "Is McLendon going with us?"

"Yeah, he said he'd meet us there at ten-thirty."

"Who's gonna handle the interview?"

"I don't know," Hager said and stood. "I guess it'll be up to Brick. It might be better if it's Brick because Rivers is black. And if he got his ass kicked like the sergeant said he did, he won't be too happy to talk to us."

Lloyd nodded. "Yeah, might be, unless the trooper was black."

Hager shrugged his shoulders. "Well..."

"You sure you're all right?"

Hager took a deep breath. "Lloyd, I'm fine. Would you stop asking me about it, please?"

Lloyd raised his hands in mock surrender and started down the hall. Hager shook his head, knowing his pain was obvious. His partner could tell he was down and wanted to help, but there was nothing he could do.

"Lloyd?" he said stopping his partner's stride. Lloyd turned around. "Thanks for yesterday, man. I appreciate it."

Lloyd smiled. "Thank Martha. She cleaned up all the puke."

CHAPTER
21

BEFORE DRIVING TO Rocky Mount, Hager called the Nash County jail and told them the two agents and McLendon were coming to interview the black male known as 'John Doe.' Hager was informed that Luther Rivers had admitted his true identity.

A good investigator always did some background on a person he intended to interview. In addition to Rivers' computerized criminal history, Hager also requested the case file from the Rape arrest that led to Rivers' most-recent prison term.

The report detailed a typical sexual assault. The victim, a young white female, her car broken down in the middle of nowhere and no help in sight, made the critical mistake of getting into a predator's car after he'd stopped to help.

The file painted a picture of a calculating opportunist who preyed upon women when they were most vulnerable. Rivers also used a knife to threaten his victim. Hager learned that Rivers was working at a Jiffy Lube, and according to trial transcripts, he was wearing a mechanic's uniform at the time of the attack.

But this victim had survived. Cynthia Craven hadn't, but the agent knew that hunters like Rivers were prone to escalate their violence over time. Had Rivers graduated to murder?

Hager was also able to get in touch with the trooper who arrested Luther Rivers. Hager spoke to him on his cell phone while Lloyd drove east on U.S. 64.

According to the trooper, he attempted to stop Rivers driving the wrecker on NC 97 just outside Rocky Mount. The trooper suspected the driver to be drunk and when he turned on the blue lights, a brief chase ensued. The wrecker ended up in a ditch bank and Rivers tried to flee on foot. The trooper was able to tackle him and a scuffle began with Rivers being doused with pepper spray.

In his drunken state, the pepper spray apparently had little effect on Rivers so he and the trooper exchanged blows—the trooper using an ASP baton—until another trooper arrived and Rivers was taken into custody.

The agents met McLendon in the parking lot of the Nash County jail. The Raleigh detective was wearing a pair of Ray Bans, a navy tie and slacks, a white shirt—stains had appeared under his arms. Not wearing a gun, he held a notebook and, as usual, he wasn't smiling.

"How you want to handle this, Hager?" the detective asked.

"I think you should lead the interview and we'll sit in, adding anything you might overlook."

McLendon glared at the profiler as if he'd insulted him. He pulled off the glasses. Beads of sweat had gathered on his forehead. "Overlook?"

Seeing the detective's reaction, Hager shook his head and chuckled in a frustrated way. "What I meant is...we all forget to ask a question or two during an interview. It's always better to have someone else in there in case you forget to ask an important question."

Brick nodded slowly. "I'm just asking about this interview. Are we gonna handle it like an interrogation or interview?"

Hager furrowed his brow. "What's the difference?"

"What I mean...Is he a suspect or a witness?"

"Good question. Technically, he's just a witness right now, but since he's in custody and possibly a suspect, we should give him his Miranda rights anyway."

"I think that'll scare him from talking."

"Maybe, but what if he confesses? What are we gonna do, then? Remember, he's in custody. If we don't Mirandize him, any confession will be thrown out. Then what do we have?"

"All right, but I don't think we're gonna get shit from the brother."

Hager shrugged his shoulders. "We may not. If he doesn't cooperate, it'll just make him look even guiltier than he already does. Either way, we continue on with the case — with or without his help. I think we need to do a suspect kit on him since we have some evidence from the scene. If he doesn't consent, we'll get a search warrant."

"You really think he's our man?" McLendon asked with a laugh.

"I don't know what to think until we talk to him. Right now, he's the only one with a record of rape and kidnapping. That looms pretty large in my mind."

McLendon shook his head. "Always gotta be one of the brothers," he whispered loud enough to hear.

Hager opened his mouth, ready to go full-force with his argument, but Lloyd interjected, "Come on. We're wasting time with this bullshit. Let's go talk to the man and find out." He opened the door.

A deputy led the three men to an interview room in the corridor of the jail. The room was small and wouldn't be large enough to safely accommodate the three lawmen and Rivers. According to the deputy, it was the only room available. While waiting for Rivers to arrive, Hager told McLendon about the key found in Cynthia's vagina. Lloyd showed it to the detective, but Hager insisted they retain possession of the evidence since it was eventually going to be analyzed by the SBI lab. McLendon asked all the logical questions and Hager answered them accordingly.

Clad in an orange jumpsuit, Rivers was escorted into the room. Hager regarded the black man's injuries. Both his eyes were swollen, his bottom lip cut, a scab beginning to form. He sat down at the table, his hands cuffed in front. Rivers' hands were also cut and swollen. He must have put up one helluva fight.

McLendon sat down in a chair and spoke first. "Mr. Rivers, I'm Detective McLendon of Raleigh PD." He jerked his head to Hager and Lloyd who stood at the door. "These two men here are special agents from the SBI."

Rivers nodded and held his head down. Lloyd stayed at the door while Hager joined the detective at the table.

The room wasn't big enough for Lloyd to stand behind Rivers—an interview technique used to make the suspect more nervous. Hager pulled his chair back and over to the side, gaining a good view of Rivers' body language, despite the table. He would serve as observer, interjecting questions when Rivers seemed to be letting down his guard.

"I know why you're here," Rivers started. "It's 'cause of that white woman, ain't it?" He looked at Hager, then returned his glare to McLendon. Rivers put his hands on the table and leaned forward. He was sweating like he was hot, but his body trembled.

"Look," Rivers said. "I don't know anything about that. I just picked up the car and took it back to the yard, that's all."

McLendon glanced to Hager, the agent perceiving the

detective wanted to know if he should continue without giving Rivers the Miranda warnings. Hager shrugged his shoulders and gestured it was okay for Rivers to continue. Spontaneous utterances were admissible.

"What do you know about a white woman?" McLendon asked.

Rivers fell backward in the chair and rested his hands in lap. He smirked and rolled his eyes. "Look, man, I ain't playing no games with you. I'm talking about the dead white woman in the car. The silver Benz?"

The detective shot a glance over to Hager again. Rivers looked at Hager, too, then returned to McLendon. This was an interesting situation because it appeared Rivers was controlling the interview. McLendon looked confused, not knowing exactly what to do.

Suspects usually waited for the police to fire questions at them; instead, Rivers was volunteering information. This was another indication of a guilty person. The best strategy at this point was simply to let him continue talking and then direct questions about what he'd said.

"Tell us about it," Hager urged after a too long moment of silence.

McLendon looked over again and cleared his throat. "Yeah, Luther, tell us about it."

Rivers leaned forward and told the group how he'd been called to pick up the Mercedes and how the next day he'd found the woman's body in the trunk of the car. Rivers made faces evident of his memory of the macabre discovery, evoking gruesome stench laden visions to Hager's mind. Hager jotted notes on a legal pad and Lloyd looked on in observation.

"Where'd you pick up the car?" McLendon asked.

"On Seventy, out near the county line. I can show you if you want."

Hager nodded. "We'll need you to do that when you get out."

"You go into the car, Luther?" McLendon asked.

"Had to. The man said the key would be under the mat."

"Did you find it there?"

"Uh-huh. Right where he said."

"You go anywhere else—other than the front? In the back maybe?"

Rivers shook his head. "Nope."

"We found some blood inside. Could that be yours?"

"No way. That's not my blood in there."

"Some hairs inside, too."

"Nope. Not mine. Look, all I did was pick up the damned car. I didn't take a nap in it."

"So you won't mind giving us a sample of your blood and some hair?"

Rivers scratched his head. "I don't know. I remember what the po-lice did to O.J. out in L.A. They took his blood and then they spread it all across where they found those two people."

"But they found O.J. not guilty, Luther," Hager told him. "If you're innocent, it'll work out."

Rivers shrugged his shoulders. "What the hell. You gonna get it anyway, with or without my permission. I'll give it."

Hager and Lloyd left McLendon in Rocky Mount while a nurse collected blood, hair, and saliva samples from Rivers. From there, the two agents headed to Durham to the Royal Fitness Center. Hager drove and Lloyd chewed on a plug of Red Man, spitting in his usual Styrofoam cup. Lloyd turned the radio to a country music station.

"What do you think?" Lloyd asked.

Hager tilted his head in doubt. "I don't know. He's lying; I know that. About what, and why, I don't know."

"You see the cut on his right hand?"

"Yeah, looks pretty fresh, but it could've been from the scuffle with the trooper."

Lloyd chuckled. "Scuffle? From the looks of him, I'd say it was a brawl."

"You've seen SHP's work before. I'm sure you've seen worse. You remember those blackjacks they carried up until a few years ago? Man, those would knock your dick in the dirt."

Lloyd shook his head and spit into the cup. "Oh, yeah. Hit you so hard, your whole family would hurt."

"I don't know, Lloyd. Rivers' story seems logical, but did you see how upset he got when we started asking him about being in the car? He could've gotten a call—maybe from Cynthia—to pick up the car. Rivers gets there. Sees Cynthia; notices how attractive she is…and he takes it from there. Perfect story—perfect cover for a sexual predator. You remember the report on his earlier Rape charge? Same thing happened. This case fits him like a glove."

"Yeah, maybe he just came up on her like the other woman."

Like they always did, the two agents continued discussing possible scenarios as a matter of conversation. It was mostly conjecture, given the limited amount of information they had at this point. But it accomplished getting the investigative juices flowing in preparation for more detours along the path of murder.

CHAPTER

22

VANESSA WAVED to Liz when she came through the
door. She bypassed the hostess, pointing toward her lunch
mate and made a straight path to the table. Liz smiled and
slid into the booth opposite Vanessa. A waiter hurried over.
He was young—about Liz's age, tall and good-looking. Like
a peacock, he flashed his pearly whites at her, his eyes beaming in hopes of making a good impression. Liz was about
to speak to Vanessa, but he interrupted, asking for their
drink orders.

"I'll have a glass of Chardonnay," Vanessa said.

He turned to Liz. "And what can I get for you?"

A mischievous grin appeared on her face. She answered
nonchalantly, "I'll have the same, please." She smiled coyly.

He tilted his head, sizing up her probable age. "You're
twenty-one right?"

"No, twenty-two. You need to see some ID?" she asked

grabbing for her purse.

The waiter smiled back. "No, I don't think that's necessary. I guess you look over twenty-one."

"You're very observant, uh..." She looked at his chest for a name badge.

"Kevin."

"Yes, Kevin." She giggled. "I promise. She's my mother," she said pointing to Vanessa. "I think she'd say something if I weren't."

He looked at Vanessa. "Your mother?" His face flushed. "Oh, I thought she was your sister. You don't look old enough to be her mother, if you don't mind me saying."

"Well, I'm engaged to her father. So I guess I'll be her stepmother when we get married. Thank you."

"Oh...well. I'll get those drinks for you," he said and walked away.

Vanessa leaned over the table. "What are you doing? You're not twenty-one yet. I could get into trouble if they find out."

Liz grinned. "Oh, it's no big deal. I do it all the time. I never get carded, especially when I start digging for the ID. It gets them every time, especially the guys."

"I didn't just hear that in case your father asks. You saw how angry he was when Owen brought the wine over the other night." Liz shook her head. "By the way, how is Owen?"

Her eyes brightened. "He's great. Other than at the office, I haven't seen him since the other night. We try to stay away from each other at work. You know, keeping business and pleasure separate."

"Yeah, those inner-office romances can be difficult, can't they?"

"I guess so. To be honest, Vanessa, he's acted kinda weird the past few days. We were supposed to go out to lunch, but he stood me up. He left the office and stayed gone for two hours. When he came back, he seemed...different."

"Different? How?"

"I can't really be specific, but he was just very nervous and jumpy. Lately he's been that way. One minute he's happy, the next he's quiet, then he says he's going for a walk and comes back acting real nervous."

Vanessa took a sip of water. "Hmm. That is strange. Do you—"

"But he's so nice most of the time. Just yesterday, he came around to my desk and gave me a little kiss on the cheek." Her eyes sparkled.

Vanessa chuckled. "When I worked with your dad at the SBI, he'd just show up in my section and say 'hello.' He was so sweet. I knew I was in love with him then. He just didn't know he loved me, too." Tears welled in her eyes. Liz smiled and then tapped Vanessa's hand.

"Has he called you, yet?"

Vanessa used her napkin to wipe her eyes. She sniffled and shook her head. Liz shook her head in frustration.

"I don't know what's gotten into him, Vanessa. I tried to call him yesterday but didn't get an answer. I called Lloyd and asked if he knew where he was. He went over there to check on him and found him passed out drunk. He said he looked terrible like he'd been doing it all night."

"Did Lloyd say he was okay?"

"Yeah, just hung over as hell. He and Martha cleaned up the mess Daddy had made of the house. But I guess he's at work today."

Kevin returned with two glasses of wine and another dashing smile for Liz. They both ordered and bid Kevin adieu.

Vanessa sipped her wine hoping to extinguish the painful fire of thinking about Clark. She sat silently, remembering the last time they had made love. He was such a generous man, so loving and tender with an unrelenting passion for everything. She was devastated by his reaction over the house plans. How could he still have such a strong connection with Kelly's memory?

How dare he accuse her of not being able to get past the comparison? Her pain quickly turned to anger as she remembered the argument. She gulped the wine and her eyes burned with tears again.

"Don't worry, Vanessa. He'll call and apologize in a few days once he realizes what a jerk he's been. You know my father as well as I do, and you know he's usually reasonable and admits it when he's wrong."

Vanessa used the napkin on her eyes again. "I'm not sure I want him to right now."

ROYAL FITNESS CENTER was situated in the middle of a strip shopping center. A large building once a Piggly Wiggly grocery store, it had elaborate features with clean, shiny equipment and an air of nobility given the fact it was a place where people came to grunt and sweat.

Hager and Lloyd entered the brightly lit interior. The layout of Royal Fitness was typical of most contemporary gyms with the room divided by the manner of exercise: free weights on the far end; Nautilus machines in the center; stair-steppers, life cycles and treadmills in the front. The place was filled with familiar gym noises—clanging of plates, the smooth humming of treadmills and stationary bikes, and music piped in from above—all to create an atmosphere conducive to exercise.

The center was crowded, and Hager looked at his watch, seeing it was just after noon. Both agents walked up to the front desk manned by a fit-looking guy wearing a blue golf shirt with the name *Lou* embroidered on the front.

Lou gave the agents a welcoming smile. "How can I help you gentlemen today?"

Hager reached into his coat and removed his badge case. "SBI. I'm Agent Hager and this is Agent Sheridan. Are you the manager?"

The friendly smile disappeared and Lou seemed to have

lost all the color in his face. He shuffled some papers and straightened a clipboard on the desk. "Yes, I'm the manager. Is there a problem?" He continued to fidget on his feet.

"Can we talk in private?" Hager asked.

"Uh, yeah, I guess," he answered. "I have an office. We can go there." He turned and motioned for the agents to follow him to an office behind the counter. Lou remained standing at the office door while they took two seats opposite a desk.

"Let me find someone to cover the front desk. I'll be back in a minute." He walked out and closed the door behind him.

"Kinda squirrelly if you ask me," Lloyd proclaimed.

"You see his face when I showed him my ID? I thought he was going to faint."

"You see him out there?"

"No, give me that key. I want to try it on this lock." Hager reached for it. "You never know."

He pulled the key from the bag and attempted to fit it in the lock—no luck. Gently, he returned the key to the bag and gave it back to Lloyd. "Remember to try the front door when we leave, okay?"

Lloyd nodded.

LOU PICKED UP A PHONE in the back of the center. With trembling fingers, he dialed a number. Simon Legard answered.

"We have a major problem. They're here," Lou said.

"Who're they, Lou?"

"Cops in suits. Two of them."

"They say what they wanted?"

"No, just asked if I was the manager and asked to talk to me in private. That's when I went to call you."

"What kind of cops?"

"They said they're SBI. One middle-aged, the other older."

"Okay. Well you know how to handle them. Just like I told you. You did take care of the changes to her membership, right?"

"Yes, I did that yesterday."

"What about Lyle's information?"

"That, too."

"Did you tell the others to make themselves scarce?"

"Yes, just like you told me. Look, I'd better get back. They're waiting in my office. They might be wondering what I'm doing."

"Lou, don't say anything stupid, ya hear? Just answer their questions the way I told you."

HAGER GOT UP and looked out the door. No one was at the front desk.

"No, I still don't see him."

Just then, an attractive blonde woman wearing a similar blue golf shirt arrived at the counter. Seconds later, Lou emerged and entered the office, taking a seat behind the desk. A nameplate on the desk identified Lou as Lou Yates. Hager could tell Yates was still nervous. He fiddled with a pen.

"Now, what is it I can do for you gentlemen?"

"Mr. Yates we're investigating the death of one of your clients, Cynthia Craven."

Lloyd opened a folder and removed a photo of Cynthia. He passed it to Yates.

"Were you aware she'd been killed?" Hager asked.

Yates looked at the photo with a genuine interest. "No, I wasn't. What did you say her name was?" he asked rising from his seat. He walked over to a large filing cabinet.

"Cynthia Craven. You don't know her?"

Yates shook his head. "No, I've never seen her before.

But there's nothing strange about that. Agent Hager, we have over two hundred members at this center. I don't know all our clients. I know some of the very regulars who come when I'm here, but not many."

He opened the top drawer marked *A-H* and fingered through a number of file folders before pulling one out.

"Here it is. Cynthia Craven. She's been a member since January 1997. We get a lot of new members after the New Year. You know, resolutions and all. People want to lose all the weight they put on during the holidays."

"Can I see that, Mr. Yates?" Hager asked.

Yates hesitated, contemplating his decision. His eyes jumped upward as if he were trying to remember something. He shrugged his shoulders.

"I don't see why not. It's not like she's going to complain about it, right?" Yates chuckled nervously and handed the folder to Hager, who passed it to Lloyd. Lloyd opened the folder and flipped through some pages.

"Do you have a staff of personal trainers here, Mr. Yates? You know, for beginners?" Hager asked.

Yates was watching Lloyd curiously. He returned his eyes to Hager. "Personal trainers? Oh, yes Mr. Legard hires only certified personal trainers. It can be a very high liability area. And contrary to what you may already know, personal trainers are not used for beginners only. In fact, many of our most devoted clients use them more than beginners. It's a common misconception."

"Who's Mr. Legard?" Hager asked, already familiar with the club's owner. Royal Fitness had their own web site and Legard's bio and picture were plastered all over it.

"Mr. Legard—Simon Legard is the owner of Royal Fitness Centers. We have six facilities in the southeast."

"Did Cynthia Craven have a personal trainer?"

Yates looked over at Lloyd, still examining the contents of the folder. "I have no idea, Agent Hager. It would be in that file your...your..."

"Partner," Hager said.

"Yes, your partner. If she'd used the services of one of our staff trainers, then it would be in there."

Lloyd looked up and shook his head. "Standard application. Paid for one year in advance on her credit card."

"Isn't that a little strange?" Hager asked. "She paid for a year in advance. Don't you usually put them on some type of payment plan?"

"Yes, that's true for people who can't afford to pay at once or those who don't want to pay the interest tacked on. Mrs. Craven was a wealthy woman. I guess she could afford the two thousand a year membership."

"Two thousand dollars a year?" Hager asked, his mouth wide open.

Lloyd nodded and smiled.

Hager continued. "That's a lot of money to join a gym, even for a wealthy woman like Mrs. Craven."

"Like I said, I wouldn't know if she were, Agent Hager. And Royal Fitness is not just a gym. We have the most state-of-the-art fitness equipment available, a staff of the best personal trainers, aerobics instruction, sauna, whirlpool, tanning, nutritional advice and development, and a strict code of ethics, and not to mention the cleanest facility you'll ever see. You could eat off this equipment."

Yates' face turned a bright shade of red. He looked offended. Hager reminded himself not to call it a gym again.

The agent also made note of lie number one. Yates said he didn't know Cynthia, but just a minute or so before, he said, 'Mrs. Craven was a wealthy woman.'

Just now he said he didn't know if she were wealthy. He wasn't a very good liar, but Hager would wait until he confronted him with it, pounce on him like an alley cat fighting for the last piece of fish.

Hager could see the look on Lloyd's face—a look that told him he was aware of Yates' mistake. He rubbed his scar and if Hager could have read his partner's mind, he would think Lloyd was trying to conjure up a witty retort to Yates' comment about eating off the equipment.

"Mr. Yates, I think Mrs. Craven may have been seeing someone here. He looked like the type to work out a lot; maybe he comes here, too."

"It's entirely possible. We've also happened to bring a few of our members together. It's all a part of the lifestyle."

"Yeah, a regular love connection," Lloyd quipped.

Yates turned to him with a cold stare. Hager was about to end the interview, but he remembered something he'd seen on the front counter. The clipboard Yates first straightened contained a member sign-in sheet.

"I noticed you have a sign-in sheet for members at the front. I'm assuming you keep those records?" Hager asked.

The blood drained from Lou's face again. The nervous twitch, the pen flicking on the desk.

"Sign-in sheets?" he asked like he had no idea what Hager was talking about.

Hager stood and started for the front desk. "Yeah, the sheets on the clipboard out there. The members sign their names when they come in."

"Oh, yes. I know what you mean, now. I'm afraid we don't keep those sheets. We just use them to keep the members honest and to prevent non-members from sneaking in. Those sheets are thrown out at the end of each day."

Yates was lying again and Hager could see it in his eyes. Logic played a big part in this fib—why would Yates be so concerned with having someone at the front desk if the sign-in sheets were there to keep members honest?

No, the register was used to keep up with member attendance, repeat names of guests, and for basic record keeping. Any legitimate business would maintain a record of at least the current year.

Hager was building some momentum for a subsequent clash with Lou Yates. The term *Obstruction of Justice* came to Hager's mind, and Yates was stretching the limits of the agent's patience. But the foremost questions remained lingering.

Why? What is he hiding?

"Do you have a list of employees here?" Hager asked.

"Employees?" Yates sighed. "Agent Hager, what do any of our employees have to do with this woman's death?"

"I don't know. Maybe one of them knew her. They may recognize the picture we showed you—might turn up this guy I think she was involved with. You have a problem with that?"

"Well," he rubbed his hands together like a fly saying, 'I've got you now.'

Hager knew he'd quote the EOC regulations about providing information about employees to outside sources. It was illegal. Trying to put him on the offensive, Hager grooved Yates one right down the middle of the plate. Hopefully, he'd try to hit it out of the park. His Grinch-like smile foreshadowed his answer.

"I can't give you any information about our employees. It's against the law."

"Right. I see," Hager said, pleased his trap was set. "Well, I guess you don't mind us going around and talking to the ones who are here, you know, show them her picture, ask questions, maybe even talk to some of your clients. And of course, we'd probably need some uniformed officers to help out since it's so crowded at this time." He looked over at Lloyd who smiled and nodded.

Hager continued. "Can I use your phone?"

Yates stood rock solid still, his eyes burning with anger. Watching the brain work was an exciting event. Seeing the eyes close, the lips purse, hands rubbing the face, all in natural response to the stress of making a very important decision. *Do I give them what they want? Or do I let them destroy my business?*

Yates looked like he'd just given up his first-born. "I can give you a list by tomorrow. I'll have to get it typed out so there won't be any record of it coming from here. Will that be enough?"

Hager smiled. "Oh, yes. That'll be fine, Mr. Yates."

As Hager walked out of the office, he managed to scan

the work out area, looking for the man Cynthia was with a few months ago. He recognized no one and the room seemed a little less crowded in the fifteen minutes it took to speak to Yates.

Leaving the cool confines of the building, he and Lloyd ventured out into the heat and humidity of high noon. Lloyd reached for his pocket and quickly pulled out the key. Hager stood at the door, blocking the view from the inside, as his partner tried the key. Again, it didn't fit. Lloyd cursed and both of them walked to the car.

Lloyd stopped at the passenger door. "You get the feeling he was putting on a show?"

"Uh-huh. Like reading a script. But he's definitely no DeNiro."

CHAPTER

23

ON THE WAY to Catherine Molderson's home, Hager's cell phone rang. It was Judy.

"Neil Baxter from Trace Evidence called with preliminary lab results for the Craven case. He wants you to call him as soon as you get in. He said he'd found a few interesting things."

"Okay, I'll do it. Thanks. Anyone else call?" *Vanessa perhaps?*

"Yeah, Phil Craven also called this morning. He wanted to let you know he wasn't able to get his wife's cell phone records from BellSouth."

"I figured as much. Judy, put a subpoena together to BellSouth for Cynthia Craven's phone records. Request the past three months' calls. You'll have to fax it to their office in Atlanta. Call them ahead of time. I have a contact number in my Rolodex. Ask for them to give it a rush and tell them it's a murder case. They usually get it back pretty quickly and make sure they fax it to us. I don't want to wait for them to mail it." He gave her Cynthia's cell number.

"Okay, anything else?"

"No, no other calls?" Hager asked hopefully.

"No, were you expecting someone to call?"

His heart sank into his gut. "No, just curious. Bye." Hager disconnected the phone and related to Lloyd what Judy had told him.

He had called Mrs. Molderson before leaving the parking lot of Royal Fitness so she would be expecting them. She lived in Treyburn, the most affluent neighborhood in Durham. Catherine Molderson's husband Jerry was a big wig for the Duke-owned U.S. Tobacco Company.

She didn't need to work—as they were filthy rich, evident of the square footage of their house, but she sold insurance as a way Hager guessed to keep busy. She worked out of her home and set her own schedule.

After navigating the long drive, Hager parked the car. The house was a mass of bricks reminiscent of a modern-day castle. Before announcing their presence, Lloyd tried the key at the front door. Slowly, the jagged edges disappeared into the keyhole. Both their eyes grew larger in eager anticipation. As deft as a safecracker, Lloyd tried to turn the key, but it remained still.

"Jiggle it a little," Hager suggested.

Lloyd jiggled, still no movement. "It's not the right key, Clark. But we're getting closer. It's definitely a house-type key." He returned the key to his pocket. "This lock is a Schlage; so that means this key probably fits a Schlage lock."

"Elementary, Watson," Hager said, quoting Sherlock Holmes. "Now all we have to do is find the correct key out of all the millions of locks this company produces."

Lloyd gave a look indicating he wasn't impressed with his partner's impression.

Hager rang the bell and waited. A minute elapsed with

no answer or movement from within, so foregoing the bell, he tapped firmly on the door. Still there was no answer. Both of them exchanged puzzled looks.

With a house the size of this one, she certainly had a maid or butler or someone to answer the door. Hager was beginning to sweat under his jacket. Lloyd pulled a handkerchief from his pocket and wiped his brow.

"Let's check around back," Hager suggested.

On such a hot day Hager wasn't surprised to find a woman clad in a revealing black bikini, sunning by the pool. She was relaxing in a chair, a book in her lap, sipping on something in a glass — probably a gin and tonic — when they breeched the gate leading to the back yard.

Upon seeing them, she immediately stood and reached for a sheer black blouse, slipped it on and walked over to greet them. Hager looked at Lloyd who pumped his eyebrows in adolescent exuberance. Hager smiled in agreement. She'd obviously just gotten out of the pool.

"Agent Hager, I presume?" she asked after removing her sunglasses.

Hager answered, "Yes, ma'am. Mrs. Molderson?"

She nodded. "Call me Catherine, please," she said with a sexy British accent. She offered her hand.

To the agent's amazement, she was considerably younger than Cynthia — probably 33 to Cynthia's 45 years — and a strikingly beautiful woman. Hager took her hand and she squeezed firmly, holding on a bit longer than normal for a first meeting. She kept his gaze with a pair of dazzling green eyes.

"Nice to meet you, Catherine," Hager said, relinquishing her hand. "This is my partner Lloyd Sheridan."

She took a step and offered her hand to Lloyd. Hager could see the excitement in Lloyd's eyes as he took her hand. "Pleasure, ma'am."

Catherine propped her sunglasses on her head, pushing back her damp auburn hair. Hager guessed her hair color wasn't natural as she had a wonderful tan, which was contrary to most people with auburn hair. Her hair wasn't the only unnatural aspect of her physique—apparent from the stature of her bikini top.

"Silly me, let's go into the house where it's cooler," Catherine suggested. "Both of you must be burning up in those suits."

She strode barefooted toward the patio door, and of course, Hager and Lloyd remained obediently behind admiring the breathtaking view. Lloyd nudged his partner and held his hands out in front of him at chest level. Hager nodded and chuckled silently.

The house smelled fresh as spring and the wave of cool air was like taking the Nestea plunge. She directed them to a small breakfast table where Hager and Lloyd took seats with a view of the pool. She remained standing and put a hand on each of their shoulders. The cool air had affected her as well, but in a way only a man can appreciate.

"Can I get you something to drink? I made some iced tea this morning."

Both of them nodded, saying, "Sure."

Lloyd kept watching her as she turned and walked the five or six feet to the refrigerator. He had stars in his eyes and Hager thought his partner had just fallen in love. It had to be her accent; it was captivating.

"I hope you like sugar in your iced tea. I never drank iced tea until I came to the States. I quite like it cold, especially when it's this hot. My husband said it's a southern tradition to make it sweet, so that's the way I make it— sweet but not too sweet."

Lloyd didn't answer, his eyes still glazed over.

"That's fine, Catherine," Hager said kicking his partner under the table.

She returned with two crystal glasses of tea garnished with a lemon wedge and a green leaf Hager presumed was mint. Class wasn't hard to ignore. She placed the glasses on a pair of coasters and returned to the kitchen to retrieve a glass of white wine, probably a Chardonnay. Returning to the table, she took a chair facing them both. Hager opened his notebook.

She smiled and sipped her wine. "So, what can I tell you about my dear friend Cynthia?"

Hager gazed into her eyes and they seemed to have lost some of their shimmering beauty. Hager guessed it was a consequence of the current subject.

"How long did you know Cynthia?"

"Oh, I don't know. I guess a year or so. Jerry and I moved from California in 1995. Cynthia and I met shortly thereafter—at the club. We both came to the pool quite often and found ourselves chatting about one thing or another."

"When was the last time you'd seen her?"

She took a deep breath and sipped her wine again. "About two weeks ago, I recall—when she came over. It was insurance business. She wanted to increase the death benefit for her and Phil's life insurance."

"I thought she was doing that so the two of you could go on a trip overseas?"

"Yes, she was. I suppose you've already spoken to poor Phil. Yes, we were planning a trip to the Bahamas this coming winter. One of the perks of this job, you know, is winning trips. You sell a certain amount of this company's insurance and so on. The other, of course, is bonus money. I have plenty of that. I simply adore the traveling."

"She worked out at a place called Royal Fitness. Did you go there with her?"

She smiled and stood, her hand reaching for the sole button on the chemise. Unbuttoning the blouse, she slid out of it, displaying her gorgeous figure. "Do I look like I need to go to a meat market fitness club?"

Lloyd's mouth opened and stayed that way. He pulled off his glasses and blinked his eyes. Catherine stared directly into Hager's eyes with a seductive allure.

"Uh…no, you don't. I just thought—"

"I don't need to go to this center to get a body like this," she said, slipping her arms back into the blouse. "I get my workouts here at home — in the pool. Swimming is the most exhilarating exercise. Do you agree, Agent Hager?"

He looked over at Lloyd; his glasses were back on, but his mouth was still open. If he hadn't seen it, he would've never believed it, but his partner actually rose from the chair to help Catherine with the blouse. How embarrassing.

Hager nodded. "I've swum a few laps before, but I was always into sports, so I lifted a lot of weights."

She gaped at him, her eyes signifying her attraction. "Oh, but being in the pool completely naked with the cool water lapping against your body..." she hesitated, searching for his reaction. "There's no greater feeling than being totally free!" She gasped and flung her hair back. "I bet you've gone skinny dipping a time or two, Agent Hager."

"A couple of times," he answered.

In her own subtle way, and for whatever reason, Catherine Molderson was trying to sway the interview. Apparently, she had a lot of confidence in her body and sex appeal — enough to make her believe she could distract two seasoned investigators.

Hager looked at Lloyd again. His mouth had closed, but he was smiling at her. He exchanged glances with his partner and the smile disappeared.

"Catherine, I'm sorry, but we really need to ask you a few more questions about Cynthia," Hager said.

She looked disappointed, but she smiled anyway. The disappointment on her face wasn't one of catastrophe, but one of respect Hager guessed. She apparently realized she couldn't influence Hager with her beautiful appearance. But, Lloyd was a different story. Hager sure had a tough job.

She took her chair again. Now, Lloyd looked disappointed.

"Okay, enough fun," she sighed. "What else do you want to know?"

"Did Cynthia ever mention being *involved* with anyone at the club?"

"Are you asking if she had a lover?" Her eyes flittered a spark.

"Well, yes. Did she?"

"Of course, she did. Why do you think she went there three times a week? Yeah, she got a bloody workout, all right. They would do their thing at the club during lunch and then they would go back to his place for dessert—and I'm not talking about strawberries and cream."

"So, he was a member, too?"

She chuckled and shook her head. "No, silly boy. He worked there. He was her personal trainer as she said it."

"Did she tell you his name?"

"Of course." She sipped her wine. "It was Colin—Colin Lyle."

Lloyd wrote the name on his pad.

"Address?"

"Somewhere here in Durham, I gathered. Not far from this fitness place."

Hager was happy with her answers, knowing he'd have another meeting with Lou Yates. He knew Yates was lying before, and now he would prove it. Hager decided the next time he spoke to Lou Yates would be at the SBI office.

Hager completed the interview, asking additional questions about Cynthia's relationship with Colin Lyle. She didn't know much more than she'd already said, but it was enough to find Cynthia's mysterious lover.

The three of them rose from their chairs. Hager closed his notebook and finished off his tea. The agents said their thanks for her information and she showed them to the front door. Returning to the heat of the day, Hager stopped on the porch, remembering to ask a very important question.

"Catherine, who do you think killed Cynthia?"

"Honestly? I think it was Colin. Cynthia told me he was extremely jealous of her marriage—wanted her to leave. Believe me, she was thinking seriously about it. She and Phil just weren't getting along and…"

"Had Lyle ever been violent toward her?" Hager asked.

"Not that I know of. She told me he wanted her to leave and they argued about it a few times, that's all."

"Okay, thanks."

"You're welcome, gentlemen. Please come back when you can stay for lunch. And remember to bring your swim trunks!" She waved as they drove away.

CHAPTER

24

THE AIR CONDITIONER blew cold air, but did little to cool off the sweltering heat inside the car. The back of Hager's shirt was wet with sweat. He checked his pager to see if it was still on.

"Vanessa should have called by now," he told himself and began to fret about his personal problems.

While he was working a case, Hager, the agent, was usually able to move his personal life into the back quarter of his mind. But the moment the action slowed, Clark Hager, the man, father, and fiancé, revealed himself and whatever problem existed. There weren't many, but this week was turning out to be one he'd rather forget.

Lloyd was driving now and he turned the Crown Vic onto U.S. 15-501 headed toward I-40. The air conditioner had cooled the car sufficiently to stop the flow of sweat dripping down his back. They were approaching Mt.

Moriah Road and traffic was backed up. Hager looked at his watch—*4:21 P.M.*

This intersection was notoriously bad for heavy traffic due to the New Hope Commons shopping center and its proximity to I-40.

"Why'd you go this way, Lloyd? You know how bad traffic is here this time of day."

Lloyd spit in his cup and smiled showing his tobacco-stained teeth. "I wanna stop by the Barnes and Noble for a minute. There's a book Martha wants. I thought I'd get it for her."

"Feeling guilty?"

A shocked look came to his face. "Guilty? Me?" he chortled. "What in the world would I feel guilty about?"

"I can answer that in one note, Johnny. Catherine Molderson."

Lloyd blushed and he rubbed his scar—probably a re-play of Catherine showing her body.

"That's two notes."

"You know what I mean. I saw you. Don't worry; I won't say a thing to Martha. It might cost you, though."

"Shit, I was just honing my observation skills is all. Re-member, I've been outa work for six months."

"Oh, okay. I see. I'll have to remember that one if I ever get caught checking someone out."

Lloyd laughed. "You think Martha cares if I look at other women? Shit, she's the one who told me, 'It's not where you get your appetite, as long as you eat at home.'"

"Yeah, right," Hager laughed. "That's what *you* say." He picked up his cell phone. "Here, let me call her and find out what she thinks about her hubby getting all goo-goo-eyed over a woman we interviewed today."

Lloyd wasn't laughing now. "I don't think so," he said sternly and then chuckled.

Hager put the phone down and laughed. As Lloyd made the turn onto Mt. Moriah Road, Hager noticed a homeless man standing at the corner. The man was holding a sign in front of him: *Just Plain Hungry*. He knew what the bum was up to and his blood pressure began to rise.

"Just plain lazy is all you are," he muttered.

It took Lloyd all of five minutes to find the book Martha wanted. While Hager bought two cups of coffee, Lloyd picked up Sandra Brown's *Unspeakable* from the discount rack. Apparently, Lloyd's guilt didn't result in expensive gifts like it did for most men. A light bulb turned on brightly in Hager's head. Maybe he should look for his own reparation gift.

They left the parking lot and turned onto 15-501, beating the traffic light and preventing a repeat performance of Hager's tirade directed toward the homeless man. Lucky him, because Hager was still in a mood thinking about the spat with Vanessa.

Just as the car merged onto I-40 east, Hager's cell phone rang. It was McLendon.

"How'd it go over in Durham?" the detective asked in an abnormally cheery voice.

"So-so. We have a name on Cynthia's boyfriend, but the manager at Royal lied to us. He's hiding something; I just don't know what."

"Good, where are y'all now?"

"On the way back to the office. The prelims on the lab tests are ready; I'd like to take a look at them. How'd it go with Rivers? Did he give you any trouble with the Rape kit?"

"Oh, no. In fact, he's been real cooperative. I took the liberty of talking good to the judge for him. Got him an unsecured bond so he could show me where he picked up the Mercedes. We're here now. You interested?"

"Oh, yeah. Where are you?"

"On Seventy, about a mile or so from the Five-forty loop toward Durham. We're right at the county line — on the westbound side. You'll see my Taurus."

McLendon's car was parked on the shoulder of U.S. 70 in one of the few undeveloped areas of the highway. Lloyd pulled behind the Taurus and stopped. The 'Welcome to Wake County' sign was just ahead, which meant they were in Durham County. Both McLendon and Rivers got out of the car; Hager and Lloyd met them between the two cars.

"He can't be sure exactly where the car was since it was night when he picked it up, but he thinks it's about here," McLendon said.

Hager looked down on the ground and then to the wooded area north of the road. "How can you tell exactly?" he asked Rivers.

Rivers pointed east down the road. "I remember turning around at the same median y'all did, and then I came back about this far. I believe it was before I got back across into Wake County 'cause I remember seeing the sign there."

Hager looked around again, scanning his surroundings. "Well, let's look around for something that may give us a clue."

Hager walked along the shoulder in a westerly direction. Lloyd walked east. McLendon walked in a circle near where he was standing. Rivers remained still with his arms crossed. The shoulder wasn't wide enough to accommodate the entire width of a car, and Hager wondered how much of the Mercedes was on the paved portion of the shoulder. He continued walking, looking for a sign — some piece of evidence from the car.

He heard Lloyd's voice from behind. The agent turned to see his partner bent over at the waist looking at the ground.

"Clark, I think I've got something here."

Hager hurried back. Both Rivers and McLendon had reached Lloyd and were looking at the ground as well.

"What is it?" Hager asked.

Lloyd pointed downward to the pavement. Three yellow pieces — similar to ones from a turn signal lens — were lying amid the mix of gravel and pebbles. "This could be something."

Hager knelt to the pavement. The pieces were scattered close to the white lane marker, indicating they had most likely come from the left front of the car. "Do you remember any damage to the Mercedes?"

Lloyd scratched his head and looked to McLendon for an answer. The detective shook his head. "Can't say as I do," Lloyd responded.

"Me neither," Hager said. "I really didn't look. How about you, Luther?"

Rivers wiped his sweaty forehead with his hand. "If I remember right, I backed up to the front of the car and when you do that, you sometimes hit the bumper pretty good. I guess I could've hit it hard enough to bust the signal lens."

Hager didn't respond; instead, he walked over to the Crown Vic, opened the door and reached for the cell phone. A voice answered, "Trace Evidence, Neil speaking."

"Neil, this is Clark Hager. I need you to check something for me."

"Yeah, Clark. I've got the prelim ready for the Craven case. I found some pretty interesting stuff."

"We'll have to cover that later. I need you to go out to the victim's car and check the left front and see if there's any damage. I'm looking for a broken lens or something with the amber plastic over it."

"Oh, okay. Hold on a sec. I'll have to go down to the garage." Neil said and put down the phone.

Hager was sweating again. He avoided touching the top of the car, as the metal surfaces were burning hot. Lloyd and the others remained in their positions, waiting for Hager to get his answer. About five minutes elapsed and Neil returned to the phone. He sounded out of breath.

"Clark? Yeah, there's damage to the left front turn signal lens. It's been busted and it's the amber color."

"Great, Neil. Thanks." He looked at his watch: *5:11.* "Can you stick around until we get back to the office? We should be back in about thirty to forty-five minutes."

Neil agreed to stay and Hager disconnected the phone. He gave a thumbs-up to Lloyd.

Hager rejoined the group. "Confirmed damage to the left front signal lens. This is the spot." He turned to Rivers. "You did good, Luther."

Rivers smiled and nodded. Hager eyed the woods in front of him. *Did it happen there?*

"What do you think? Would it be worth the effort to do a search of the woods from here around? We might come up with a crime scene."

McLendon shrugged his shoulders. Lloyd rubbed his scar. Rivers just stood with his hands in his pockets.

"We don't have a clue where she was killed," McLendon said. "We don't even know it happened here. This could've just been a drop-off point. I don't know."

Lloyd nodded. "I have to agree with him, Clark. It's such a remote possibility, we'd be looking for a needle in a haystack."

Hager eyed Rivers suspiciously. He didn't want a potential suspect and convicted rapist to be privy to their investigative processes.

"Luther," Hager said. "Why don't you have a seat in Detective McLendon's car while we talk."

Rivers took Hager's request as an affront and his scowl showed it.

McLendon's words seemed to calm him. "Luther, it's okay. Just go on back to the car. He's right. This is police business."

Rivers bowed his head and walked back to the car.

As soon as Rivers returned to the car, Hager continued, "Remember, Doctor Clemmons said he found some leaves in her hair. I bet they're from these woods."

"But those leaves could've come from anywhere. Finding anything in those thick woods would be almost impossible," Lloyd said.

Hager frowned. "Okay, I'll go with you for now, but we need to mark this spot in case we need to come back. Has it rained lately?"

Lloyd looked up in thought. McLendon pursed his lips.

McLendon answered, "I think it rained late Monday night. I remember getting up Tuesday morning and my grass was wet because I was gonna get my son to mow it."

Hager looked at Lloyd. "Lloyd, there's a can of spray paint in my trunk. Would you get it for me?"

"Yep," he answered, and started toward the car.

"After you drop Rivers off, meet us at the SBI lab so you can turn in that Rape kit. We can take a look at the preliminary evidence report. Will Phillips be available to come over?"

McLendon nodded. "All right. I'll get in touch with Phillips."

Holding a can of spray paint, Lloyd crouched over the pieces of plastic. Seconds later, a white mist floated from the road with the hissing sound of aerosol as Lloyd marked the spot with a *V.* He picked up the three pieces and put them in a plastic baggie.

CHAPTER
25

NEIL WAS WAITING in their office when Hager and Lloyd returned. He had a large envelope in his hand, thick with papers. A cardboard box was at his feet. The lab specialist followed the agents back to the conference room. Hager stopped at his office, hanging up his jacket, picked up the phone to check his messages. The smooth dial tone indicated there were none.

Still no call from Vanessa.

A fax lay on his desk. He put on his reading glasses. There were three pages, the top one, a cover page from BellSouth. Hager thumbed to the second page, revealing an itemized list of phone calls. The list was in descending order beginning with July 15, 1997 at 12:44 A.M. all the way back to April 1, 1997.

Hager noted the number and looked one number down to the second most recent call. He recognized the number for Capital City Towing, called at 11:53 P.M.

A noise in the lobby indicated McLendon had arrived. Hager picked up the pages, crossed the hall and followed McLendon into the conference room.

"You get in touch with Phillips?" Hager asked McLendon.

"Yeah, but he can't make it. They got a DB call. Phillips was the only de-tect in the office."

"Shit. I guess he's gonna be tied up with that for a while?"

"Probably. From what he said there's not much to go on. Some white guy was found dead in a townhouse."

"Okay, Lloyd, did you get anything back from DMV on Lyle?"

Lloyd held a sheet of paper. "Yeah, Colin Michael Lyle, white male, 4/17/64, with an address of 7431 apartment K, Latta Drive, Durham. I ran a CCH and he's got a conviction of Misdemeanor Possession of Schedule four drugs. I've got a picture from DMV being faxed over right now."

"Schedule four? Could be anabolic steroids. All right, Neil, let's see what you have."

Neil opened the envelope and removed a stack of papers, latent fingerprint cards, sketches, and photographs. He put the papers in three separate stacks, then opened the box and removed small clear plastic envelopes, a cell phone, and the black leather bag belonging to Cynthia Craven. All contents of the box either had a label or were tagged. He dispersed stapled copies of a report to each of them.

What made Neil such an asset to Hager and the rest of the SBI, and such a good forensic specialist, he was fastidiously organized—every report, every item collected was properly labeled and in discernible order.

"I'll start with the cell phone first. We were able to power it up and get the number. It's the same number as you provided for Mrs. Craven."

Hager held up the list of calls. "I've got her cell phone

calls for the past three months. The last one was made at a quarter to one, the morning of July fifteen, *after* Rivers supposedly picked up the car. What number did you get from re-call?"

He read the number. It matched the last number called on his list. The call was local—a Raleigh exchange. The number didn't sound familiar to Hager. Lloyd jotted it down on his pad. McLendon had a weird look on his face— a look of recognition.

"That number ring a bell, Brick?" Hager asked.

The detective was flipping through papers in a folder. He stopped. "Here it is. I thought I recognized that number."

"What is it?"

"It's Rivers' home number."

A smile appeared on Hager's face. "Uh-huh. Well, that makes things a little more interesting, doesn't it? I knew Rivers was lying this morning. He used that cell phone and the fucker stood right there with us on the road listening to us. He'll have some explaining to do with this."

Lloyd looked surprised. McLendon shook his head.

Hager stepped to the aluminum board and wrote three names across the top:

Phil Craven   *Luther Rivers*   *Colin Lyle*

Under Rivers' name he wrote: *cell phone call*

The agent crossed the room and wrote on the other board:

Evidence From Car

"Okay, let's run down the rest."

The specialist continued. "Okay, we found numerous fibers, hairs, and pieces of dirt from the interior of the car. All the fibers were cotton and polyester, which are typical carpet and clothing fibers. The dirt—normal dirt—but we also found traces of a strange metallic substance in the back from the floor and seat. Every item is bagged separately." He picked up one of the envelopes.

"Metallic? What type of metal?" Lloyd asked.

"They're aluminum shavings. The source I haven't an idea. But since they were found on the floor, I'd guess they came from someone's shoes."

He handed the evidence to Hager who had taken his seat again. The agent brought the envelope close to his face. The shavings were very small, a variety of colors from silver, gold, and black. Some were clumped together, reminiscent of Hager's experience with bumping into the brake lathe machine at Capital City Towing.

"This looks like the same metallic substance I had on my hands the night we found Cynthia's body," Hager said. "If so, that's another link to Rivers. I think we need to collect some of that stuff and make a comparison."

McLendon reached out for the envelope. Hager handed it to him.

"What else?" Hager asked Neil.

"The contents of the bag are as follows: a pair of women's spandex tights — size six; a spandex top; a pair of white socks; women's panties; a towel; a pair of Nike tennis shoes — size seven; a hair brush; and some make-up. There was a small bloodstain on the panties, very close to the elastic waistband. We typed it and it matched the blood found in the front seat. We can send it to DNA Analysis to confirm it, but I didn't know if you wanted to wait until you had some suspect blood to make a comparison."

Hager immediately reflected back to the cut on Rivers' hand. "Yeah, let's wait. McLendon collected some blood from the wrecker driver."

"There was also an empty water bottle and a pad lock — probably used to secure a locker of some kind. Now, for the details. We recovered a variety of hairs from the bag as well — three different ones to be exact."

"Three?" Hager asked.

"Yes, some long ones that match the victim. A short brown hair from a Caucasian, and a short black hair from a Negroid."

McLendon shot the specialist an offended look.

"What was that?" McLendon scowled.

Neil blushed and was about to explain the term he used when Hager interjected.

"Easy, Brick. He's using the anthropological term. He didn't say what you think."

McLendon leered at Hager. "Whatever. How does he know the hair's from an African-American?"

Hager shook his head and Lloyd rolled his eyes.

Neil began to explain, "It's a process of elimination, detective —"

"Trust me, Brick," Hager interrupted. "Neil here is an expert in analyzing trace evidence. When he says it's a hair from an African-American, it's a hair from an African-American. We'll also compare that hair to Rivers'."

The specialist made notes on a pad. "There were some other things we found, too," Neil said.

"Yeah, let's keep moving. It's getting late," Lloyd said.

The specialist pulled another envelope out of the box. "The key recovered from the trunk isn't an original key. It's a duplicate. I don't know if it means anything, but it might. Also, there was a compact disc player in the car, but I couldn't find any CDs. I thought that was strange."

Hager furrowed his brow. "Are you sure?"

Neil nodded. "Yeah, I even double-checked myself. No CDs inside. Whoever killed her might have taken the CDs."

"I guess it's possible. Her purse is still missing. Maybe she was ripped off as well. Lloyd, make a note to ask Phil Craven if he knew what CDs his wife had in her car. We still have the key the M.E. found inside her. It has to have something to do with who killed her."

Lloyd wrote in his pad.

"What about any prints?" McLendon asked.

Neil cleared his throat. "We collected several latents

from inside the car. We dusted the outside, but we didn't get anything other than smudges and overlaps. There are two sets of prints from the victim, from the driver's window. Others from the same window were matched from AFIS to a Luther Isaiah Arthur Rivers, black male, 10/4/52."

Hager grinned. "From the driver's window? Any other place?"

"No," Neil shook his head. "Just from the window."

"That makes sense," McLendon said to Hager. "Hell, he picked up the car. His prints are going to be there."

Neil looked confused. His eyes shifted from the three cops, back and forth, wondering about the recent exchange.

Hager shrugged his shoulders. "Just another point toward Rivers."

He stood and wrote on the board the words *prints in car* under Rivers' name, then crossed to the other board and addressed the specialist. "What else do you have, Neil?"

Neil looked into the box, and flipped through the report. "That's about it for now."

Hager scribbled terms relating to the evidence found in the car. He looked at his watch. *6:40.* "Okay, Neil. We appreciate you sticking around for this. It was a big help."

Neil stood, gathered the papers and returned the evidence to the box. He left the room.

"So, what's next?" McLendon asked.

Hager returned to his seat. "Well, first, we need to have that blood and hair compared to the evidence Rivers gave today. Then we work on Rivers. I was looking at this list and guess what number was called before Luther made his call?"

"Okay, what number?" Lloyd asked.

"The number for Capital City Towing just before midnight."

"So," McLendon snapped. "That's what time Rivers said he'd received the call about the car. What's so important

171

about that?"

"Why would a killer use his victim's cell phone to call a wrecker to pick up the car? Plus, how would he know Capital City Towing's number off-hand? I think it's Luther covering himself. The call was made to give him a reason to have picked up the car, or it was Cynthia who made the call."

"And then Rivers calls his house after he kills her? It doesn't make sense." McLendon argued.

"What about Rivers lying? He said he only went into the front of the car but his blood and hair are in the back."

"You're not positive it's Luther's blood or hair back there. That's just what you want to think!"

Watching Hager and McLendon, Lloyd's head turned like he was watching a tennis match—from side to side. Hager thought he was actually enjoying the debate.

"It's his. Who else's would it be? I don't know why you're closing your mind to Rivers being the one who did this. He's a convicted rapist for Chrissake! Now, the lies, the cell phone call, the hair and blood, and the metal shavings. What else do you need to convince you?"

McLendon jumped from his seat. "The same thing goes for your boy Phil Craven. Remember? I said the same things about him you're saying about Rivers and you expect me to be convinced just because you said it?" His eyes were bulging.

"That's different," Hager announced, almost pompous-like.

"Different? Ain't no fuckin' difference other than Rivers is black and Phil is white; that's what's different!"

Hager stood and closed the gap between himself and McLendon. He was shouting and he pointed his finger at the detective. "No! Rivers is a fuckin' sexual predator. No, correction—convicted sexual predator! And Phil Craven isn't. Rivers' blood and hair is in that car and on her fuckin' panties! Not Phil's. Those aren't Phil's prints all over that car, either! We didn't make up this shit in front of us. It's the facts. If you'd open those eyes of yours, you might be able to see what I'm talking about!"

McLendon moved forward and now they were chest to chest. Lloyd was still seated, amused at the display of testosterone.

McLendon growled, "And if you'd open that racist mind of yours, you'd see that somebody white killed that woman. You can't blame the death of every white woman on a black man, Hager!"

"Don't hand me that shit, McLendon. I could care less if Rivers was black, white, or yellow. If he's a killer, then I'm out to get him—period! I know what it is. You just can't stand to see one of your *brothers* fall for this. Well, I could give a rat's ass if you feel that way. I'm gonna get him if he's the one!"

McLendon stuck out his chest as his anger grew. Hager had a couple of inches on him, but the detective was stocky. During his last words, Hager bumped him with his chest, which McLendon apparently took as offense. In complete reflex, the detective pushed Hager back. Hager's eyes raged, and he stepped forward with his own shove and McLendon flew back.

Papers and folders scattered. The furniture clunked noisily. Seeing the debate escalate from an argument to the imminent exchange of blows, Lloyd sprang from his seat and put himself in between the two combatants.

"Goddammit, you two!" Lloyd exclaimed. "Now both of you simmer down. Damn, this case is touching off some serious personal issues with the both of you. Both of you sit down and shut up for a minute. Jesus Christ!"

McLendon and Hager stood fast and immobile; their eyes deadlocked in what probably looked like the typical "pre-fight stare" in boxing.

Lloyd tried again. "If y'all don't sit down, I'm gonna have to knock the shit outa both of you." As strong as he ever was, Lloyd's meaty hands shoved both of them away from each other and back to their neutral corners.

"Now," Lloyd began in a calm voice. "Both of y'all just sit there and listen to what I have to say about this. Y'all been runnin' off at the mouth so much, you've forgotten that we have another person to consider in this, huh?"

He eyed both of them, looking for the realization.

"Did you forget about Colin Lyle?" Lloyd asked.

Both Hager and Brick's eyebrows rose—in essence, the light bulb had turned on.

"He could've done this as easily as the other two, and y'all are standing there about to punch each other out because both of you have this big chip on your shoulders. Well, I'm here to tell ya, both of you need to get the fuck over it and concentrate on all the suspects in this case instead of your personal favorites!"

Hager was stunned. He'd seen his partner go off on people before—those blue eyes turn fiery red during one of his outbursts, but he'd never been a target of Lloyd's temper before. Maybe both he and the detective needed for Lloyd to knock some sense into them so they could solve this case. Hager looked over at McLendon. They both smiled at each other, realizing Lloyd was right.

CHAPTER

26

HAGER ARRIVED HOME at eight o'clock. The sun was setting, casting brilliant shadows from the trees in his front yard. The big orange ball was creeping its way below the horizon now centered perfectly in Hager's mirrors as he pulled in the driveway. He stopped briefly at the mailbox to gather the day's delivery of bills and junk mail.

Thankfully, the box was empty and the feeling of dread quickly turned to disappointment, seeing it absent of any correspondence.

The day had been a long one with the trip to Rocky Mount, then over to Durham, and back to the SBI office, culminating with the heated argument with McLendon. Hager was tired.

A truce had been established and Lloyd was playing the part of Henry Kissinger—the diplomat. It had taken an eye-opening event like nearly punching each other out for the two men to realize they'd fallen victim to their own personal biases, making judgments based on how they perceived the facts.

What made it even more interesting to Hager, always the eager student of human psychology, was that both he and McLendon had been given basically the same set of facts; however, they came to two different conclusions, which was manifested from their own preconceptions. In its simplest form, each of them saw this case a different way.

Eye of the Beholder.

This recent disclosure went a long way toward Hager's understanding of McLendon's conclusions and also of the detective's defensive reaction to those theories being contradicted.

At the same time, Hager had also come to terms with his own prejudices and understood they were products of many variables. If only every person could have such a revelation. The agent always believed that the biggest hindrance to improving race relations was the lack of either side's ability or willingness to understand each other. How simple a concept.

Roscoe was waiting excitedly at the door when Hager entered his home. He snorted and rubbed his nose on his master's leg, beckoning to go outside. Hager opened the back door, allowing the dog to exit. The agent turned back to the kitchen and opened the refrigerator looking for a cold Ice House. Disappointed, he recalled the past weekend's fiasco, which led to his two-day drinking binge, hence, the reason his fridge was void of beer.

Instinctively, he picked up the phone to check his messages. He heard the static dial tone that indicated a message was waiting. He hoped the call was from Vanessa. His fingers quickly punched the codes to access the system: one message.

Hager's heart thumped, hoping for a détente in this mini war with Vanessa over a new house. When he heard

Elizabeth's voice on the other end, he felt a pang in his gut like he'd been punched. His daughter didn't want anything; "just checking to see how you were doing" were her words. No questions nor did she mention Vanessa at all. She didn't even ask for him to call her back. His thirst for a beer increased.

Hager's conscience began interior conversation.

Call Vanessa. Tell her you're sorry, try to get past this obstacle.

The hardheaded portion of his psyche argued with the more rational one.

Don't crawl back! She's the one who stormed out and got so angry. She's the one who can't get over Kelly's memory.

This interior dialogue went back and forth, each side making valid arguments, but Hager's rational side — the one that desperately needed to hear her voice, feel her touch, say her name, won out. Hager reached for the phone and dialed the number. His hands trembled, Hager as nervous as a teenager asking for a first date.

One ring, two rings, three rings later, his heart calmed, realizing the machine was going to pick up. Her recorded voice came on, so soft and sweet. He cleared his throat, trying to act as normal as possible — not wanting to tell her he was hurting. He didn't realize Mr. Hardhead had sneaked up and taken over the minute Hager opened his mouth.

"Hey, it's me. Uh, I just wanted to say hello and see if we could talk about what's bothering you. I really don't understand what happened or what I did to make you so mad. I'll be home the rest of the night."

The statement came out so quickly, as smooth as if it had been rehearsed, that Hager hadn't realized exactly what he'd said until it was already said. His words were like a bullet — he could never take it back.

When he hung up, he knew he'd said the wrong thing. Disgusted with himself, he rested his arms on the counter and buried his head in shame. He felt like someone was wringing his insides like a wet towel.

VANESSA HUNG UP the phone after hearing Clark's message. Tears welled in her eyes as she sat on her couch. She couldn't believe or understand the way Clark was acting, evident of his recent words. He'd actually placed the blame on her for their argument, for wanting to make a fresh start in their new life together as husband and wife. She replayed his words in her mind.

I just wanted to say hello and see if we could talk about what's bothering you. I really don't understand what happened or what I did to make you so mad.

"What's bothering me, Clark?" she asked wiping a tear from her cheek. "If you don't know what you did, then you're more clueless than I thought."

She reached for a tissue with her left hand. Sparkling on her finger, the diamond ring that signified their commitment and promise to each other. She gazed at the gem, its brilliance radiating light, shimmering like a star. It didn't have the same effect as it had before.

A few days ago, she'd looked at the ring while watching Clark sleep, feeling the genuine warmth and love of its meaning. It was truly a treasure, a reminder of her love for the man when they were apart—a symbol of finding what she'd waited for all of her thirty-four years.

He was her Prince Charming. Tears dripped down her cheeks as Vanessa realized their fairy tale romance had come crashing down more like *Humpty Dumpty* than *Cinderella*. Where was her fairy godmother when she needed her?

CHAPTER

27

HAVING GONE TO BED early the night before, Hager arrived at the office early, carrying coffee and bagels. It was only a little after seven; Judy hadn't even come in yet, so Hager relaxed in his office, reading the paper while he ate. Judy arrived about fifteen minutes later, surprised to see her boss. Judy walked back to Hager's office and stood at the door. Hager took a sip of coffee, looked up, seeing Judy wearing a concerned look.

"You're here early, Clark. Is there something wrong?"

Hager chuckled. "Why does there have to be anything wrong if I'm here early?" he asked, trying to shield the pain he was feeling over Vanessa. "I just went to bed early; that's all."

Her mouth turned up for a warm smile, but her intuition wasn't convinced, and her eyes showed it. "There doesn't have to be. You just don't look the same, Clark."

Judy's eyes narrowed. "I'm not sure what it is. You seem...distracted? Are you sure you're okay?"

Her voice was sweet and motherly, her concern sincere and intuition right on the money, but Hager wasn't going to admit it—certainly not to her.

"I've been tired the last few days. We worked late on the Craven case last night and I haven't been sleeping well of late."

She smiled. "I thought you said you went to bed early last night?"

"Oh, uh, I did. Uh, what I meant was that we worked late and when I got home, I went straight to bed."

The lobby door opened, and Judy walked toward the front. A familiar jingling and whistling indicated Lloyd had arrived. Hager heard muffled voices, Lloyd and Judy's. With Judy out of the way, not asking all the questions, Hager returned to the paper and a small headline located in a sidebar about halfway down the page:

CAR STOLEN DURING CARJACKING RECOVERED

Early this morning, Raleigh police recovered a car stolen from a Triangle woman. The 1994 Pontiac Grand Prix, taken during an apparent carjacking Friday evening, was found by officers in the 6100 block of Western Avenue after they received a call about a suspicious vehicle.

The car was taken after the woman discovered a man hiding in the back seat of her car as she left the parking lot of Crabtree Valley Mall. She escaped unharmed, but later said the man, a white male in his early 30's, threatened her with a knife.

The case is still under investigation and detectives are urging anyone with information about this case to call Crimestoppers.

Lloyd walked in just as Hager finished the article.

"Man, here I thought I was late when I pulled in and saw your car already here. You sick or something?" He pulled up a chair.

Eye of the Beholder

Hager handed him the bag and coffee cup. "No," he snapped. "What's the big deal with me being early? Both of you act like I'm always late or something."

"Just an observation, Clark. Now don't get sassy with me. You still steamed because of McLendon last night?"

"No, that's water under the bridge. I think we needed that blow-up. You know, clear the air a little. It kinda put things in a better perspective for me. Opened my mind up a little."

Lloyd chewed his bagel. "Speaking of that, what's the game plan for today?"

"I called McLendon this morning, and he's gonna run down some other information on Cynthia's credit cards and then give our friend Luther a call again. I looked at her cell phone bill last night. The last call made before the calls to the tow company and to Luther's house was made at seven fifteen, to this number."

With a pen, Hager pointed to the number and then down the page. "And here again, earlier at four twenty-one. I called it and no one answered, but the machine picked up. It was one of those generic voice box greetings. You know, like it came from inside a toilet. I checked the phone book and the reverse look-up, but the number's apparently unlisted. I thought I'd call the phone company this morning and see who it belongs to."

"I was thinking about those last two calls," Lloyd said, tapping his finger on the paper. "One thing we didn't think about…what if she and Rivers had something going on?"

Hager made a disgusted face. "Cynthia and Luther Rivers? No way."

"I know it's a long shot, but she called the tow company and then his house. It's possible they had something going on, they fought and he killed her."

Hager shook his head. "Nah, I see what you're talking about, but Cynthia and Rivers?" He shook his head again. "She wasn't the type—"

"I thought you said your mind had opened up a little."

Hager chuckled. "I said 'a little' not that much. No, it

181

didn't happen that way. You didn't know Cynthia; she wouldn't do something like that."

Lloyd shrugged his shoulders. "Well, how do you explain it, then?"

"Either Rivers or her killer made the call. My bet's on Rivers. You know that."

"Why would Rivers call his own company? That would be pretty stupid."

"No one said Rivers was a rocket scientist, Lloyd," Hager said with a laugh.

"Yeah, I guess you're right. What else did you find?"

Hager looked at the phone bill again. He pointed to a number. "In between the calls to that number, she called this one at six-thirty. It's the number for Nikko's Restaurant."

"The nice Italian place downtown?"

"Yep. I think whoever this number belongs to, she met them at Nikko's the same night she was killed, and I'm thinking it's our personal trainer."

"Oh, that reminds me." Lloyd got up, crossed the hall to his office and returned seconds later with a piece of paper in his hand. He offered it to Hager. "Does he look familiar?"

The paper was a faxed copy of the driver's license photo of Colin Lyle. The agent eyed it carefully. "Hmm, it could be the same guy. It's hard to tell with just the face."

"What did you look at? His ass!" Lloyd asked jokingly.

"Fuck you, Lloyd." He handed him the paper. "We need to get up with this guy today and see if it was him."

"We got an address. Why don't we find out?" Lloyd asked rising from the chair.

"All right. Let me call the phone company and see about the number. Do you know where Latta Drive is?"

Lloyd shook his head. "No, but I've got a map. I'll find it while you make the call."

Hager's suspicion was confirmed when his contact at the

phone company informed him that the number came back to Colin Lyle of the address on Latta Drive. With map in hand, Lloyd navigated while his partner drove.

"Catherine the Beautiful was right about Latta Drive being close to Royal Fitness. From the map, it's just around the corner," Lloyd said.

A half hour later, they passed the Royal Fitness Center. Hager eyed the business as he drove. "Don't forget we need to have another word of prayer with Mr. Yates after we confirm some things from Lyle."

Lloyd nodded. "The turn should be coming up soon." He pointed out the windshield. "There it is. Latta Drive."

Hager turned the Crown Vic looking for the 7400 block. They continued for several blocks and an apartment complex appeared on his left. Hager stopped the car in the middle of the road.

"I think this is it," Hager said and turned into the parking lot.

The numbers *7461* were displayed prominently on the front of the brick building. Hager pulled into a vacant space, noticing a blue Chevrolet Lumina and a silver Ford Taurus, both with blue lights on their dashboards — unmarked police cars. The cars were empty.

Normally, there would be nothing unusual about the presence of detectives in an apartment complex. But this group of apartments was located in a fairly nice neighborhood. Hager gestured to his partner in the direction of the cars. As they approached the building, Hager grew uneasy. What were the chances the two agents would cross paths with local cops?

"Which apartment is it?" Hager asked.

"It's 'K'." Lloyd looked up. "It should be upstairs."

They both climbed a narrow staircase fixture outside the building. When they reached the door, Lloyd pulled out the mystery key. The key slid into the lock as easy as it did at Catherine Molderson's house. It didn't move when Lloyd tried to turn it.

Suddenly, the door opened almost pulling Lloyd's hand with it; the key remained in the door. Hager jumped back against the wall, his hand reaching for his pistol. Lloyd crouched and moved to his right and away from the door.

Hager peered around the edge of the doorframe. Standing at the door was a man wearing a tie and holding a gun by his side, a badge clipped to his belt, *Detective — Durham Police Department*.

Hager swore to himself when he recognized Detective John Ventura from Durham PD's Crimes Against Persons Unit.

"Well, look what the cat dragged in, Larry?" the detective smiled, calling to the room behind him. "I didn't think they'd call in the dynamic duo this soon." Ventura offered his hand to Hager.

"How's it going, Ace? What are you doing here?" Hager asked.

"I guess I should be asking you the same question. What were you trying to do? Pick the lock?" He stepped back allowing the two agents to enter. They both stepped inside. Ventura shook Lloyd's hand.

"No, we were trying to see if this key worked," Hager said.

"Hmm," Ventura said. He tried the key. "It doesn't work here." He pulled the key and handed it to Hager. "I guess I'll find out why in a minute. So, what brings you boys out?"

"We're looking for a guy named Colin Lyle. Is he still…" Hager's mouth remained open as Detective Larry Phillips emerged from a room. "Shit," he whispered.

"Hey, Clark. What are you doing here? Did I hear you say Colin Lyle?" Phillips asked.

"You did. I thought you caught a homicide yesterday?"

"Yep. Just looking through my vic's apartment to see if I can get an idea who offed him. That's my vic — Colin Lyle."

Hager's gut sunk to his feet. "Shit. I don't believe this."

"You're shittin' me?" Lloyd said.

"What?" Phillips asked. "What's the problem?"

Wearing a look of confusion, Ventura's head moved from Hager to Phillips.

"Colin Lyle's dead?" Hager asked, hoping it wasn't true.

"As a doornail. Y'all still working on that case with McLendon, right? What's he got to do with it?"

Hager shook his head. "He *was* a suspect. Damn!"

CHAPTER
28

STILL INSIDE Lyle's apartment, Larry Phillips gave the agents what he knew at this point. The former Colin Lyle was found strangled in a town house in River Glen, an upscale development in Raleigh near the Cameron Village shopping center. Whoever killed him used a thin nylon garrote, which almost severed his head.

At present, Phillips was trying to find out why Lyle was inside the luxury condo. The detective was checking real estate records to find the owner, but since the home was recently purchased, the paperwork had not yet been filed with the Register of Deeds.

From what Phillips had observed, clothes and property apparently belonging to the young personal trainer were found in the luxuriously furnished town home now stained bloody from a grotesque murder.

"Did you check to see if he had a key to the condo?"

Hager asked, now sitting on the couch in Lyle's apartment.

"Yeah, there was a single key in his pants pocket when we found him. It fit the front door," Phillips answered.

"What led to the cops being called?" Lloyd asked, seated at a dining table taking notes.

Phillips shook his head. "People are so stupid sometimes. The day before yesterday, a neighbor who lives next door to the townhouse said she saw two men knocking on the door. Apparently, they were allowed inside and then a few minutes later, she heard a commotion that sounded like a fight going on. She said a minute or two later, the noise stopped and then she saw the same two guys leave."

"Did she call the police then?" Hager asked.

Phillips answered with a facetious chuckle. "Hell, no. She didn't think about it until the next day. Shit, two goons come to a house, you hear a fight next door, then the same two goons leave in a hurry, and you don't think anything's wrong?" He shook his head in disgust. "I wanted to slap her for being so stupid, but it turns out, Lyle couldn't have been saved anyway."

"Did she give you a description of the two goons?" Lloyd asked.

Phillips nodded. "White males, one about forty, the other younger. She said they were driving a big black car. She didn't know what make."

Hager shook his head. "Figures. You been able to find anything useful here?"

"Nothing much, just some check stubs from his employer. He worked at a place just down the street called Royal Fitness."

Hager looked around the room. A copy of the *News & Observer* was lying on the coffee table in front of him. The edition was from the previous Friday and the page was folded, revealing the article detailing Cynthia Craven's death.

"Look at this. It's Friday's paper and it's turned to the article about Cynthia's body being found."

"You think it means anything?" Phillips asked.

"I'm not sure. If he killed her, he could've just been confirming her death." Hager stood. "But, if he didn't, this article has just told him that his girlfriend's been killed and if I'm screwing someone else's wife and she turns up dead in her own car, I'm thinking I may be next, so I get the hell outa here."

"Or he might be scared the cops are gonna come looking for him," Lloyd added.

Hager nodded in agreement. "Larry, this is your case so will you call over to the M.E.'s office and get Lyle's blood sent over to our lab? And see if they can get a few hairs from him, too. We're doing a DNA comparison from the victim and crime scene and I want his put in there, too." His temper was boiling. "Damnit! Just when I thought we were getting a step closer, this had to happen. We find the guy who was probably the last person to see Cynthia Craven alive and now he's dead. Lloyd, let's go talk to Yates again."

The two agents argued as they walked to the car. Hager wanted to go to Royal Fitness and arrest Lou Yates for Obstruction of Justice. Lloyd disagreed and tried to convince his angry partner that it would be useless.

"What would it accomplish, Clark?" Lloyd asked.

"He lied to us and if he hadn't we may have been able to talk to Lyle before this happened. He's gonna learn not to fuck with me." Hager was sweating and his face was red.

"Clark, we only talked to Yates yesterday. Lyle was already dead. Remember, he was killed on Sunday according to what the lady said. Yates lying to us didn't kill Lyle." Hager took off his jacket and placed it in the back seat.

"Well—" Hager began.

"Plus, what else would we learn that we don't already

know? We know who Lyle is. We know he worked at Royal Fitness. We know he and Cynthia were having an affair. What else can Yates tell us? Phillips is gonna have to talk to him anyway."

Hager hesitated, trying to come up with a logical reason for snatching up Yates and throwing him in jail. A few seconds of pondering and still the profiler couldn't answer. Only visions of the smug Lou Yates spilling his bullshit story the other day flashed in the agent's mind. He smiled, realizing his partner's wisdom.

Lloyd wasn't finished, however. "What we still don't know is…who killed her and also we don't know if it was Lyle who had dinner with her the night she was killed."

Hager sighed. "You sure are right a lot this week. Did Martha knock some sense into you or something?"

Lloyd smiled and fingered his scar. "It's wisdom of the ages, partner. Sometimes you just have to turn on the switch."

Hager chuckled. They both took their seats in the car. Hager started the engine and looked over at his partner who was loading up his mouth with Red Man.

"Thanks for setting me straight, Lloyd—last night and today. I guess I'm not working on all cylinders. I don't know what I would do without you."

"Ah, you're not gonna kiss me or anything, are you?"

Lloyd had said it with such a straight face, Hager burst out laughing. "Not with that shit in your mouth!" Hager shouted.

CHAPTER

29

HIS FINGERS GLIDED across the books' spines on the shelves. The helpful librarian had told him the True Crime books were in this section, but he hadn't found what he was looking for. He continued his search, his eyes peeled for the numbers he remembered.

A musty odor permeated the walls of the old library building. Hundreds of books stood lifelessly on shelves, waiting for someone to open their dusty covers and flip through the yellowed pages.

He heard whispering voices two aisles over. A lady about forty sat at a table scanning the contents of an old volume; she looked up nervously at him, then quickly averted her eyes downward. He smiled as he felt the aura of her anxiety — the smell of fear.

As he walked slowly down the aisle, the numbers passed by in ticker-tape fashion, his eyes focused on the search.

He stopped quickly when he'd found his mark. He started at the top shelf, using his index finger to scan the different titles. When he located a book he wanted, he pulled it off and tucked it under his arm.

Satisfied with his selection, he approached the check-out, plopping four books on the counter. The woman smiled in a motherly way as she took his library card. She picked up the books and scanned them on the computer, stopping at the last one. She flipped open the cover, then turned it over, examining the spine. A frown appeared on her face. She sniffled and gave him a peculiar gaze, staring a little too long for his liking.

"Is there a problem?" the man asked.

The woman shook her head and smiled in an insincere way. "Oh, no. There's no problem, sir. I've just never seen anyone take that much of an interest in such a subject." She shivered. "Serial killers. Why would anyone want to read about them?"

He smiled at her and looked directly into her eyes, holding it longer than she liked, since she looked away nervously. "You ever hear the saying 'The evil that men do'?"

She nodded, still avoiding eye contact.

"Well, I'd just like to know how I stack up. You know?" He snorted a chuckle.

She tried to laugh with him, but didn't fare well. She cleared her throat and her hands were trembling as she gave him his card. "Yes...well. I hope you enjoy them, sir. They're due back August sixteenth."

"Yes, I will," he said, sliding his library card back in his wallet. "Yes, I will."

When he left the library, he caught the same woman watching him leave. She looked away again when his eyes met hers. He grinned, knowing he'd scared the living shit out of her.

CHAPTER
30

MCLENDON CALLED on their way over to Nikkos Restaurant. Hager told him that Colin Lyle was dead—and coincidentally, the dead body Phillips was working on. Of course, they speculated whether the trainer's death was related to their case.

The reason the detective had called was that he'd received Cynthia's credit card statements and confirmed a $94.00 charge to her Visa card on Monday, July 14 at Nikkos. Two other charges appeared on the same card on July 14: a $132.50 charge from Victoria's Secret at Crabtree Valley Mall, and a $2.00 charge from Mid-Town Locksmiths in Raleigh.

"Locksmith?" Hager asked. "What the hell can a locksmith do for two dollars?"

"I don't know," McLendon answered. "Maybe she got locked out of her car and needed a key made."

"For only two dollars? No, they charge a helluva lot more than that." He sat thinking.

Lloyd offered, "Maybe she got a key copied. Locksmiths make duplicate keys, don't they?"

The proverbial light went on in Hager's head. The smile on his face revealed the discovery and Lloyd had realized the same thing.

In harmonious unison, both agents declared, "The key!"

Hager told McLendon what they had figured out. Hager's heart thumped at the excitement of adding another piece to the puzzle.

Before disconnecting, McLendon said he'd checked with the airlines to get a name and address for a passenger on the same flight as Phil, but they had no one by the first name of Yvette on the list. Apparently, she'd given Phil a false name as well. The detective said he'd called the Sheraton and the clerk who checked Phil in would be working the next day; he was going to interview her about the mystery woman.

Hager recognized an enthusiasm in McLendon's voice—something he'd never heard from the detective. It was amazing what a little 'clearing the air' will do to a relationship. Hager could finally see a light at the end of the tunnel.

Nikkos was a fine Italian restaurant, decorated with original Mediterranean art, exquisite lighting, and the most elegant table settings in the area. Besides the charming atmosphere and ambience, Nikkos' menu was first rate.

Hager had taken Vanessa there a few months back, the memory a painful one in light of recent events. But Hager ignored his pain—shelved it away, allowing his eagerness to pursue this case to take precedence. His repression was a natural defense mechanism. When he was working, Hager would put aside his personal problems in his quest for the truth.

The Maître d´ sat the two agents at a table. It was a little after eleven so they decided to have lunch. Hager scanned the menu and found the lunch version of a wonderful dish he'd tasted during his previous visit. The seafood pasta dish had provided the inspiration for what he was going to prepare for the *Cooking Light* contest. It was called Seafood Mediterranean.

The meal consisted of a plate of penne pasta covered with generous helpings of fat scrumptious sea scallops, jumbo shrimp, crab, lobster, and mussels, their shells acting as garnish, all mixed with a wonderful marinara. Hager had already decided to put a personal touch to this recipe and add fresh portobello mushrooms and proscuitto. His mouth watered in remembrance and his pallet called for a glass of their best Chianti or Merlot to accompany the meal. Unfortunately, they still had the rest of the day ahead of them.

Lloyd ordered the lunch lasagna. After ordering, Hager asked the waiter to speak to the manager. The manager, a woman named Isabel, came over minutes later. Hager showed her his badge and asked if she could help find a record of a credit card purchase on July 14. The agent also asked for the name of the waiter who served those customers.

Their plates were piping hot and accompanied by a basket of warm rolls. They both dug in and Hager ate slowly, savoring the taste of his meal. The seafood blended perfectly with the marinara. He wished he'd ordered the dinner portion. Lloyd practically inhaled his lasagna, saying it was the best he'd ever tasted. Both of them utilized the remainder of the rolls to sponge up leftover sauce on their plates.

Just as they finished, Isabel returned with a few slips of paper, which looked like a restaurant tab with a receipt stapled to the front. She handed them to Hager. The writing was in restaurant code, but at the bottom was a computerized printout of the details of the order. There were two guests; they had dinner and a bottle of Chianti totaling $73.69 with Cynthia leaving a twenty-dollar tip.

"Does it say who the waiter is, ma'am?" Hager asked.

She nodded. "Yes, Dominic was their waiter. He's here now if you'd like to speak to him."

"Great."

Isabel snapped her finger at their waiter. "Dominic," she beckoned. The waiter could have been Andy Garcia's twin with a boyish grin. When he came over, she said something in Italian Hager didn't understand. She showed him the ticket and said the words *signor* and *signora,* which Hager understood — man and woman. He nodded his head and looked at the bill, shrugging his shoulders. Isabel faced the agents.

"Dominic said he doesn't remember this. I hope you understand, he serves hundreds of people a week."

Dominic remained behind his boss. He raised his hands gesturing, "I don't know."

"Doesn't he speak English?" Lloyd asked.

"Only a little. But since he's worked here, he understands more than he can speak."

"Oh," Hager said. "Well, we have pictures of the two people we're asking about. Does he think he could recognize them?"

She turned and asked him in Italian, he shrugged his shoulders again and nodded. Lloyd handed the pictures of Cynthia and Lyle to Isabel. They both looked at the photos. Dominic pointed to one photo, nodding and saying something in Italian. Isabel looked at this picture and nodded as well, the Italian exchange continuing to the frustration of both Hager and Lloyd. He tapped his finger on the bill and said, *Sí.*

"He remembers the woman. She's been in here several times. She was here with a man the other night and he believes it was this man, but he isn't sure."

Isabel handed the pictures back to Hager. "Does he remember anything about them?" Hager asked. "You know, did anything unusual happen?"

Again, she acted as interpreter. He shook his head quickly, saying, "No." She was about to deliver the message when he touched her arm like he'd remembered something. He went on in Italian for about thirty seconds, using vivid hand gestures commonly associated with Italian people. Her pointed at the table and the only word he caught was *chiave*. She nodded and returned to Hager.

"Dominic said he remembers the man and woman arguing at the table. The man got angry and left the restaurant leaving the woman to pay the bill. Dominic said she'd left a key on the table and he had to catch her in the parking lot to give it back to her."

Hager and Lloyd met eyes, both raising their eyebrows. "Did he see the man after that?" Hager asked.

Isabel turned, but Dominic had apparently understood the question. He shook his head.

Hager sat deeply in thought for a few seconds, not wanting to forget something important to ask.

"Should we show him the key we have?" Lloyd asked. "You know, to see if it looks like the same one."

Hager shrugged his shoulders. "I guess it couldn't hurt, but remember Phillips said they found a key on Lyle when they found his body. Plus, how is he going to tell one key from the other?"

Lloyd reached into his pocket and pulled out the key. It was still in the plastic bag; he passed it to Dominic. The waiter examined the key. He returned it to Lloyd and spoke in Italian. Isabel translated.

"He said it looks like the same key."

Hager thanked Isabel and Dominic for their help. When the agent picked up the bill, Isabel held out her hand. "I will take care of that. It is our treat today."

Hager tried to refuse, but the woman insisted and not wanting to offend her generosity, he humbly accepted. Since the meal was paid for, both Lloyd and Hager left generous tips, putting a big smile on the face of Dominic.

In the car Hager sat down and glanced at his watch. It was five after twelve. He said to Lloyd, "We have almost two hours until the service for Cynthia. You know, I hadn't thought of it before, but that key might be to that townhouse. You think?"

Lloyd stuffed tobacco in his mouth again and nodded. "I was thinking the very same thing, partner, but if they found Lyle's key on him, whose key is it? Cynthia's?"

Hager shook his head. "Nah, I don't think she would've stuffed the key inside herself."

Lloyd grinned.

"Don't answer that, Lloyd."

"Did she have the bucks to afford one of those luxury condos?"

"Oh, yeah, and then some."

"If it's hers, that makes it kinda hinky for old Phil."

"Hinky?"

"Yeah, she buys a new house and gives the key to her boy toy. It only means one thing; she was going to leave Phil."

"Or, it could've been *his* house and *he* gave *her* a key. And that's what they argued about. Lyle demanded she leave Phil, and she refused. He gets pissed, storms out of the restaurant, and waits for her in the parking lot where he jumps her. He drags her into the car and you know what happens after that."

"He drags her into her own car?"

"Maybe, I don't know. Maybe he followed her. I'm just speculating."

"You know where the house is?"

"Yep," Hager said and pushed the accelerator.

CHAPTER
31

AS A COURTESY, Hager called Larry Phillips while they were on the way to the town house. The house may have been still secured and the agents didn't want to infringe on Raleigh PD's crime scene without being accompanied by one of their detectives. Phillips agreed to meet them in ten minutes.

Phillips' Taurus was parked in the driveway when Hager's Crown Vic arrived. The Raleigh detective got out to meet them. His clothes were disheveled, tie undone, and his sleeves rolled up.

"I appreciate you meeting us, Larry," Hager said. "I didn't know if the scene was still secured or not."

"Nah, we released it as soon as the lab got finished. We locked it up as well as we could. The officers had to go through a window to get in, so the door's still intact."

"Well, let's see if we're right, Lloyd."

Lloyd dug in his pocket, and out came the key. He held it up in the air like he was trying to attain some divine intervention. Hager and Phillips followed closely behind Lloyd as he bent over, inserting the key. He turned his wrist and the key moved to the right and a click indicated the lock was disengaged. The door fell open. Lloyd turned around. "Well, that's it."

Phillips entered first with the two agents following. Although the town home had just recently been purchased, it was completely carpeted and furnished.

Phillips started, "Let me take you through what we think happened."

He walked toward the wall and pointed to a sunken in spot about head high in the sheet rock. "We think a struggle of some sort started here at the wall. Probably due to someone's head hitting it."

He directed his hand to the floor at some blood spots in the carpet. "This trail leads all the way back to the back bedroom," he said walking toward the back.

Lloyd and Hager followed the detective, noting small bloodstains. A room opened to the left at the end of the hall. Phillips motioned for them to step in.

He pointed down to the carpet—stained crimson in contrast to the beige color. "This is where we found him. He was face down; his head was in the corner as you can see by the blood. Since it all started in the living room, we think the killer jumped him from behind, and Lyle took off, trying to get away. Hell, as big as he was, the killer probably rode him all the way with the wire around his neck. Hence, the blood trail to here."

Hager looked around the room. A king-sized bed with a lot of frilly stuff, lace and flowers. New polished dressers and curtains adorned the room. This was the bedroom of a woman.

"Did you find anything here?" Hager asked.

"Nope," Phillips said. "There were a couple of empty soft drink cans, Subway wrappers, and a Chinese food box in the trash. The fridge was empty, nothing in the dressers or closets. Whoever bought this place hadn't moved in yet."

"What about a phone?" Lloyd asked. "Is there one here?"

"There's a cordless in the kitchen, but it's not turned on."

Hager sighed and then looked at his watch — *1:13.* "Once you find out who owns this place, give me a call, Larry. I think it's going to belong to Cynthia Craven, but you never know. Come on, Lloyd, we have a funeral to attend."

NANCY LAPINSKI read the written report — a requisite of her job as Special Agent-in-Charge of the newly named Molecular Genetics Unit. Formerly called DNA Analysis, Lapinski's unit was responsible for examination and analysis of evidence in crimes where DNA analysis is a vital component in identifying the perpetrator. Specialists in the unit also made entries of DNA into the SBI's DNA database, which, similar to an AFIS computer, contained DNA evidence in solved and unsolved crimes. In essence, what AFIS does to fingerprints, the database does to DNA.

She heard a tapping on the door to her office. It was Specialist Paul Koen. Nancy looked up and motioned for Paul to enter. He was carrying some papers and wore an excited look on his face.

"What can I do for you, Paul?"

"I just finished the analysis on the Craven case. I think you're going to be surprised at what I found." He gave her the report.

Nancy took the papers and sighed. Her eyes scanned the first page, a list of the evidence submitted. She flipped to the second page, then to the third. The fourth page had words printed in bold letters across the top: DNA DATABASE HIT

She turned a page back and read again. She looked up

over her glasses. "Are you sure this is correct?"

He nodded and smiled again in an exuberant way.

"I'd better call Clark."

CYNTHIA'S SERVICE was reserved for family and close friends, so only about twenty-five people were in attendance — one being Catherine Molderson. Lloyd had seen fit to choose their seats beside the vivacious woman. When he saw her weeping, Lloyd put his arm around her in consolation. He was in heaven.

After the service and while Lloyd played his role as Mr. Placate, Hager visited with Phil and members of his departed wife's family. Phil seemed solemn, but didn't waiver in his emotions. He seemed to have gotten past his animosity toward the agent, greeting him with a grateful smile. Phil excused himself and pulled Hager to one side, away from Cynthia's family.

"What's the word on the investigation?" Phil muttered.

Hager didn't want to give him any vital information so he decided to keep it brief. After all, the victim's family had just as much right to be kept abreast in an investigation — even if Phil were still a suspect.

"We're making progress. Some of the pieces are coming together, but it's still too early to say."

Phil's face turned sour. "That sounds like something you'd tell the press, Clark. Don't give me riddles! I want facts. You found the wrecker driver. What did he say?"

Hager took a deep breath. He perceived that Phil was sensing a disavowal of some sort when it came to his involvement in the case.

"We're still looking at him. He said a man called saying he was Cynthia's husband and asked for him to pick up her car by the side of the road."

"Me? Where did he say it was?"

"He actually showed us and it appears it was there because we found part of her turn signal lens on the ground. We're still checking out his story. There are some other angles that I don't feel comfortable discussing right now."

"It involves me, doesn't it?" Phil asked with a defensive look.

Hager shook his head. "No, not really, Phil." He turned to look for his partner, who was comforting Mrs. Molderson. "Look, I really can't get into this. There's just not enough concrete information at this point. I'll let you know something soon. I promise."

"What about the DNA tests? Have they come back yet?"

"Not yet, but it should be soon. My cases get the highest priority at the lab."

The agent noticed Phil hadn't mentioned the mystery woman from the plane. Maybe she wasn't a mystery at all. "Have you heard from Yvette, yet?"

Phil seemed caught off guard with the question. "Yvette? Oh, yeah, her. No. Why? Did you find out who she is?"

"Not yet," Hager said, deciding not to tell Phil what the detective had discovered. "McLendon's checking with the airlines to get a name and address. He hasn't heard anything back yet."

Phil rubbed his eyes and in a whiny voice, he said, "I just want this to be over, Clark. I need to get on with my life. I can't do anything while this black cloud still hangs over my head."

Hager thought Phil would break down right then. He continued to rub his eyes. When he removed his hands, he looked Hager dead in the eye. "You know?"

Hager kept his gaze for a second or two; his friend's eyes exhibited a diabolical haze—wickedness. His voice was different than the previous whining; the tone was normal in a calculating way.

Hager nodded in agreement. "Yeah, I know."

He turned. "Keep me posted, Clark," he said and walked away.

Lloyd left Catherine's side and joined Hager at the front door.

"Did you make her feel better?" Hager asked his partner.

Lloyd grinned. "I sure hope so. Man, she smells so good."

Hager laughed. "You're gonna run out of guilt presents to give Martha if you keep this up."

Before leaving the chapel, they both turned and spotted Phil talking with Catherine. She wore the appropriate black dress, black hose, shoes, and purse. Everything but her lipstick and nails were black, both of which were an auburn color like her hair. She gave him a reassuring hug that seemed to last longer than normal for acquaintances.

"Lucky fucker," Lloyd whispered seeing the embrace. "I give all the comfort, and he gets all the reward."

"Those are the breaks, partner."

The heat was miserable as they walked to the car. Just as Hager unlocked the door, his pager vibrated.

Vanessa, maybe?

He sat down, fired up the engine, and pulled the pager from his belt. It was Judy at the office with the tag— *911* beside it.

"It's Clark. What's up, Judy?"

"Nancy Lapinski from Molecular Genetics called. She needs to see you right away—about the Craven case."

"The DNA tests must be done. Did she say anything else?"

"No, that's it. Are you coming right now?"

"We're just leaving Cynthia's funeral. We should be there in about twenty minutes."

"Okay, I'll call Nancy and tell her."

Hager disconnected and dialed the number for McLendon.

"Who are you calling?" Lloyd asked.

"McLendon. The DNA tests are done and Nancy wants to meet with us right away. I figured he should be there, too."

"Must be something good."

Hager brought the phone to his ear. "I just hope it doesn't have Phil's name all over it."

McLendon answered in a brusque voice.

"McLendon? It's Hager. The DNA tests are done and the agent-in-charge wants to meet with us at the SBI lab. You wanna join us?"

"Damn right, I do. What time?"

"As soon as you can get there. We're about twenty minutes away. Just meet us at our office."

"You got it. Hey, I got some news for you. One of the property guys showed me a pawn report and guess whose name showed up on it?"

"Not Phil Craven, I hope."

"Nope. Luther Rivers. You remember your trace evidence guy said that they didn't find any CDs in her car? Well, just happens that Luther pawned ten CDs on July fifteen."

"Very interesting."

"Yes, it is. I called the pawnshop to see what kind of discs they were and they told me they were Shania Twain, Alan Jackson, Celine Dion, Frank Sinatra, and others like that. I don't think Luther's the type to listen to that, do you?"

"Not likely. Did you get in touch with him? We still need to ask him about that phone call and now this."

"Yeah, I called over to his house and left a message with his wife. He's supposed to be back in a little bit. You know he got fired from the towing place?"

"I figured as much. Rivers will have to wait until after we meet. I'll see you later."

"Hey, what did you find out from the Italian place?"

"Oh, I almost forgot to tell you. Yeah, it was the personal trainer guy—same guy I saw her with a few months ago. The waiter remembered them. He said they argued and he stormed out of the restaurant."

"Really?"

"That's not the best part. The waiter had to chase her down in the parking lot because she left a key on the table."

"A key? You think?"

"Yep, we think it's the same one. And we finally found out where the key belongs. It opened the front door of the same townhouse where Lyle was found. We think the townhouse belonged to Cynthia."

"Hmm. That wouldn't look good for Lyle if he were still alive.

"No, it wouldn't. Brick, you may be able to clear this case without charging a soul. See you in a few minutes," Hager said and disconnected the phone.

CHAPTER

32

THE CONFERENCE ROOM rarely looked so crowded. Including the investigative trio, six people were seated around the rectangular table; Nancy Lapinski and Paul Koen from the lab and Bob Maxwell joined the group.

"All right, Nancy," Hager started. "We're all here. Let's hear what you have."

She nudged Paul who picked up a sheaf of papers, stood and distributed stapled copies of the report.

"Paul's passing out the DNA analysis reports and also the information on the database hit we got," Nancy said.

"Database hit?" Maxwell asked.

"Yes, we got a hit back on one of the suspects' DNA."

"Which one?" Hager asked.

"Luther Rivers," Nancy said. "The hit came back to a Rape case in Louisburg back in 1987."

Hager resisted the urge to smile, to rub this new information in McLendon's face. After all, they'd overcome their animosity towards each other, but to Hager, it had become a competition of sort.

"What happened in that case?" Hager asked.

"A copy of the SBI Lab Request form is attached. I think it's the last page."

Everyone flipped to the last page. Hager scanned the synopsis of the case. A young black woman was attacked in the parking lot of a night club. Although the crime appeared to be a date rape, the woman wasn't able to identify her attacker.

"There wasn't a H.I.T.S. packet filed because we didn't have it back then. Apparently there was a Rape kit submitted at the time and the DNA was entered into our database."

H.I.T.S., the acronym for Homicide Investigation Tracking System, was instituted early in the 1990's. The system established a statewide database documenting violent crimes in response to the ever-increasing problem with multi-jurisdictional crime.

Law enforcement agencies are encouraged to submit information packets on their cases to increase the possibility of apprehending criminals who move from city to city, town to town.

"How do you usually handle notifying the investigating agency when something like this happens?" Hager asked.

"Usually with a phone call. We haven't had a case we were actually involved with before, so I didn't know if a call to them would create a problem."

Maxwell spoke, "Call them right away, Nancy. We'll need a complete report and talk with the investigating detective."

Nancy nodded and Hager added, "Nancy, I'll give them a call. I think since we're looking at this guy, too, it'll be good to tell them what we're working on."

Nancy nodded again.

"What about the rest of the tests?" Hager asked.

She flipped back to the first page. "Okay, the items submitted from the crime scene are marked by the letter 'C', the known items have a 'V' for victim and 'S' for suspect, depending on whom it came from."

The group followed along in their reports. She looked up to see if everyone was on the same page and when their eyes met hers, she was ready to proceed.

"First, we'll start with the blood. All the blood in the car is from suspect number two, Luther Rivers."

Hager slowly nodded his head, holding back a joyous grin. He looked over at McLendon, who kept his head down focusing on the reports. Lloyd's eyes caught Hager's attention. His eyebrows were raised above the rim of his glasses.

"The Caucasian hairs we found that didn't belong to the victim are still not identified. The Negroid hairs also belong to Luther Rivers. Those were matched from the samples collected in the suspect kit. Now for the semen," she said, turning the page.

This was the big moment — the final nail in Luther Rivers' coffin. Knowing the answer to this question, Hager didn't bother looking at the printed results; instead, he watched the group for their reactions.

Nancy continued after her dramatic pause, "And this is what baffled me and Paul."

Hearing the word 'baffled' caused Hager to look down at the report. Next to the item referencing the semen collected from the victim during the autopsy, NO MATCHES.

"The semen wasn't from Rivers?" Hager asked, dumbfounded.

Both Paul and Nancy shook their heads.

"No," Nancy said. "Once we matched the blood and the hair to Rivers, we figured it was a done deal that the semen would belong to him, too." She shrugged her shoulders. "But it's not."

Now McLendon gazed over at Hager with a triumphant beam.

"What about the unknown hair?" Lloyd asked. "The

Caucasian one."

Nancy looked over to Paul. "What about it?" Paul asked.

"Does it match the semen?"

Paul was about to answer Lloyd's question when McLendon spoke up. "What about the husband?"

Paul looked confused and lowered his head to the report. Hager scanned the paper and recognized Phil's identifier. "Suspect number one. That's Phil Craven, the victim's husband."

"No, he didn't match either the hair or the semen."

Maxwell said, "Lloyd asked about the unknown hair. Did it match the semen?"

Paul shook his head. "You didn't request for us to compare that. You only asked for us to compare the semen with the known samples from the Rape suspect kit."

Maxwell frowned. "It should have been done with or without it having been requested, Paul."

Nancy blushed at her subordinate's mistake but like any good supervisor, she came to his defense.

"Bob, we usually only do the analyses that are requested on the form. Paul didn't know enough about this case to decide on his own, to make a comparison that wasn't requested. They should've made the request clearer."

Maxwell looked over to Hager for an answer. He didn't know what to say. He'd completed the lab request form himself so the mistake fell back on him.

The agent raised his hands in surrender. "I guess I forgot to put it on there. It's my fault."

The assistant director frowned again—this time, it was directed at his star agent. Lloyd kept his head down. Maxwell stood, leaving the report on the table. He didn't look pleased.

"Well, let's get it done, people. If that semen came from the person not yet identified, it looks like you've been wasting your time looking at Rivers and the husband."

As his boss chastised the group, Hager remembered the evidence from Colin Lyle's autopsy. "Nancy, Larry Phillips from Raleigh PD should've brought over a suspect kit from a Colin Lyle. I don't know if he's gotten it here yet, but we'll need to make that suspect number three."

"Who's this Lyle?" Maxwell asked.

Hager explained Lyle's involvement while Paul left the room to see if Phillips had delivered the kit.

"You think Lyle's death is related somehow?" Maxwell asked Hager.

"I'm not sure. It could be, but from the way he was killed, I'd say it was done by a pro."

Hager suddenly remembered the autopsy report on Cynthia's death. Single stab wound — military-style knife. He recalled Dr. Clemmons' words: *Whoever did this knew exactly what he was doing.*

He thought about Phil's involvement — or lack thereof in the results. Was it proof of his innocence? Or was it a clever coincidence that meant he'd arranged for the two deaths to happen?

CHAPTER

33

HAGER DROVE HOME with a sinking feeling in his stomach. He didn't know whether it was from the embarrassment of his earlier mistake with the lab request form or from his most recent revelation that his old friend Phil may have been the killer he was hunting.

For a brief minute, Hager had almost banked on Luther Rivers being that man. Most of the evidence pointed to him — some more than a coincidence — with the blood, hair, and his irrational behavior after the body's discovery.

What else could anyone think? The evidence coupled with his record; Rivers was the most likely perpetrator, but all of it was circumstantial.

Looking at the case from a different point of view — with another pair of eyes, perhaps — every piece of evidence did as much to prove Rivers' innocence as it did to substantiate his guilt.

His story made sense: the call from someone claiming to be Cynthia's husband about the car; Rivers' natural curiosity of the contents – the CDs he ended up stealing; and later, his reaction to finding that he'd transported a dead woman in the trunk. With a record like his, who wouldn't run?

On the other hand, Phil's involvement could be described similarly – aside from his lack of criminal record. He'd lied to Hager and McLendon concerning his whereabouts, the display of behavior associated more with the guilty than a grief-stricken husband, and most damaging, the likelihood that Phil discovered his wife was having an affair with a man who was now dead – his DNA Hager believed would match the semen recovered from Cynthia's body.

Colin Lyle was just as likely a suspect, but it all seemed too perfect – too complete – like it had been arranged to happen that way.

As Hager pondered the identity of the killer, he also silently wondered why he'd been so blind to these facts in front of him. The uncharacteristic tunnel vision, the bad moods, and the mistake he'd made on the lab report. It was no wonder the case had taken such a turn. He was just going through the motions.

Usually able to detach his personal issues from his work, Hager had found himself distracted over his lingering ordeal with Vanessa. A pain squeezed through his shoulders – the distraction he was carrying – *Vanessa*.

Hager arrived at his house without remembering anything about the trip. Trapped in his thoughts, the agent's own navigational system guided his car home safely. As the car slowly rolled down the driveway, Hager made a decision to put an end to the distraction, to achieve a capitulation of sorts. No more childish games of waiting for her to call and apologize. The phone loomed near, which caused Hager to push the accelerator.

The sinking feeling suddenly disappeared as Hager

quickly pulled himself from his car. Almost bouncing, he strolled through the doorway past Roscoe, directly to the phone. He put his jacket on the counter, briefcase on the floor, and picked up the receiver. With dialing finger poised to punch the numbers, his eyes caught the glimmer of an object atop a white envelope on his dining table. At second glance, Hager recognized the shiny object, a diamond ring.

Hager's heart sank, mired in quicksand with no escape. He stood frozen in place, his eyes focused on the horror on the table. Inscribed on the front of the envelope in her unmistakable handwriting was his name. Except for his heart, which was thumping, Hager's entire body moved in slow motion.

The receiver made a loud cracking sound when it hit the floor; the dial tone had changed to the annoying clamor of high-pitched tones. Roscoe barked softly, following with a growl, sensing his master's stress. Hager's eyes remained fixed on the ring—the symbol of his undying love, his utter devotion—so callously abandoned by the object of his affection. Tears welled in his eyes as he slowly collapsed to the floor.

The cold nose of Roscoe stirred Hager's sleep thirty minutes later. The phone still screeched its deafening tones on the floor. His head still hazy, he rose to his knees; managing a handhold on the counter edge, he pulled himself to his feet. He looked to the table; the horror remained.

Although he already knew the contents of the envelope, it beckoned his attention. Seconds later, he picked up the ring, cold without the heat of her finger, and held it in the palm of his hand. Vanessa's key to his house fell from the envelope, clunking on the table. The paper unfolded slowly, dread mounting in his chest. His hands trembled as he read:

Dear Clark,
This is the hardest decision I've ever had to make. I'm
so confused right now. I don't know what to do. You've
hurt me deeply and I can't seem to figure out why. Why
do we have to go through all of this again? All I wanted
was for us to be happy together. A new life—a beauti-
ful new house. Just like I thought you wanted. I have to
go away for a while and I'm not sure if I'm coming back.
I love you, Clark—with all my heart and soul, but I just
can't do this again.
   I'll love you always,
   Vanessa

As he read the note, his grip tightened on the ring, piercing his skin. Gently, he reached out and touched the paper,
caressing the words as if they were her face. He slowly
shook his head in disbelief and closed his eyes. The pain in
his chest seemed cavernous, so deep it felt empty, leaving
only his guts tied tightly into knots.

He read the note again, not believing his eyes. The words
conveyed the same message, but Hager wanted to gain a
sense of hope from them; instead, all he read were words
of hopelessness and surrender. The pain wrenched his chest
again. He wanted the pain to go away—to be restored to a
healthy bliss somehow—to feel connected to her again. He
stood, the letter and ring still in his hand, and stepped into
the kitchen. He opened the refrigerator door for the pain
relief he needed.

With his fridge being void of the painkiller known as Ice
House, Hager found himself behind the wheel of his Explorer with an unknown destination. He'd never been much
of a drinker and wasn't familiar with any place where he
could just be alone with his pain. So, he set out to find such
a place. Again, he drove a course he didn't know and

wouldn't remember, but when he stopped, he was parked in front of Jillian's.

Sitting at the bar, he quickly downed three shots of Wild Turkey, chasing them with Ice House longnecks. It didn't take long for the alcohol to kick in. The alcohol hadn't affected the throbbing pain of loss in his heart but did a paralyzing number on his mind as the shots and beers continued to flow. The pool tables on the far side of the place caught the agent's impaired attention. Maybe the violent breaking of balls would drive out some of his pain.

Before walking over, he ordered another round and tottered over to a young guy behind a counter where he asked for a table. As he stood, his brain was flowing like the Pacific—back and forth like waves crashing down in his forehead. The first break of the balls was successfully achieved, much to his impression of himself, and he proceeded to pound the balls around the table in no discernible sense.

The striking felt good—a release of violent tension consequential of his own behavior. He leaned over the table, eyeing his next shot when her voice came from behind. Startled, he jumped and looked over his shoulder.

"Of all the people I thought to find in this place, you were the last," she said in her sexy British accent. The voice belonged to Catherine Molderson.

Hager didn't know what to say. He smiled wanting to return to his shot, but he couldn't take his eyes off her. She was still wearing black, but had changed from the elegant frock of the funeral to a cocktail dress with a hem well above her knees. Her green eyes were blazing at him. She tilted her head and smiled devilishly.

"Well, won't you at least say 'hello,' Agent Hager?" she asked taking a step closer.

Hager closed his eyes; once she came closer, he smelled that wonderful perfume Lloyd had raved about earlier today—he thought it would be great for Vanessa. But Vanessa was gone, and the pain of her leaving still groaned within his body.

Vanessa was gone.

"Hello, Agent Hager," he responded, trying to be witty. He was able to peel his eyes away from her long legs and to the shot at hand.

She giggled like a schoolgirl. "Oh, I was right about you. You *do* have a sense of humor!"

The cue ball cracked against the fifteen, slamming it into the corner pocket.

"And an accomplished billiard man as well," she added.

Proud of his shot, he stood by the table now clear except for the white ball, and admired his work. He turned and faced her. She held a gin and tonic.

"Not really," he said. "I think the more I have to drink, the better I get in this game."

Her wild green eyes peered inquisitively around him. "Would you care for another?" The smile produced a gleaming set of pearly whites. "My treat."

Catherine turned and grabbed the attention of a nearby waitress. Hager's eyes started at the back of her dress, cut mid-way down, her tanned skin unblemished from her bouts of worshipping the sun. Then his eyes traveled from her back, down to the hem to her long legs with well-formed calves; a pair of black high-heeled sandals covered her pedicured feet, her toes painted the same rose color as her fingers.

"What are you drinking?" she asked catching Hager's examination. She gaped in a flattered way.

Hager quickly brought his eyes to hers, realizing he'd been caught in mid-glance.

"Ice House, please."

He turned toward the table and collected the balls for the next game. With the balls racked, he picked up the cue and worked his way around the table to its opposite side. Catherine had taken a seat on a stool next to a small table, apparently eager to watch him play.

"Are you celebrating or just out here for some fun?"

she asked stirring her new drink with her finger.

Hager chuckled. "Celebrating? No, not that."

She removed her finger from the glass and brought it to her mouth, her tongue reached out for it, her eyes glued to his as the digit disappeared in her mouth. "Hmm," she purred. "I do love the taste of gin." She ended her sentence with a seductive grin. "What then? Agent Hager. What brings you out all alone tonight?"

As much as he needed to talk to someone about his current problem, Catherine Molderson was certainly not the right person to hear about it. He decided to play it cool.

"Oh, I'm just blowing off some steam, I guess. I've been working on Cynthia's case pretty hard lately. I guess I just needed a break. And you can call me Clark. What about you? You don't seem to be the Jillian's type."

The ogle again. She removed his beer from the table and held it out for him to take. "I believe this is yours," she said coming to her feet. Their fingers touched lightly as if she'd meant for it to happen. Her touch was electric and didn't go unnoticed.

"Oh, I was supposed to meet a friend down the street, but they didn't show up, so I thought I would drop in and have a drink."

"Thanks for the beer," Hager said. He took a swig. "The next one's on me."

She held up her glass in toast. "Cheers." Again, she fired those sexy green eyes at him.

Her perfume wafted in the air as she brushed by him, scanning the pool table. Walking slowly beside the table, her fingers glided along the smooth mauve colored felt, careful her matching nails didn't rip the cloth. She stopped at the opposite end and turned to face him, obviously establishing her opponent.

"Would you care for some friendly competition?"

Catherine suggested Nine-ball. Five games and five drinks later, Hager emerged as champion. Catherine's pool skills were above average; seeing this, Hager felt himself fortunate to have beaten her. Each game was fiercely competitive, Catherine displaying a fiery Irish streak and a few choice words to boot.

They laughed and teased one another, both taking the opportunities to make casual contact as they exchanged cues or places at the table — each time, the touch sustained longer than before. Hager's mind buzzed, and for the moment, the pain had faded. She was seducing him — he was letting her. This was trouble.

It was all Hager could do to walk without bumping into a table. He returned the balls to the same young guy, who despite his youth appreciated Catherine's striking beauty as she stood waiting. As they headed for the door, she hooked her arm in his; a minute later, he felt the thick summer air on his face.

Strolling like lovers, they traveled the sidewalk along a row of cars until Hager reached his Explorer. He stopped, reaching in his pocket for the keys.

A concerned look appeared on her face. "I don't think we should be driving, Clark. Let's catch a taxi."

He swayed on his feet, trying to decide what to do. He could call Lloyd and have his partner drive him home. He strained to keep his eyes open. She touched his arm and looked into his eyes.

He didn't see her move forward, but in a second her lips were firmly planted on his, her tongue in gentle discovery. His eyes closed unconsciously as she pulled him closer, but all he could do was fall backward into his car, taking her with him. With the solid support of his car, their mouths became a hot and wet game of exploration.

Kissing her felt as natural as drinking a glass of water — soft and moist without any effort. Her opulent perfume now a steadfast memory in his head — the scent surging through his nostrils, making him hungrier for more.

They made out like teenagers against the car for the better part of fifteen minutes, each taking short breaks to tease the sensitive skin on their throats, nibble on ears, and grind their pelvises together like kindling making a fire.

When they finally separated, both their faces glistened with sweat. He wiped a flowing drop from his cheek; she caught his wet hand and brought it to her lips; her tongue emerged and she tasted his sweaty fingers. Hager thought he'd faint.

"We can go to the Marriott downtown. Why don't you ring for a taxi?" she murmured.

Hager almost fell opening the door to the Explorer. He sat down and reached for his cell phone. His body was surging with sexual excitement. On the seat lay the diamond ring and Vanessa's letter. The pain hit him again.

"Oh, shit," he said to himself. "What the hell am I doing?"

He gazed out the window at Catherine. She was facing the side-view mirror, ruffling her hair back into place. The diamond called to him from the seat. A flicker of light reflected on the marquis cut, casting pointed daggers of light like the crown of a queen.

The ring only served as an inanimate reminder of his loss—his catastrophic vise-grip of obstinacy. It was simply a bauble without the essence of her hand keeping it alive—the ring symbolic of never-ending love and desire.

Looking at Catherine, he realized he was severing the significance of the ring—betraying the indestructible faith it represented. He unfolded the letter again and read her last words: *I'll love you always—Vanessa.*

"But Vanessa is gone," he said to himself, his eyes focused on Catherine's legs. *Damn!*

She smiled curiously at him. "Clark, dear. Is anything wrong?"

Vanessa is gone...

...I'll love you always—Vanessa.

Catherine's gorgeous body...

...the diamond ring.
Catherine...
...Vanessa.
Wild green eyes...soft sensuous lips...her perfume...

He returned her smile and held up his cell phone. With a trembling finger, he dialed the number. His decision was made.

CHAPTER
34

THE AIR WAS THICK and soupy as he made his way down Glenwood Avenue. Despite the stagnant breeze and heavy humidity, he felt refreshed and alive—powerful. Cars with bright lights cruised past him as he walked in the grass. The cicadas sang their dreary song until he approached in his dew soaked tennis shoes. This time he'd been successful in his mission and he felt good about it.

The knife in the waist of his jeans felt heavy and cool against the skin of his back. He reached around and reverently massaged the knife, readjusting its position in his pants. It felt good to have it there. It gave him the power, the strength he needed to survive.

His breath came in pants as he thought about how easy the knife pierced through the outer layer of skin, deep into the flesh with only a slight thrust and the grunting moan of pain from his target.

Succumbing to the will of his blade never came slowly. An accurately placed stab caused a quick collapse, their eyes rolling back in their heads, the desperate gasps of air while they bled to death. He'd hold them in his arms, stroking their hair, seeing life escape their bodies. Watching them die was the biggest rush of them all.

He'd sit patiently, hovering over their mouths, waiting for their souls to abandon the soon rotting flesh. The last gasp of breath was when the soul left the body.

He wanted to catch that breath—the soul of his victims—so he could feel their pain, their fear. Once the eyes did somersaults, the last life-sustaining breath would come and he'd clamp his lips over their mouths in his kiss of death.

Suddenly, he stopped walking; he closed his eyes and his lungs filled with air remembering his latest victim's face. He smiled and opened his eyes. Across the span of pavement that made up the parking lot of Crabtree Valley Mall, he scanned the darkness, now void of cars—a peaceful silence that only hours before was a bustling mass of moving metal and people oblivious to the danger lurking near.

Like an animal, he sniffed the air and smelled the opulence of perfume. Maybe he was reflecting again. The sound of a door closing grabbed his attention. He looked to his left. Movement caught his eye.

A small bright light—a flashlight, and two headlights, the beams broken as someone crossed their paths. He squatted behind a tree, peering in the distance at the Barnes & Noble parking lot.

A man in uniform—his light blue shirt vivid in the darkness and silhouetted in the headlights—was standing at the rear of a car. It was *his* car and the man was a cop.

Clutching the tree and now standing, he remained still watching the show. From his position at the rear, the cop was probably running the license plate. It was part of the routine to see if the car was stolen. He laughed to himself.

If only that cop knew what he was investigating.

A minute later, he watched the cop return to the front seat of the police car. The interior light illuminated his face. He was young—a youthful soul so vibrant and alive. He'd be a nice addition to his collection. It would be easy. He was only about a hundred feet away and separating them, only a black sheet of darkness. Seated in his car, partially blinded by the dome light above, he would never see or hear it coming.

The killer's heart began to thump, the sweat beading on his brow in anticipation of the hunt. The soul called to him, heart beating faster, pounding in his chest, his breaths rapid, tongue swelling dry. He clenched his hand around the knife. An awesome strength emanated from the handle to his fingers, down his arm, through his chest and into his heart.

He took a step forward and he froze. The car turned dark, the face no longer visible. Seconds later, he heard a thumping of the transmission and the car rolled slowly backwards. He took a deep breath to calm his nerves. God had saved the officer, preserved his soul.

For now.

Once the patrol car left the area, he slowly meandered forward. An epiphany struck him in the head.

"Son of Sam," he said to himself. "That's how they got him. His car."

He remembered the book *Confessions of Son of Sam* he'd read about serial killer David Berkowitz. How police were able to link him to one of the killings in New York because his car had been given a parking ticket the same night. It was such a stupid mistake—a mistake this killer wouldn't make.

CHAPTER

35

THE PHONE RANG on the other end of the line. *One ring...two rings...three rings...four rings...*before someone answered. Hager paused, reconsidering his decision. He looked Catherine directly in the eyes and smiled. A frustrated voice on the phone beckoned and Hager finally spoke into the phone.

"Lloyd? It's Clark. I need you to come get me. I can't drive." He knew Lloyd would detect his partner's slurred words and realize he needed help.

"Where are you?" Lloyd asked.

Hager told him and Lloyd promised to be there within an hour. He hung up, relieved he'd made the right decision. His feet touched the sidewalk. He locked and closed the door. Catherine was still smiling when he turned around. She nuzzled close to his chest and licked her lips.

"Are they coming?" she asked.

Eye of the Beholder

In all his 46 years, Hager never believed he would have been in this position—unfortunate in one aspect, fortunate in another—of rejecting one of the most beautiful women he'd ever laid eyes on. He remembered an old saying, "Don't let one night of pleasure ruin your whole life."

A smile came to his face as he said to himself, "I'm not sure I'd even make it to the room before I passed out anyway, much less have sex with Catherine, who would have surely been quite a ride."

"Clark?" she purred. "Well, are they coming?"

He offered his cell phone to her. A deep breath later he told her, "I can't do this, Catherine." Her smile disappeared and a glimmer of anger touched her eyes. "I'm sorry," Hager continued. "Look. You're a very beautiful woman, and under different circumstances, I'd be falling all over myself to be with you. But..."

She rolled her eyes. Hager didn't think Catherine had ever been turned down before. He was probably right.

"What the hell happened to you?" she asked angrily, stomping her foot. "Who did you ring then?"

"I called Lloyd. He's coming to take me home. I suggest you call a cab," he said extending the phone to her again. "I think you've had too much to drink."

"Me? A cab—by myself?" she shook her head. "Surely, you're joking?"

She decided to give it another try. The seductive grin appeared and her eyes glowed and she moved closer touching chest to chest. Her breath was hot and sweet.

"Forget about your partner, Clark. Once we get into bed, you'll forget all about what's bothering you. I promise. You won't be able to think about anything else but the two of us."

The heat was rising in Hager's gut again. Catherine was so beguiling—so tempting—so...near. She wrapped her arms around him, putting her head against his pounding chest; she began to whimper.

In soft tones she pleaded, "Please, Clark. Make love to

me tonight. Please, I need someone. I need you."

He could feel himself melting in the summer night's heat. His knees started to buckle — so did his resolve. Holding this warm, beautiful, sensual woman, who smelled so delicious, who wanted him desperately — the hypnotic trance was powerful to resist.

The image of the diamond ring — lonely without its rightful owner — appeared in his head. He'd left it in the front seat along with Vanessa's letter. He shook with a start and gently pushed Catherine away, reaching into his pocket for the keys.

"Clark! What are doing?" she asked, crying real tears.

He handed her the phone. "Call a cab." He reached into the Explorer, his fingers touching the ring. Coming out of the car, he grabbed the letter and put them both in his pocket.

"Clark, why do I have to call a taxi? Why can't Lloyd give me a lift home then?"

Watching her lips move was mesmerizing. He chuckled thinking of Catherine in between he and Lloyd in the front seat of his truck. He envisioned her hands groping through the darkness and between his legs, torturing him like Vanessa would do when she was especially amorous. He shook his head.

"I don't think it would be such a good idea, Catherine. Just call a cab, please."

Catherine apparently got the hint, sighed, and with a hint of aggravation, she punched in the number for information. She didn't speak to him after she'd called the cab.

Thirty minutes later, the taxi pulled to the curb. She sauntered over to the car, turned with a dreamy smile that told him to "eat shit and die," then blew him a kiss and took her seat.

Lloyd's truck pulled directly behind the cab and stopped. The cab pulled away and Catherine didn't even look over at him as she went by. He laughed, knowing he'd never get the chance to have her again.

Lloyd opened the door with an excited smile. "Was that who I think it was?"

Hager nodded. "One and the same, partner."

"Holy shit, Clark!" Lloyd did a series of double takes. "You didn't?"

Hager could only manage to shake his head slowly.

"Oh," he said, disappointed. A proud smile appeared on his face. He slapped Hager's shoulder. "Good boy. You did the right thing. Now tell me what the hell is going on?"

Lloyd pulled forward and during the twenty minutes it took to get to Cary, Hager showed him Vanessa's ring, read the letter, and related how Catherine Molderson happened along.

"This ain't good, partner," Lloyd declared. "We need to find Miss Vanessa and talk some sense into her. But first, it's bedtime for you."

CHAPTER
36

TWO TABLETS DROPPED into the glass. The fizzing began as the Alka-Seltzer blended with the water. Hager watched the effervescent bubbles rise in the air. Although he'd taken the requisite dose of Advil and a glass of water before bed, his head still throbbed, feeling as thick as a pumpkin. He looked at the clock on his office wall— *8:30 A.M.*

Lloyd's whistling started just as the lobby door closed. The jingling from his pockets grew nearer as he approached, stopping at his office door. Hager rose from his chair, checking on the status of the headache remedy, and walked out the door and down the hall. He leaned against the doorframe. Lloyd was hanging up his jacket.

"Mornin'," Hager said.

Lloyd looked up surprised. "Hey, I wasn't expecting you in so early this morning. How are you feeling?"

Hager smiled and shook his head. "Not too bad. I have some Alka-Seltzer brewing on my desk. That usually does a good job on a hangover."

"You had breakfast yet?" Lloyd asked, taking a seat.

"Not yet. My stomach doesn't feel so hot."

"You wanna grab something on the way to get your truck?"

"Truck?" Hager asked forgetting he'd left his Explorer in front of Jillian's. "Oh, yeah. Sure, that sounds good. You can follow me back to the house after that."

"Okay."

Lloyd gave his partner a quizzical look. He could see the pain in Hager's eyes. After a moment of silence, Lloyd asked the question. "Well, have you heard anything from her?"

Hager's eyes narrowed, the frown on his face, his response. He clenched his jaw and shook his head and whispered, "No."

Lloyd sighed in frustration. "Damn. Did you call her?"

Hager nodded. "Yeah, first thing this morning. All I got was her machine. I didn't know what to say so I didn't leave a message."

"Did you try Liz?"

"Nah, I don't think she'd know anything."

"Try her anyway. She and Vanessa are close. Liz may know more than you think. If that doesn't work, we'll drive over to RTP and see if she's at work."

"I already called over there. I spoke to one of the other doctors and he said she's taken a leave of absence."

"Shit. Did he say for how long?"

"No, just that the leave was indefinite. I have a feeling she's gone up to Pennsylvania to see her mother."

"What does she normally do when y'all have a tiff?"

Hager shrugged. "I don't know. We've never had a fight like this. I guess it was a long time coming."

Judy appeared from behind Hager. "Clark, Nancy Lapinski's on the phone for you."

"The DNA tests must be done. Good."

Lloyd picked up the phone and accessed the line. He handed the receiver to Hager who had taken a chair next to the desk.

"Okay, Nancy. I hope you have something good for me."

Nancy chuckled. "This case gets better every day. You're gonna love this." Her tone was sarcastic.

"Uh-oh. Come on, Nancy. I don't need any more surprises with this thing." Hager took a deep breath, waiting for the news.

"Well, it's pretty much a surprise to me. We got the suspect kit from Phillips on the dead guy Lyle. His semen is present in the evidence collected from the victim."

Hager exhaled. "Okay. This is good. It's what we expected. What else?"

She sighed. "This is the part you're not going to like. We rechecked the samples recovered from the victim, vaginal, anal, and mouth swabs, and residue found on her thigh. Most of the semen was collected from her pubic hair and that was what we'd originally tested and that's what came back to Lyle. We used that part because it was the sample with the greatest volume. We probably should've done this before, but I guess we thought it wasn't likely that there'd be two different samples."

"Oh, shit!" Hager swore, causing Lloyd raise his eyebrows. "Two different samples? You've got to be kidding me."

Nancy sighed again, her frustration evident. "No, I'm not kidding and I'll tell you before you ask. We did comparisons of the two samples to all the suspects and neither of them matched so that means..."

"We have someone else to consider. I can't believe this." He looked at Lloyd who shook his head and chuckled in disbelief.

Hager continued, "Damnit, Nancy! Why didn't you all check all the samples from the autopsy? Isn't that standard procedure?"

"Clark, our protocol states that we have to type match each sample and we did. They're the same blood type—O positive and we stopped there thinking it was from the same person."

Hager returned to the seat and rubbed his throbbing temples. "This is great. Just when we probably had a definite link to Lyle being the killer, we find this shit. Damnit."

Hager hung up the phone and stood. "Goddammit, my head hurts," he snapped and walked out of the office.

Lloyd followed and Hager picked up the glass from his desk. He downed the liquid in a couple of gulps, not tasting the chalky painkiller. Lloyd pulled off his glasses and began to clean them with a handkerchief.

"So, we're back at square one, then?" Lloyd suggested.

Hager took his chair, licking his lips wishing the Alka-Seltzer would work quickly.

"I guess. I can't believe this. I need to call Maxwell."

"What about Louisburg?"

Hager closed his eyes. He'd forgotten to notify the small town's police department of the DNA hit.

"Shit, Lloyd. Can you call them for me? I need to get in touch with McLendon, too, so he can have Rivers picked up."

"No problem, partner. I'll make my call and you make yours; then we'll get something to eat. I'm starving."

An hour later, a turkey and Swiss bagel sandwich chased with a cup of hazelnut coffee in his belly, Hager began to feel normal again.

The temperature had already risen to a humid eighty-five degrees with a forecast of highs near ninety-five. The car's interior felt like an oven when Hager sat in the passenger seat. Lloyd cranked the engine and flipped the A.C. to high, warm air turning quickly to cool.

Hager's pager vibrated as soon as Lloyd turned up the volume of country music on the radio. McLendon's phone number appeared on the display. Hager turned on his cell phone and dialed the number.

"McLendon," the detective answered.

"Hey, it's Hager. Any word on Rivers?"

"No, a detective from Louisburg is coming up later. We'll pick him up then. I just found out something pretty interesting."

"Oh, shit. I don't need any more surprises after this morning's discovery."

"What now?"

Hager told the detective about the DNA test results and that they were probably looking for another suspect.

"Hell, I don't know if that makes what I found out more important or less."

"Do I want to hear this?"

"I think so. I just left the Sheraton. I talked to the clerk who checked in Phil Craven the other day."

"Did she remember anything about Phil?"

"No, she didn't remember him, but she did remember the woman he was with."

Finally some good news for Phil. "She did? Any lead on who she is?"

McLendon chuckled. "Not really, but she gave us a description."

"Anything to go on?"

"Nothing other than she was a redhead with a British accent."

Hager took a deep breath and his heart thumped. *Catherine.*

"Really? Nothing else?"

"One more thing. She said she'd seen the woman before, a couple of times actually. You know what I think? I think your boy Phil was lying again. The woman he met with is from here and he doesn't want us to know about her."

So much for good news for Phil. His friend had lied again. Hager shook his head. Phil and Catherine? He quickly reminisced to the night before—her kisses were addictive. He snapped back into reality.

An affair between Phil and Catherine was another co-incidence too strong to overlook. Their involvement with each other amounted to a classic motive for Cynthia's murder.

He remembered seeing them together at Cynthia's funeral service. The looks exchanged and the sustained hug were all part of the subtle communication of secret lovers.

This case looked too easy to pin on Colin Lyle. The evidence was stacking up on the trainer as of late, which caused the agent to wonder if it had been prearranged.

Being Cynthia's friend and also aware of her affair with Lyle, Catherine was perfect for the role of co-conspirator. She was probably aware of Cynthia's activities, thus a link where Phil could wait for the right opportunity to put their plan into action. A plan? Hager thought how well thought out the plan for Cynthia's murder had been.

It was Catherine's suggestion that Cynthia increase the value of her life insurance, which would provide a substantial money pool when she and Phil finally decided to be together.

Currently living off her rich husband, Catherine probably wouldn't have anything to fall back on if she left; therefore, she would need to be with someone who could provide for her extravagant tastes.

The thought of Catherine's husband flashed through Hager's mind. Maybe he was next—maybe he was already dead, but the body not yet discovered. It would be perfect—a perfect murder.

But Hager had failed to see it. Although it was right in front of his face the entire time, he was looking at Phil through the eyes of a friend rather than the eyes of an investigator.

That was why Phil had contacted the agent in the first

place. He'd thought of this before—that Phil had attached himself to the agent to divert the eye of suspicion. After all, Phil wouldn't be so dumb as to kill his wife and then contact the state's best expert in murder investigations to help him. It was Phil's own rationalization and it made sense. His plan to get away with killing his wife began with contacting Hager.

Almost convinced his friend was responsible for Cynthia Craven's death, Hager still felt a nagging sensation in his stomach. One piece of evidence still didn't make sense—the unknown semen. Presumably, Phil had followed Cynthia and Lyle from the restaurant, probably to the new townhouse where the two lovers had sex, consequently providing Lyle's semen. Then, the two parted ways and Phil waited for Cynthia to get home where he killed her, then drove her car to the highway and called Rivers.

But how would someone else's semen be present on Cynthia's body? What was the link if it happened that way?

"You still there?" McLendon asked after the several moments of silence.

"Yeah," Hager responded. "I was just thinking about who this woman might be."

"You know who she is?"

"I'm not sure. Let me make a call and I'll let you know."

Hager disconnected the phone and relayed to Lloyd what the detective had told him.

"Catherine and Phil," Lloyd said softly with a nod. "Yeah, it adds up to a lot of what we've been seeing."

"Yep, but now I'm worried about Mr. Molderson. He may be next on the hit list. With him gone, she and Phil can live happily ever after."

"Yeah, it's like a fairy tale—a regular *Beauty and the Beast.*"

CHAPTER

37

THE OFFICER STOOD in his living room holding a clipboard. After each question, the cop eyed him suspiciously waiting for a response, looking for a hint of deception from his *victim*. Clad in the standard uniform, the young patrolman — according to the nametag, his name was Richards — scribbled with his pen on a piece of paper attached to the clipboard.

"Okay, Mr. Cherner," the cop started. "Now let me read this back to you to make sure I've got the whole story." He tapped the pen on the paper. "You said you parked your car in your driveway last night around eleven P.M. and you woke up this morning and it was gone. You think you may have left the car unlocked, but you still have the keys, right?"

Cherner nodded with a smile holding up a huge ring with a large array of keys. He jiggled his hand, causing the keys to jingle like sleigh bells.

Officer Richards rolled his eyes and continued. "You didn't hear anything last night while you were asleep? Dogs barking—car doors slamming?"

Cherner shook his head. "No, sir. I sleep like a baby most of the time—especially last night." He placed the key ring down on the table.

"Why last night?"

Cherner grinned proudly. "I wasn't alone if you know what I mean." He ended with a childish snicker.

An almost silent groan came from the officer this time. "Oh, okay. Do you keep a spare key in the car? Just in case you get locked out."

He picked up the key ring again and fingered through the mass of metal. There had to have been at least fifty keys all together. He stopped and held up a silver key.

"This is the only spare I have, Officer. I haven't had much use for it, you know because of where I work."

Richards nodded. "Right, the locksmith shop. I guess if you got locked out, it wouldn't take you long to get back in, would it?"

Cherner smiled and shook his head.

"Well, Mr. Cherner. I think I have everything we need to file a report. I'll run your name through DMV to get the license plate number, and then your car will be entered into NCIC as stolen. If someone comes across it, we'll let you know."

Richards clicked his pen closed and turned toward the door. "Oh, Officer. Do you think this has anything to do with those car thefts around the mall recently?"

"Excuse me?" Richards answered.

"Yeah, at Crabtree Valley Mall. The man who's taking the cars from there."

Richards rolled his eyes and smiled at the naïve man. "No, I don't think so, Mr. Cherner. Those cases are car-jackings and so far, the only victims we've had have been women. I don't think your car has anything to do with that."

"Oh, thank goodness. I wouldn't want to know that my car had been stolen by someone like that. Do you have any idea who's doing these car-jerkings?" Cherner asked playing the role of dummy perfectly.

The officer started to laugh, but held it after a single grunt. He held his lips together and managed a smile usually reserved for children.

"It's a car-*jacking*, sir. And no, we don't have any leads I know of yet." Richards reached into his shirt pocket and removed a business card. He wrote on it and then handed it to Cherner. "Here's my card. On the back is your case report number. You'll need that to get a copy of the report for your insurance company. We'll call you if your car turns up." Richards pushed open the door and walked out to his patrol car.

Cherner stood at the open door and waved at the officer when he pulled away. His mouth turned into a diabolical grin once the car was out of sight. Acting like an imbecile, he was able to eke out some important information not released to the public about his activities. Cops had such huge egos; they dropped their logical guards when they dealt with people of lower intelligence.

HE KEPT HIS EYES peeled at the door, waiting for Phil to emerge. Hager and Lloyd were parked in the employees' parking lot of Bayer Industries poised to confront Phil Craven with the latest news in this bizarre case. Previously, Hager's effort consisted of finding the killer of his friend's wife while silently ignoring the plausibility that Phil could be the person he was looking for.

This effort Hager concluded had manifested itself akin to the state's top agent working in the capacity of a private investigator when, instead, he still worked for the State of North Carolina.

Phil had lured his college buddy into this case; for what

reason, he didn't know, but since Hager had found himself mired deeply in a personal conflict where he was forced to make reason of his own prejudices, he'd decided to take his investigative efforts to a different level.

For the past week he'd done as much work trying to prove that Phil didn't kill his wife as he had looking for a killer. Now, he would grab the proverbial bull by the horns and get to the bottom of the mess it had become.

Anger had fueled Hager's energy since they'd discovered Phil's recent indiscretion. He wasn't going to be nice to his old friend. This was business — serious business. He worked the muscles in his jaw, his eyes focused on the door as they waited for Phil to appear.

Hager glanced at the car's digital clock — *12:02.* Just then, Lloyd tapped his shoulder as Phil emerged into the heat. Adrenaline kicked into overdrive as he watched Phil approach his Navigator. The car eased forward as Lloyd took his foot off the brake, turning in Phil's direction. Unaware he was being followed, Phil strolled through the rows of cars, his jacket propped over his shoulder, a brief case down by his side.

"Pull right along side him," Hager told Lloyd.

Hager's heart was jumping as the car slowly overtook his target. They were alongside him now. Like a flash, Hager pushed open the door and jumped from the car. In what seemed like one motion, the agent grabbed an arm and introduced his old friend to the back end of a blue minivan. With a thump, Phil's forehead crunched against metal — the look on his face was one of surprise and shock.

In less than a second, Hager had Phil's left arm secured behind him, his chest pinned to the minivan. Both the brief case and jacket fell lifelessly to the pavement.

"What the fuck!" Phil screamed. The pain was evident in his voice. "Clark, what the hell are you doing?"

"How ya doin', old buddy?" Hager asked, lodging his own foot at Phil's heels to keep him off balance and stuck to the van. Lloyd made his way around the car, flashing a worried leer to his partner.

"Clark," Lloyd said. "Maybe we should—

"Just found out another little white lie you told us, old buddy. This is getting fucking old, Phil. I'm tired of your shit. It's time you and me had a little word of prayer."

"Lie?" Phil exclaimed. "What lie? I don't know what the hell you're talking about. If you don't let go of my arm, you'll be sorry, Hager."

Hager wrenched upward on the arm. Phil shrieked in agony. "Goddammit, you know exactly what I'm talking about, you lying fuck! The hotel—it wasn't some whore you picked up on the plane. It was Catherine!"

The image of Catherine's face appeared in Hager's mind. He quickly imagined Phil and she together and it sickened his stomach. He jerked up on Phil's arm and slammed his head against the van again.

"Clark!" Lloyd shouted, placing his large hand on Hager's shoulder. "Get a hold of yourself. What the hell is wrong with you?"

With a surge of strength, Hager pulled Phil by the arm and shoulder swinging him around and tossed him like a child into the side of the Crown Vic. Phil stumbled and braced himself against the car. He looked up. His eyes were full of rage. He clenched his fists and rebounded from the car straight toward Hager, determined to fight.

The punch swung wild and Hager parried it easily, countering with a quick snapping left hook to Phil's chin and a right to his solar plexus. Hager heard the air escape from Phil's lungs and watched him collapse to the ground. Reeling and fighting for air, Phil's arm easily came behind him as Hager placed a cuff around his wrist.

"Clark, what the hell are you doing?" Lloyd asked, a look of utter shock on his face.

Hager's eyes were wild like an animal. He'd tasted the sweet nectar of adrenaline—like blood, he wanted more. The primitive flair to his eyes quickly changed to a smile. "I'm arresting him. That's what I'm doing," he answered as the second cuff ratcheted closed.

"Arresting him? For what?"

"He assaulted me. Didn't you see him?"

"Clark, you can't—

"The hell I can't," he said with clenched teeth. "I was trying to detain this suspect for questioning and he resisted and then assaulted me." Hager winked at his partner. "Are you gonna help me get him up or what?"

Lloyd sighed and shook his head. "Shit."

CHAPTER
38

VANESSA WAITED in a parking lot in view of Liz's car. She looked at her watch — *11:52.* Liz would have finished her last class before lunch and, hopefully, return to her car.

Desperation and confusion were feelings Vanessa had rarely experienced. She had no idea what to do — whom to turn to. The tears just wouldn't stop. Her anger wouldn't go away. She needed to talk to someone. She had no family here, other than Clark and Liz and the former was the root of her problem.

Liz was her only choice — other than her mother who lived four hundred miles away in Pennsylvania — and seemingly her intended stepdaughter was her brightest choice.

During the almost eighteen months she and Clark had been together, she and Liz had become more than friends. They'd sealed an unbreakable bond in the absence of her mother and during the ordeal with "The Strangler."

Now, she had to tell Liz she'd broken off her engagement with her father—to tell her she needed her help to mend the fences. She sniffled and wiped a tear in her eyes as Harry Connick, Jr. crooned from the CD player. Harry always made her feel better when she was sad but it wasn't working very well this time.

A movement caught her eyes and she glimpsed up seeing Liz approaching the car. She was walking with another girl, both of them toting backpacks over their shoulders. They stopped at the rear of Liz's Neon. Vanessa tooted the horn and stepped from her BMW. Liz spotted her and apparently seeing Vanessa's tear-filled eyes and somber face, the smile she'd displayed with her friend quickly disappeared, turning into a look of motherly concern.

Liz excused herself and walked toward the BMW.

"Vanessa? What are you doing here? What's wrong?"

Vanessa suddenly thought Liz may have seen the despair on her face and automatically attributed it to a tragedy involving her father. "Oh, Liz," she said, bursting in tears.

Liz's wrapped her arms around Vanessa's shoulders. She joined her father's fiancé with her own tears. "Vanessa, what's wrong? It's not Daddy, is it?"

She stood back and used the tissue again. "No, your dad's okay, I guess."

"Then what's the matter? Why are you so upset?"

"I gave your dad his ring back. I've been so angry about this entire argument." A tear rolled slowly down her cheek. "I think I've made a big mistake," she said and wept uncontrollably.

THE TWO DETECTIVES sat with a view of the front of the house. The sunlit sky burned brightly on the front windshield of the car. McLendon was the driver and Detective

Henry Barnett from Louisburg sat beside him as they waited for everyone to get into their positions around Luther Rivers' house. Two other teams of detectives were covering the back and sides of the duplex on Tate Street. Rivers lived in apartment 'A', which was on the left side of the building from the street.

With the assistance of Nancy Lapinski of the SBI lab, McLendon had obtained a DNA warrant ordering the arrest of Rivers based on the database hit. Barnett had not been the investigating detective at the time of the incident, but he was able to find the case file with all the information.

The rape had occurred in the back parking lot of a bar in Louisburg after the victim had left with an unknown man. The only suspect information she was able to provide officers was that he'd been a black man she'd met at the club. Apparently, after dancing and a few drinks, the two decided to go outside and "get some fresh air." According to the victim's statement, the two began to get romantic, but the male forced her to his car and raped her.

This case was a classic date rape, which made sense in the large scheme of Rivers' escalation of his crimes. First, he started with the date rape, then the attack on the young woman, and possibly the murder of Cynthia Craven. McLendon knew Hager would agree with him in his assessment.

The radio squelched, the other members of the arrest team indicating they were ready. He and Barnett would go to the front along with a uniformed officer to make the arrest. McLendon reached for his cell phone and dialed Rivers' number.

"Hello?" a woman's voice answered. McLendon recognized the voice of Rivers' wife.

"Yes, this is Gerald Young from the Unemployment Security Commission. Can I speak to Luther Rivers please?" McLendon nodded at Barnett and they both climbed out of the car.

"Can you hold on? I'm on the other line," she said.

Still on the phone, McLendon led the way with Barnett and the uniform following closely behind. He read the young officer's nametag: *Candler*. A minute went by and still Rivers had not come to the phone.

They entered the front yard and quickly traversed the walk and ascended the four stairs leading to the front door. McLendon disconnected the phone and returned it to his pocket, the hand returning instead with his pistol. The stoop was small, only large enough to accommodate one person. Barnett and the officer placed themselves adjacent to the door and waited. McLendon knocked loudly, the pounding reverberated through the walls.

"Police department!" McLendon shouted.

His voice was followed by muffled voices—both male and female and a baby's cry. Footsteps sounded from one side of the apartment to the other. McLendon spied the front window and saw the curtain moving. Rivers was either trying to hide or find an avenue of escape.

"I've got movement from inside the house," an officer declared over the radio.

McLendon's heart thumped inside his chest as he stood braced against the house waiting. He heard more muffled voices, much like excited whispers. The baby cried again, then the footsteps, followed by a thumping noise that sounded like a door slamming. McLendon shook his head at Rivers' futile effort in trying to hide.

Remembering the cell phone in his pocket, he re-holstered his pistol and brought the phone out. He pushed the redial button and seconds later, the phone rang inside the house. The baby cried again accompanied by another song of muffled voices. The phone continued to ring and McLendon put the phone back in his pocket, hoping the incessant ringing would add to the already mounting stress of the occupants.

Barnett looked up and shrugged his shoulders.

McLendon pounded on the door again. "It's the police, Luther! Open the door!" He slammed his fist against the door again.

The house suddenly grew quiet. McLendon tilted his head toward the door, listening for any movement.

"Are we gonna kick the door?" Barnett asked.

McLendon took a deep breath. "I'm not sure we should with the wife and kid in there."

"Did you see if the door was unlocked?"

McLendon shook his head. He reached down and turned the knob. The door eased open. He took cover behind the door and peeked inside. There was still no movement or sound from the house. McLendon pulled out his portable radio and pushed the talk button. "We're going in the front. All units stand by."

He put the portable back in his pocket and came back out with the pistol. The house was silent—peculiar in light of what they had heard before. Slowly, he took a step inside. Two more steps and he was completely in the house.

Suddenly, a pink figure appeared from the hall to his right. It was a woman and she was screaming, wielding a long kitchen knife and advancing toward the detective. She was wearing a nightgown, her hair in curlers and the knife raised over her head.

"What the hell are you doin' in my house!" Trenesa Rivers shouted.

Seeing the armed woman, McLendon focused the pistol in her direction, stopping her in her tracks. Barnett appeared from behind along with Officer Candler.

"Where's Luther?" McLendon shouted.

The woman remained in her place and continued to scream. "You get the fuck outa my house!" She took a step toward the detective. McLendon brought the pistol directly in front of him. "Don't!"

She stopped and dropped the knife, still shouting obscenities and ordering them out of the house. McLendon shouted again, "Where's Luther?"

"Ya'll motherfuckers get the hell outa my house!"

She lunged toward Barnett, grabbing at his arms. Barnett scuffled with her as she flailed her fists, shouting, "Get outa here, you white motherfuckers!"

McLendon and Candler reached Trenesa at the same time and the three of them struggled with the hysterical woman. McLendon heard a loud growling from behind and before he could turn around, the force of Luther Rivers' body slammed him to the floor, the four combatants toppling over like bowling pins. His pistol fell from his hand.

The struggle became a mass of arms, hand, and horrible smells of fear and body odor. McLendon felt a strong hand groping his waist and then a hammer like object crashed down on the back of his head. McLendon saw nothing but blackness.

When McLendon awakened, he smelled the familiar smoky aroma of burning gunpowder. Trenesa Rivers was still screaming. Officer Candler stood in shock, his pistol clutched in both hands in front of his belt. Barnett was struggling with the woman, whose legs and arms were swinging wildly. Luther Rivers lay on the floor near the front door; lying at his feet was a pistol. Blood was leaking from his bare chest. He wasn't moving.

McLendon reached for his gun. It wasn't there. Two other detectives from the outside arrived after hearing the apparent gunshots. McLendon looked at the young officer; his eyes were glassy and fixed. He was the shooter. He was in shock. The two other detectives helped Barnett handcuff the woman and McLendon stood and walked over to Candler.

The officer jumped quickly in response to McLendon's touch. The detective backed away, raising his hands in surrender. "Hey, it's okay, man," he said in soft assuring tones. "It's over. Just put the gun down. It's okay."

Candler lowered the gun, seeming to return to reality.

He holstered the pistol and looked at the fallen Rivers.

"Rivers is dead, Brick," said one of the detectives.

The baby cried again, long fearful wails. McLendon looked over and acknowledged the statement. Still screaming and fighting, Trenesa was then taken outside. "My baby!" she cried. "I've got to get my baby!"

CHAPTER

39

THE DOOR TO THE OFFICE slammed open, startling Judy as she sat at her desk. Hager entered first, one arm interlocked with Phil's. Lloyd followed Phil, holding the door open until they all cleared the breach. Judy stood, a look of amazement on her face as if the two agents had never brought a handcuffed prisoner into the office before.

In fact, this was a rare occurrence. Usually arrestees were taken to the local police department or SBI field office for questioning. But this was no normal arrest—more like a compulsory interview with a stubborn subject.

Phil was no longer struggling—he'd given up trying physically to resist the restraints; instead he'd resigned himself to making threats of lawsuits and other allegations of mistreatment.

They walked quietly back to the conference room and gave Phil a seat. He was still cuffed and his face displayed painful expressions as he twisted his shoulders, trying to ease the tightening caused by the unnatural position of his arms.

"Can you take these damned things off?" Phil asked sounding more like a demand than a request. "They're killing me."

Hager threw his keys on the table and took a seat next to Phil.

"I don't know, Phil. You already took a swing at me earlier. I'm not sure we'd be safe with you unrestrained. What do you think, Lloyd?" Hager asked with a smile.

Lloyd frowned and shrugged his shoulders.

"You know me, Hager," Phil said, wincing in pain as he worked his wrists. "I'm no danger to you or your partner. Just let me go and I'll tell you the whole story. Come on! I'll come clean—completely this time."

"Oh, Phil, stop the whining. You sound like a baby," Hager said.

The agent looked over to Lloyd, who had crossed over to the end of the table. Lloyd nodded his head and held up a handcuff key.

"All right, Phil," Hager agreed. "You have my partner convinced so I guess we'll accommodate you this time. Stand up and he'll get those cuffs loose."

Phil stood and faced away from Lloyd, who quickly removed the cuffs. Sighs of relief came from Phil as he returned to his seat, rotating his shoulders and massaging his wrists. "I never knew how bad those things were."

Phil actually smiled and managed a chuckle. "Clark, you're something else. You know that? Throwing me against the car and all. I didn't take you as the abusing type of cop. I have a good mind seriously to sue the shit out of you for this…but, I think I know what's going on and you might be misinformed about a few things."

Hager furrowed his brow. "Misinformed, Phil?"

"Well, maybe not misinformed, just misinterpreted."

"No, I know one thing. You're a fucking liar and a cheat

and you've been giving us a bunch of horseshit for the past two weeks. And we're gonna get to the bottom of it—right now!"

"You're right, Clark. I've lied and I'm sorry about that. But you don't understand why I had to do what I did." He took a deep breath and his head fell back. "Yes, Catherine and I were…are having an affair. We've been involved for about a year now. It's mostly a sexual thing, you know? I knew Cynthia was getting some on the side and so I figured why not? What's good for the goose and all."

"But why lie about it, Phil? You knew we'd find out sooner or later."

Phil fidgeted in the seat. He shook his head. "No, not really. I knew Catherine wouldn't say anything because she had as much to lose as I did. And plus, it wasn't a big deal until Cynthia was killed. I knew what you'd think if you'd found out about Catherine and me. It looked bad—really bad."

"Yep," Hager agreed. "It does and I still need some answers because I'm starting to believe our black friend from Raleigh PD about you being guilty. What once pointed at someone else is now pointing directly at you, my friend."

Phil held his head down and slowly shook his head. Was this the sign of submission? Was he ready to confess?

Phil looked up with a confidence in his eyes. "Yes, it sure looks like it is. And I'd be a fool if I were in your shoes *not* to think I was guilty." He took another deep breath. "But I'm not. I didn't kill her."

Hager stood, not buying Phil's explanation. He crossed to the window and stood gazing out at the parking lot. His mind drifted to Vanessa. He saw her deep brown eyes and her long lashes batting unconsciously at him, smiling with her perfect teeth. He felt a pain in his gut. She was out there somewhere—where she was and what she was doing he didn't know. He knew one thing, however. He desperately wanted her back.

Lloyd's voice interrupted the daydream. "Clark, you

all right?"

Hager turned around. Phil was staring at him. Like turning on a light, the agent snapped back into reality. He took a chair directly in front of Phil and moved it closer to his friend. He began with clenched teeth. He was going in for the kill. Phil had a fearful look on his face.

"You'll pardon me for not believing a goddamned word you say, Phil. You remember the old saying, 'Fuck me once, shame on you, and fuck me twice, shame on me'? Let me run this down for you, Phil. First, you call me because Cynthia's missing. You wanted me to help, right?"

Phil nodded and his eyes brightened a little. "Yeah, that's right. I did."

Hager slapped the table so hard it stung his hand. "Bullshit Phil! You wanted my help—not in finding your wife, but my help in putting you out of the eye of suspicion. If I was on this case and you being my friend, the grieving husband, no one would suspect you had anything to do with this."

"No! You're wrong—"

"Quiet! I'm not finished, yet. Second, you and Catherine are getting it on at the Sheraton probably on the day your wife was killed and then you fucking lie about it. You knew about the life insurance and the affair Cynthia was having."

Phil nodded in agreement.

"And to top it off, you knew about the townhouse she bought and knew she'd be leaving you soon—"

Phil looked like his eyes had just popped out of his head. Shocked would have been an understatement. "What the fuck are you talking about? What townhouse?"

Hager looked at Lloyd, who was carefully watching Phil. Lloyd's eyes met Hager's with a subtle *I don't think he's bullshitting us* look.

"Clark, what townhouse are you talking about? Cynthia bought a townhouse? Where?" Phil kept looking from Hager to Lloyd, trying to get an answer.

"I'm talking about the townhouse at River Glen. Come on, Phil don't fuck with me now. You said you'd come completely clean with us." Hager held up his hand, bringing his thumb and forefinger close together. "I'm about this close to getting a murder warrant on you and you still wanna fuck with us."

"I'm not fucking with you! Goddammit, Clark! I'm telling the truth. I don't know a damned thing about this townhouse." Beads of sweat had appeared on Phil's upper lip. The pressure was mounting.

Hager leaned back in his chair, steeling himself to go in for the kill one final time in his effort to illicit a confession. Quickly, he lurched forward, almost touching nose to nose. "Then what about the key you shoved inside Cynthia's vagina after you killed her, huh, Phil? Tell us all about it." Hager was screaming now.

"Tell us how you found out about the key and how you followed Cynthia and her lover from Nikko's Restaurant to the house and then how after he left you killed her and drove her car to the highway and had it picked up by the wrecker. Come on, Phil! Tell us."

Hager's face was red as he returned to his chair.

Phil's eyes were full of fear and dismay. He looked to Lloyd for help — for support. Lloyd just stared, waiting and watching Phil's reaction.

"You're fucking crazy, Hager! I didn't know shit about this townhouse. And what the hell is this about a key in Cynthia's vagina? Is this some sick joke?"

Hager shook his head purposefully. "No, it isn't, old friend. Not even close." His voice grew softer — more assuring. "Come on, Phil. I know that's how it happened. Believe me, I understand what you were going through. Your wife was going to leave you for a younger man. She'd bought a townhouse with your money, and she was fucking him inside it. It would lead anyone to do what you did. I understand, Phil. It's over buddy."

Phil laughed and tears streamed down his face. "What

about him? Cynthia's lover. Why aren't you brow beating him like you are me? Have you found him?" He looked from Hager to Lloyd.

Hager frowned. "Yeah, we found him. He was Cynthia's personal trainer at Royal Fitness."

A curious look planted on his face, Phil leaned forward and placed his hands on the table. "So, what did he have to say about this? When was the last time he saw her?"

Hager cleared his throat. He looked to Lloyd for advice. Lyle's death and its connection to Phil was an issue the agent had wanted to spring on him when he had him on the ropes. It was going to be his knockout punch. Lloyd furrowed his brow and gestured for him to continue.

"We didn't exactly get the chance to talk to him, Phil."

"Why not? Is he missing? There," he pounded the table. "You see? He's probably on the run because he killed her. I don't know, some kind of jealous rage or something. He's the one. You have to find him, Clark."

"He's dead, Phil. Colin Lyle — that was his name. He was killed in Cynthia's townhouse the other day. Someone used a cord to strangle him — almost cut his head completely off."

Hager waited for a reaction from Phil but he simply shook his head.

"Who do you think killed him?" Phil asked. "Did it have anything to do with Cynthia's death?"

"We were thinking you could help us out with that, Phil."

Phil frowned, confused. "Me? What kind of help could I be to you with that?"

Once his lips stopped moving, an angry look of realization materialized on Phil's face. "You think I killed him?"

Phil laughed. It wasn't a nervous chuckle, but a ludicrous laugh. Hager shot a glance to Lloyd. His partner smiled, then they joined Phil in his frivolity.

About a minute later, Phil composed himself. "I don't believe this shit. You think I killed Cynthia and this Lyle asshole?"

Hager shrugged his shoulders. "Well, who else?"

"Who else?" Phil shouted. "Who else? How the fuck am I supposed to know who else? You're the fucking expert, Clark. Not me."

"Phil," Hager said almost in a whisper. "I understand, man. A thing like that can drive you crazy. Come on, Phil. Tell us about it. It will make you feel better to get it off your chest."

Phil jumped out of the seat, startling Hager. Lloyd moved forward in defense of his partner, who was trying to increase the distance between himself and Phil.

"Aren't you listening, Hager?" Phil shouted, his fists clenched, temples throbbing. "I didn't kill her! Goddammit, I didn't kill her!"

The tears continued to flow down Phil's face as he fell down in the chair and buried his head in his hands.

A moment of eerie silence was interrupted by the ringing of the telephone. Judy was the only person who could call into the conference room and she had been instructed not to interfere with an interrogation unless it was an emergency. Lloyd was closer to the phone and he walked over, quickly removing the handset.

Phil continued to whimper as Hager listened to Lloyd.

Hager's partner groaned and cleared his throat. "All right, I'll tell him. Tell Maxwell we'll be over as soon as we can." He hung up the phone.

When Lloyd turned around, Hager knew it was bad news. Hager said a silent prayer.

Please don't let anything happen to Elizabeth or Vanessa.

"Well?" Hager asked.

Lloyd looked at Phil, and then returned to Hager. "It's Rivers. He's dead. Killed by the cops about two hours ago."

"McLendon?"

Lloyd nodded. "He's okay. Maxwell said some agents from the field office are on their way over. He wants us to go over, too."

Hager sighed. "Shit!"

Phil had raised his head, curious of the news. "Rivers? Isn't Rivers the wrecker driver who picked up Cynthia?"

Hager answered, "Uh, huh. He is...well, he was." He stood and put his hand on Phil's shoulder. "We're not going to arrest you today, Phil. I guess I'll overlook that punch you threw at me. We'll drive you back over to Bayer."

Phil managed another smile. "Does that mean you believe me, Clark?"

Hager frowned. "I don't know what to believe, Phil. You've lied so much, but there are a few other things about Cynthia's murder that don't point to you, so I guess I can say that I'm still on your side." Hager offered his hand. "No hard feelings?"

Phil took the handshake and looked Hager directly in the eyes. He shook his head. "No, Clark. No hard feelings."

CHAPTER
40

VANESSA WAS AMAZED that Liz, a twenty-year-old woman with almost no experiences in life—much less in serious relationships could come up with such a wonderful idea. In retrospect, the idea made perfect sense, knowing her father the way she did; it was as simple as making her bed.

Since Vanessa had returned her key to Clark's house, Liz gave her a spare so she could surprise him when he arrived home from work. The plan was to go armed with all the instruments of rekindling a romance—candles, wine, and some sexy new lingerie—knowing Clark would be ready to make amends.

Vanessa was currently browsing through the racks in Victoria's Secret at Crabtree Valley. She'd come across a new scented bubble bath called Cotton Blossom, and was carrying the bottle in her hand, trying to decide between the sheer white chemise with the low cut neck and support bra, or the black paper thin teddy with garters and stockings.

She felt an exhilaration surging through her body — more than her typical excitement in anticipation of their rendezvous. It was akin to the natural anxiety of a first date, with sweaty palms, flushed skin, and goose bumps.

Her eyes spotted a long white satiny gown with a beautiful transparent robe. The hem was sliced all the way up the side to the waist, making for some great leg shots. It was very elegant, and she thought she'd get that one for their wedding night — if the plan went accordingly. She brought it up to her chest and glanced to see the fit when something in front of her caught her attention.

Outside the store, a man stood watching her. He stared for at least two or three seconds before realizing he'd been caught; then quickly he averted his eyes and walked away. A cold chill crept up her spine and she immediately shook it off. She returned the gown to the rack.

Vanessa smiled in an embarrassed but flattered sort of way. It was always nice for men to look at her, but the way the man was peering had given her the creeps. Unshaken, she took the two outfits into the dressing room for her final approval.

HAGER TURNED THE CAR onto Tate Street, a quiet dead-end road with only four or five houses. As he made the turn, he saw the numerous police, fire, and rescue vehicles parked along the street. Down the street, waiting like a serpent for his prey, was a white van, satellite affixed to the roof bearing the call letters, *WRAL News Channel 5.*

"The vultures are circling the carcass," Lloyd said pointing in the van's direction.

Hager nodded. "It's good that they wait until the scene is done. There's nothing worse than pushy news people…"

Hager caught a glimpse of a pair of long shapely legs find-ing the ground just outside the van's side door. When the woman stood, he immediately recognized Shelley Broschard, *Channel 5*'s newest, brightest, and most beauti-ful field reporter. She pulled her long blonde hair back into a ponytail, straightened her blouse, and brushed lint from her black skirt. Undoubtedly, she must have been prepar-ing for a live feed from the scene. It was a little after six o'clock, so the story was timely.

Hager hadn't had the pleasure of meeting 'Ms. Won-der-Legs' as she was called by the local men in blue. Now Hager guessed was his opportunity.

"Whoa!" Lloyd exclaimed. "You see what I see?"

Hager smiled. "Hmm, hmm. I try not to miss something as lovely as that, partner."

Hager stopped behind another unmarked police sedan. As the two agents got out of the car, Hager's cell phone sounded.

"This is Hager."

"Daddy?" Elizabeth asked.

"Hi, honey. I hope this is important. I'm right in the middle of something. What's up?"

"Oh, well. It's not really important. I was just wonder-ing when you'd be home tonight. I thought I'd come over and eat dinner with you — my treat."

Hager almost fell over. The likelihood of his college stu-dent daughter treating him to dinner was about as likely as being attacked by a shark.

"Your treat, Elizabeth?" He gave a suspicious moan into the phone. "What's the matter? How much do you need?"

Her father's immediate allegation that she wanted money apparently hadn't offended her, which made the agent even more leery of her offer.

"Oh, Daddy. You're so funny sometimes. Money, very funny. No, that's not it. I just haven't seen you in a few days and...I don't know, with you and Vanessa having problems, I thought you might be a little lonely is all. Do you not want me to come over?" She spoke in her little girl voice—the kind of voice that melts the hearts of all men and dads around.

Shelley and a cameraman were walking slowly toward the house. She walked like a model, perfectly erect, her head held high, her hips swaying. She was a distraction Hager didn't need at the moment.

"No, of course I'd love for you to come over, honey. Ah…is Owen coming with you?"

She chuckled. "Yeah, right. I don't think so. What time you think you'll be there? I was gonna get some Chinese."

"Oooh. That sounds good. I'll have the shrimp with Chinese vegetables, okay? I'm not sure when I'll be home, though. Like I said, I'm right in the middle of something." His eyes found Shelley again. She was standing in the street facing the camera. "It shouldn't take too long. It's a little after six now. We should have this wrapped up by eight—eight-thirty at the latest. Is that too late?"

"No, that's perfect. Look, Daddy. I have to go. See ya later!" she said and disconnected before he could say 'goodbye.'

Hager turned off the phone and put it in his pocket. Always aware of his public relations obligations, Lloyd was ahead chatting with Ms. Shelley Broschard. Like always, his partner wore a charming smile.

VANESSA STROLLED DOWN the mall corridor toting the red, gold, and white bag from Victoria's Secret. She'd opted for the black teddy since she knew Clark liked the garters and stockings. Busy patrons walked by in columns; classical music played overhead.

She turned her wrist to see the time—*6:45 P.M.* She had almost two hours before she had to be at Clark's house. She still needed to go by the grocery store and get the wine and some cheese and crackers for snacking when they weren't snacking on each other.

When the automatic door opened, the warm humid air rushed to her face. The sun was working its way down toward the horizon, and some flat gray clouds indicated another North Carolina thunder boomer was on the way. As she walked through the parking lot, Vanessa imagined the look on Clark's face when he got home finding her in his bed.

She smiled, envisioning the mischievous grin emerge on his face, seeing herself slowly removing his clothes, seducing her lover with her hands and tongue. Warmth filled her body in response to her thoughts.

Still engrossed in the fantasy when she got to her BMW, she casually pulled the keys from her purse. Her cell phone rang; it was Liz.

"Hey, girl," Vanessa said. "Did you talk to him?"

"Yep. Sure did. He's in the middle of something right now, but he said he'd be home around eight or eight-thirty. That should give you plenty of time to get *read-ay*."

"All right. I'm just leaving the mall now. I just picked up this sexy little teddy. It's black and paper thin—very see-through. Your Dad will—"

"Ugh, I don't think I want to hear this, Vanessa. I mean, come on. He's still my Dad, for God's sake. That's a little TMI for me, babe."

Vanessa chuckled. "Yeah, I guess you wouldn't want to hear how wonderful and dynamic your father is in bed, would you?"

"Ohhh Vanessa! I think I'm going to throw up. Please don't say anything else. Please?"

"Okay. I'll give you a break. Listen, thanks a lot for the advice. I think it's going to be a big night for the both of us—"

Suddenly, a hand emerged around her waist. Vanessa felt a cold object at her throat. "Oh, my God!" she gasped, the phone still at her ear. She took a step forward, the arm now firmly wrapped around her waist, pulling her backward. She heard the crying pleas from Liz on the phone, "Vanessa? Vanessa? What's wrong?"

Fueled by the adrenaline dump, Vanessa attempted to turn around, the sharp edge of a blade tearing into the side of her neck, the strength of his grip upon her body.

An evil voice came in her ear. "Don't even think about screaming, bitch!"

He pushed her forcefully against the car, causing the phone to crash to the pavement. Her face hit the side window and she tasted blood. His arm was still tightly around her stomach, the other fumbling with the car door. It was hard to breathe; she was pinned to the car, unable to move.

He ripped the keys from her hand. Maintaining the vise-like hold around her, he was able to unlock the door. Of the many thoughts flashing through her mind over the few seconds, the most prominent one was: *Don't get in the car with this man!*

With superman-like strength, he whisked her off her feet and forced her into the driver's seat. The door was still open; he wrenched the back of her hair, twisting her neck.

"I'm getting in behind you," he said with a clenched jaw, the knife at her throat. He had a sickening sweet odor about him. "I have a gun and I'll shoot you if you lock the doors. Understand?"

She nodded obediently; her eyes were wide open in horror. The tension eased on her hair and he backed away, moving behind her. In seconds, she smelled him again and she saw the knife. The door slammed shut. He tossed the keys on her lap.

"Drive!" he ordered.

HAGER AND LLOYD were seated at the kitchen table with Officer Candler. The officer looked sullen, but lucid and under control. A Raleigh PD captain, who had arrived shortly after the shooting, had already seized Candler's

pistol—a normal procedure after an officer shoots someone. The house was secured and the two agents were getting a preliminary statement from the young officer.

A sergeant peeked in and frowned at the sight of the
agents. "Candler, remember you don't have to say anything
right now if you don't want to."

Candler looked at Hager. He had such a youthful look
in his eyes—a naivety no doubt Hager believed would be
gone by the day's end. He nodded to the young officer.
Lloyd growled under his breath.

"He's right, Candler," Hager said. "You don't have to
say anything now. But remember, if you're right, you're
right, whatever happened."

Candler's portable radio blared loudly. Two ear piercingly loud alert tones were followed by a woman's voice:

*Attention all units. Tact units working surveillance at
Crabtree Valley Mall report a kidnapping in progress. A
woman was just abducted and forced into a dark blue BMW,
headed west on Glenwood Avenue. Any unit in the area,
respond to assist. Suspect is a white male; victim is a white
female. Stand by for further.*

Candler brightened at the news from the radio. "I bet
that's the car-jacking suspect who's been hitting over there.
Damn, I wish I could go."

Hager chuckled at the officer's enthusiasm for his job.
"Well, you're kinda busy right now, don't you think?"

He nodded and reached for his radio to turn down the
volume. The portable blared again:

*All units—further on the kidnapping at Crabtree Val-
ley. Tactical units are in pursuit of the dark blue BMW with
10-28 of Henry-Mary-Frank, 4-3-2-2. Vehicle is still westbound on Glenwood Avenue. Suspect is a white male occupying the back seat. Victim is a white female and she's
driving the car. Suspect is armed. Use caution.*

Candler frowned. He looked frustrated. "Damn. I just recovered a stolen car from over there this morning. I'd like to be in on that arrest."

Again, Hager grinned at Candler's zest for doing his job. The radio squelched again. This time a male voice asked for the dispatcher to run the license plate of the BMW the officers were pursuing.

Hager remembered the plate number: *HMF-4322.* For some reason, the letter and number combination sounded familiar, but he couldn't place it.

BMW…HMF-4322?

He turned back to the officer, who kept an ear leaning toward his radio listening to the action. Hager leaned forward, also interested. The radio was quiet, everyone waiting for news. The cell phone ring startled Hager, almost moving him out of the seat.

BMW? Dark blue?

He pulled the phone from his pocket and pushed the button. A sickening feeling surged through his gut when he remembered from where he knew the plate number.

Vanessa!

The line was open, but Hager couldn't speak. He heard a female voice screaming from the phone.

"Hager!" he shouted.

"Daddy! Oh my God! It's Vanessa. Someone's got her. Oh my God!" Elizabeth cried.

CHAPTER

41

VANESSA'S HANDS TREMBLED as she gripped the steering wheel. The left side of her neck was burning, and she touched the spot, her fingers returning tinged red with blood. The initial tears of horrific fear were gone, now replaced by the overwhelming sinking feeling associated with knowing she was going to die.

Vanessa could feel him behind her, his breath and the body odor so nauseating. She shot a glance to her right, seeing the rusty blade by her shoulder. Not wanting to be caught looking, she quickly returned her eyes to the road. She drove slowly as instructed, her eyes moved from side-to-side looking — searching for an opportunity to escape. She needed a diversion of some kind so she could move quickly away from the knife before it could cut her again.

"Just keep driving," he commanded in a raspy voice. "Don't do anything stupid that may attract attention to you.

I'll cut your throat if you try anything."

She nodded again, feeling the burning on her neck from the cut and knowing how much more it would hurt if he really wanted to cut her. Tears welled in her eyes. As she wiped one eye, she glanced in the mirror. It was tilted so *he* could see behind them.

All she could see was his face: unshaven, eyes glazed, an aquiline nose and his tongue slithering around thin lips. Their eyes met and she quickly returned her focus ahead, then to the side mirror where she noticed a car following peculiarly close.

A dishearteningly evil laugh came from his mouth, one that starts low and slow, then increases in volume in a crescendo of diabolical laughter similar to a devilish cartoon character. The dam of tears broke, and they rolled down her cheeks.

He whispered close to her; she felt his breath on her cheek. "Don't worry, my sweet. I'll kill you quickly. I promise you won't feel anything but my undying love."

His head lurched forward, his lips poised to give a kiss. Instead, his tongue emerged touching her throat. She felt the wetness of his tongue and it sickened her. He laughed again, smacking his lips. "Hmm. You taste so good. I can't wait for us to be alone."

HAGER VEERED THE CAR in and out of lanes, around cars and trucks, through traffic lights, narrowly avoiding collisions. Tires screeched, horns blared, and the Crown Vic's engine roared as he and Lloyd raced toward Glenwood Avenue.

In the back seat sat Officer Candler, whom Hager had enlisted for help—for his portable radio mostly, which he held across the seat, the volume at full blast.

Still waiting for assistance to arrive, the unmarked tactical car still followed Vanessa's BMW as it headed toward

U.S. 70 on Glenwood Avenue. According to Candler, the tact car had no lights or siren; therefore, they couldn't make a stop without a marked patrol car.

Hager made the exit off the 440 beltline onto Glenwood Avenue, Crabtree Valley Mall directly in front of them. He made a quick right, his own siren blaring, a single blue light flashing on the dash. After several minutes of silence, the radio squelched again. It was the same male voice, evidently one of the pursuing detectives:

Suspect vehicle still traveling west bound approaching Duraleigh Road at a speed of thirty-five. I don't think they're aware we're following.

Hager stepped on the accelerator harder, moving around rows of cars stopped at a light. His heart pounded. He had to get to her in time. He wasn't going to lose her.

VANESSA THOUGHT SHE was going to vomit right in her front seat. The slimy feel of his tongue on her neck almost made her lose it. She knew she had to remain calm and under control. Her eyes searched the horizon for a way out—a window of opportunity.

She felt his breath on her throat again. He was making sniffing noises, his nostrils flaring like a dog's. "Hmm, you smell so good," he moaned, touching his pointed nose to her skin.

Her skin crawled in response. She looked up and traffic had stopped for a light. She began to slow, his nose still at her neck. This was her opportunity. One sudden move, and she could escape.

She tapped the breaks, his nose now buried under her hair. He kept moaning, savoring her smell. She saw the knife. Slowly, his hand lowered. The more he smelled, the lower the knife. Lower…lower…*Step hard!*

She stomped on the brakes. He fell forward, the knife completely out of view. With one quick pull on the handle, she pushed open the door, leaving the car rolling as she struck the pavement. *She was free!*

STILL LISTENING to the radio, Hager thought they were only a few blocks away, and still no car from the PD had arrived to help the tact unit.

Where the fuck are all the cops?

The radio barked again. The detective sounded excited and out of breath:

Headquarters, the female has jumped from the car. She's down. Get me an ambulance at the corner of Glenwood and Duraleigh. The BMW's been involved in a hit-and-run; it's still westbound. The male is now the driver. We're stopping to assist the victim.

"Thank God!" Lloyd shouted. "She got away. That's my girl!"

Vanessa had escaped. The man who abducted her was fleeing in her car, despite having been involved in a crash. Hager took a deep breath and closed his eyes. "Yes, Lloyd," he whispered. "Thank God."

Hager could see the mass of cars at the intersection as he approached. To the left of the road, two men crouched beside Vanessa, who was lying on her side, a blanket draped over her. Hager stopped the car about a hundred yards back, got out and sprinted toward her.

When he reached the group, the detectives rose to their feet keeping their barrier intact. They were in jeans and T-shirts. Out of breath from the run, Hager identified himself.

He knelt down beside her. Her eyes were open, but they were unwavering, the pupils fixed and dilated. She had a bleeding abrasion on her forehead, and the left side of her neck was cut. He turned to the detectives. "I think she's in shock!"

They both nodded. One of them spoke, "Yeah, she jumped from the car as it was going pretty slow. She's real lucky no one ran her over."

Hager touched her cheek. "It's okay, baby. You're safe now. It's okay." She didn't move and her eyes remained still.

Lloyd and Candler walked up and Lloyd took a knee at Vanessa's other side. He held her hand. A siren approached with red and white flashing lights. The ambulance pulled alongside the group and two men in light blue uniforms jumped out. Hager and Lloyd backed away, letting the paramedics do their work.

Hager looked at Lloyd and then behind him, he saw the distinct figure of his daughter. In a slow trot, she approached her father, a look of fear in her eyes.

"Is she okay?" Elizabeth asked.

Hager nodded and opened his arms where she fell in. "Yes, honey. She's gonna be okay."

CHAPTER

42

VANESSA SLEPT PEACEFULLY. Beside her hospital bed, Hager lounged in an uncomfortable chair watching a *Seinfeld* rerun. Only the antics of Kramer could make him laugh after a day like today. He covered his mouth when he snickered, not wanting to disturb her sleep. Elizabeth and Lloyd had left about an hour ago, both of them knowing she was in stable condition and in good hands at Wake Medical Center.

Although Vanessa escaped the ordeal absent any serious physical injuries, she suffered a psychological trauma. There were no broken bones, just some bumps and bruises—a result of the leap from the moving car. The doctor said that she would be released in the morning. Hager decided to stay with her, for he wanted his face to be the first she would see when she awakened.

A commercial flashed across the TV screen and Hager

looked at her. She was so beautiful, and to think he'd almost lost her for good. Elizabeth had told him of her plan that night. He got up from the chair and leaned over to give her a kiss when he saw her eyelids flutter. His lips touched her cheek and her eyes opened.

She flinched, withdrawing from him. She blinked a few times. In the semi-darkness of the room, she may not have recognized his face. Fear filled her eyes and she blinked again. Then her eyes brightened and a smile of recognition came to her face.

"Hey," he whispered. "How you doin'?"

She licked her lips and adjusted her position. "My head hurts." She touched the abrasion on her forehead.

"Yeah, you got a nasty bump on your head, but the doctor says you're gonna be all right. You had us scared for a while."

"What happened—what happened to him?"

Hager shook his head. "I don't know. The officers who were following you stopped when you jumped out. He took off, crashing a few cars along the way. There's no sign of him or the car. Don't worry about that right now. We're just glad you're safe."

She took a deep painful breath. "My ribs hurt. Are they broken?"

"Uh-uh, the doctor said they're just bruised. He said you were very lucky. I guess you're pretty tough when you wanna be, huh?"

She closed her eyes and smiled, nodding. "I guess so," she whispered.

"Vanessa?" he asked caressing her cheek. "I'm so—"

"Don't say anything, Clark. I love you. That's all that matters," she whispered and drifted off to sleep.

After Vanessa was discharged from the hospital the next morning, Hager drove her directly to his house and put her into bed with all the comforts of home.

While he was taking care of the patient, Elizabeth, escorted by Lloyd and Owen Harrison, went to Vanessa's town house and gathered clothes and other 'female' necessities. Knowing her attacker would have access to personal information from her car, Hager insisted that Elizabeth not go unguarded.

After he made Vanessa comfortable, Hager quizzed her about what had occurred. At first the agent believed the attack might have been just a simple car jacking. As customary in his investigative procedures, he allowed her to relate the crime from beginning to end, without interruption. Then, he asked questions—focusing on specific behaviors and statements in order to improve his understanding of the psychological makeup of the offender.

But, as she explained the incident, the physical attack, his words, the threats with the knife after the abduction, and also the peculiar behavior indicative of a sexual predator, Hager began to see it as being a much more complex event than he'd initially thought.

He listened to her words, saw the fear in her eyes as she recalled the terrible feeling when he touched her. With every word, she painted a picture of what he'd feared existed: a correlation of this attack with Cynthia Craven's murder.

Although she'd not seen her attacker very well—fear has a way of causing a person to focus on certain aspects of an event—Vanessa was able to give Hager a basic description of the man. He was a white male, late 20's, clean-shaven, and had short dark hair. The man wore a baseball cap, the team or logo Vanessa couldn't recall. She related the strange body odor emanating from the man and also said his hands were dirty with black caked underneath his nails. She'd paid closest attention to her biggest threat, the hand that held the knife.

When she finished, Hager sat on the edge of the bed in silence. How could they have been totally unaware of any similar crimes occurring in the area? From the beginning they'd focused their investigative efforts on the three people most closely associated with the victim, and failed to consider the possibility that the killing could have been the random work of a sexual predator.

Once again, the age-old problem in law enforcement had sneaked up and bitten the agents in the butt: lack of effective intradepartmental communication. It was the Achilles heel for all investigative entities, and had been a major reason many serial criminals — serial killers especially — had been able to avoid capture for long periods of time.

All the indications of a sexual predator at work were present: the body was found nude; sexual activity; the use of a knife as the instrument of death; and lastly, the symbolic placing of the key. What was it about Cynthia and the key to her new town house that meant so much to this killer? Was it a clue to the killer's identity, or a message sent to the victim explaining why she had died?

It could be both, Hager thought. Usually, the motive for a murder was directly related to the identity of the killer. In essence, once he discovered why someone was killed, the identity of the perpetrator became clear.

Two pieces of evidence remained that could be the positive link between killer and victim: the semen up to that point wasn't yet identified and the key. In a perverse usage of irony, this killer knew the key, and its purpose was the necessary link to the truth — the *key* to solving this case. There also remained the unsolved murder of Colin Lyle.

Did this recent epiphany mean that Colin Lyle's death was simply a coincidence? Was he involved in something that got him killed? Could this involvement have gotten both he and Cynthia killed? Was this the angle he needed to explore?

"What's the matter, Clark?" Vanessa asked in a sleepy voice.

"Nothing," he mumbled, avoiding her eyes.

"Nothing, my you-know-what." She sat up and leaned toward him, her fingertips touching his arm. "What are you thinking? I can tell when those wheels are turning up there."

He remained silent for a minute, chastising himself for wearing blinders. He'd let a killer remain loose and that same monster had come so very close to taking Vanessa away from him.

"Come on, Clark. Tell me what you're thinking."

He looked at her and smiled. Her eyes had regained their once lustrous beauty. They were hard to resist. Hager had always been candid and honest with Vanessa when he discussed his work. She functioned as more than just a sounding board, for her incredibly high intellect and logical reasoning gave him a resource to use when coming up with a theory. She'd heard many detailed stories, seen dozens of crime scene photos, and provided an assurance to the validity of his hypotheses. Why exclude her now? She was safe and seemed to have gathered herself emotionally.

"I'm just thinking this guy had other things on his mind than taking your car." He took a deep breath, massaging his tired eyes. "I think he's the same person I've been hunting for killing Cynthia Craven."

CHAPTER

43

VANESSA PURRED SOFTLY as she slept, her arm resting gently across Hager's chest, her head propped on his shoulder. She felt so good and warm lying next to him. He looked at the alarm clock on the nightstand — *4:25 P.M.*

They'd slept for three hours and the nap had made him feel better. Trying not wake her, Hager slid his shoulder from under her head and as he eased his back off the bed, her arm fell easily to the mattress. He padded to the bathroom, pulled a washcloth off the rack and soaked it with cold water.

The coldness of the cloth on his face brought him to complete lucidity. When he came out of the bathroom, he saw Roscoe lying at the foot of the bed. The dog looked up lovingly at his master, then he shut his eyes, returning to his nap.

When Hager got downstairs, he found a leather duffel

bag below the dinette table. On the table and underneath his set of keys, lay a piece of paper emblazoned with Elizabeth's handwriting. He moved the keys and picked up the note.

Daddy,
I put the rest of Vanessa's things in my closet. I think I got what she'll need for a few days. Call you later.
Love,
Liz

Hager returned the paper to the table and picked up the keys. He flipped through the aluminum jagged edges. There were six keys in all on a ring and silver chain connecting a sterling silver rendition of the SBI logo. Elizabeth had used Hager's key to Vanessa's house to get her things since the attacker was still in possession of Vanessa's car.

"Keys," Hager whispered. "What does it have to do with keys?" He shook the ring, making a jingling sound. He replayed Vanessa's words in his mind. The monster's hot breath, the knife, his tongue licking her, his unusual body odor—"like something sickeningly sweet," she'd said.

The phone made him jump back from the table. He walked over to the kitchen counter and picked it up. "Hello?"

"Hager, is that you?" It was McLendon.

"Yeah, what's up?"

"I got some good news and some bad news. Which do you want to hear first?" McLendon sounded happy again.

"Hmm. I'd like to hear Vanessa's car was found. If so, that would be good news."

McLendon chuckled. "Well, you're right. We found the car over off New Bern Avenue near downtown—a small street called Governor's Hill Road. It was abandoned, keys gone and the front end cracked up a little. Our lab techs are doing their thing on it now. So far, it looks clean. We'll stick around if you want to come down."

"Yeah. Give me about thirty minutes to get there. What's the bad news?"

The detective groaned. "It's not good."

Hager changed ears. "How bad could it be?"

"Another body. A woman found in the back seat of her car. Her throat was cut."

"Fuck," Hager whispered. "Where?"

"You know where Chili's is on Glenwood? There's a lot behind it. Car was parked like normal."

"Any idea how long ago?"

"Don't know. Sarge said it was bad, but not as bad as ours."

"All right, I'll see you in a half-hour," Hager said and hung up the phone.

He picked it up again and dialed Lloyd. Hager relayed the news and asked him to meet at Vanessa's car. After disconnecting, he called Elizabeth and asked her to come to the house and stay with Vanessa. He then walked upstairs where Vanessa was stirring awake. He told her about the car and the recent body, gave her a kiss and in ten minutes he was in the Crown Vic on the way to meet McLendon.

When Hager arrived the lab techs had finished their processing of the car. McLendon was standing in the street next to the BMW talking to one of the techs. He was holding a paper grocery bag that had the word *EVIDENCE* printed in black letters on the face. Lloyd pulled behind Hager as he was getting out of the car. Both agents walked to the car together.

"How's our girl?" Lloyd asked.

"Good. She seems to be her old self again."

"What do you think about this other D.B.? Is it the same guy?"

"No tellin', Lloyd. I hope to hell not. I don't need another 'Strangler' problem this soon."

When Lloyd and Hager reached McLendon, the lab tech walked away.

"What's the deal?" Hager asked.

"They lifted some prints from the car. Some of them look pretty good. I guess AFIS will get a crack at them." He held up the bag. "Her purse and contents are in here. I don't know what's missing, if anything. I guess she can tell you that. As far as anything else, they didn't get much. Vacuumed the seats and floors. It's kinda hard to see anything with the seats and floors being black."

"What about the keys?"

McLendon shook his head. "All we got is this," he held out his open hand where a gold key lay. The teeth were mangled and bent. "Found it jammed in the ignition. We had to get a pair of pliers and a screwdriver just to get it out. From the way it was stuck, I don't think it's the car key."

Hager frowned and held his hand out for the key. McLendon gave it to him. "I wish you would've left it alone. We could've taken it out without doing so much damage." He handed it to Lloyd.

"I'd like for whatever your lab recovered to be forwarded to ours. I can have them on it by tomorrow morning." He reached for the paper bag.

"No problem."

Lloyd asked, "What do you know about this other body?"

McLendon shrugged his shoulders. "Nothing other than what I told your partner. Erickson's the lead on it."

"Are they still out there?" Hager asked.

"I don't know," McLendon answered, pulling the portable from his pocket.

He talked into the radio, asking for a unit to go to another channel. After switching channels, the detective conversed with another male voice. McLendon asked if he was still on the scene and the voice replied that he wasn't.

"Tell him I'll call the office later," Hager requested,

which the detective did.

"What did you get from your boy Phil Craven?" McLendon asked.

Hager answered, "Nothing but a bunch of denials, which seem like they're turning out to be true. Especially considering these recent events. We've been looking in the wrong direction from the beginning."

CHAPTER
44

NEIL BAXTER sat in a chair in the office of Trace Evidence. Hager and Lloyd took chairs at a table facing him, ready to be updated on the evidence recovered from Vanessa's BMW. Neil had a small stack of papers lying in front of him. A small paper sack sat adjacent to the papers. Hager checked his watch. It was three-thirty.

"Okay, everyone's here who needs to be," Hager started. "What've you got?"

Neil pursed his lips and picked up a paper at the top of the pile. He cleared his throat. "Just like the last time, they collected some hairs, fibers, and a similar metallic substance."

Neil continued, "We determined there were three separate strands of hair in the car. Two are unidentified, but the other is a match to the first case, which is still unknown."

"What kind of hair was it?" Lloyd asked.

Neil opened the bag and removed a plastic envelope containing a strand of brown hair. "Caucasian. It was found in the back seat so that means it belongs to the assailant."

"Was that the only hair found in the back seat?" Hager asked.

Neil shook his head. "No, another one, a little darker Caucasian was back there, too. They were found in both the front and back."

"You might want to get a hair sample from Agent Hager on that one," Lloyd quipped with a chuckle.

"Very funny," Hager said. "What about the prints?"

"No matches. But I asked them to try again, if that's all right."

"Sure," Hager said. "I appreciate it. Anything else?"

"That's it."

Hager and Lloyd left Trace Evidence and hopped on the elevator back up to the fifth floor. The new evidence had confirmed what Hager had suspected: Cynthia Craven was the victim of a sexual predator. In essence, both agents were facing a possible serial killer situation if this recent victim was found to be related.

After almost two weeks of work, they were thrown back to square one. At least Hager had more information available to construct a viable criminal profile of the killer. With Vanessa, he had a living witness who had already provided some insight into the psychological make-up of this monster.

The previous afternoon Hager had made contact with Alan Erickson, the detective in charge of the most recent murder. He was still working on a time line from the victim's family and associates, but it appeared that the woman, Marla Hill, a twenty-five year old white female and resident of Raleigh, was killed a day prior to her body's discovery.

There were some similarities to Cynthia's murder; the murder weapon appeared to be a knife and it appeared that Marla wasn't killed in her car. Other resemblances to

Cynthia's murder would be revealed during the autopsy and from the SBI lab reports.

As in his case, Hager asked Erickson to turn over all evidence from his investigation to the SBI lab so that he could expedite the return of the results. Whether or not Marla Hill's and Colin Lyle's murder were related to Cynthia's death, Hager needed to organize his resources and formulate a joint effort. He was about to pick up the phone to call Bob Maxwell when it rang.

"SBI, Hager."

It was McLendon. "Clark, I forgot to tell you about this Crimestoppers tip we got the other day. With the Rivers shooting and everything else going on, I just forgot to tell you."

"What is it?"

"Some lady called in to pass along some information. This happened about a week or so ago, but apparently she works at the library downtown—I think it's the New Bern Avenue branch. Anyway, she said this guy came in and was acting weird. He'd checked out some books on serial killers and homicide investigation. She also said that the guy smelled funny and was carrying a bunch of keys on his belt. She'd guessed he worked at a gas station or something from the way he smelled and his hands were so dirty."

Keys? Smelled funny?

Hager replayed Vanessa's words, "his hands were dirty and he had this sickeningly sweet body odor."

Keys!

Hager's heart began to thump. Adrenaline flew through his veins; his palms started to sweat.

"That's him!" he exclaimed. "It's got to be him! It's the keys, Brick. The goddamned keys!" Hager stood and paced around the desk to the phone cord's limit. "This lady—did she say this guy's name?"

"No she didn't but I'm sure they have it if he checked out some books. You want me to give her a call?" The sound of his voice indicated McLendon was also getting excited.

Jeff Pate

"Yeah, call and find out the name and call me back. I want to see if we can get anything from DMV."

Hager hung up the phone and walked hurriedly to Lloyd's office to inform his partner of the news. Lloyd was on the phone. He told the person on the other end to hold on when Hager entered the room.

"Hey, that's great, partner," Lloyd said in response to the news. "I've got Candler on the phone. You remember, the officer who shot Rivers? Remember he mentioned recovering a stolen car near Crabtree Valley the same day Vanessa was attacked?"

"Yeah. What about it?"

"He thought it was strange at the time, but the guy who owned the car was a real loser. He said he had this big ring of keys and he had this funky body odor. He heard about what Vanessa had said about her attacker and put two and two together."

Hager raised his eyebrows. "No shit. What's his name?"

"Hold on a sec. He was just telling me when you came in," Lloyd said and returned to the phone.

Lloyd's hand moved quickly with the pen. Hager read over his shoulder.

Reid Joseph Cherner WM28 143 Blount St. Raleigh.

Lloyd was still talking on the phone when Hager heard his own line ring. He cut out the door and scampered into his office, snatching the receiver. It was McLendon again.

"I gotta name. You're not gonna believe what I found in our computer."

"It's Reid Cherner from Raleigh and he reported his car stolen and it was recovered from Crabtree Valley the same day Vanessa was attacked."

McLendon remained silent. He groaned and stammered. "Huh, how the hell did you know that? What are you, some kinda mind reader?"

Hager laughed. "Sorry, no. My partner just got a call from Officer Candler. He remembered recovering the car and the guy matched the scum bag who attacked Vanessa."

282

"There's something else. This fucker works at Mid-Town Locksmith downtown. I took the liberty and gave them a call to see if he was there. He called in sick today."

"Locksmith? Hmm, that seals it then! The metal shavings. That's where they came from. The grinding wheel in a locksmith shop."

"Yep. And you remember Cynthia had a credit card charge there? That must've been when he first saw her. Damn! That's why he put the key inside her. He was telling us."

"In his own personal way, yes, he was. I'm thinking he was also symbolically chastising her."

"Crazy bastard. Well, are you on the way?" McLendon asked in a zestful tone.

"As soon as Lloyd gets off the phone we are. Can you get a couple of your guys to go with us?"

"Yeah, both Phillips and Erickson are here. I think the sarge'll want to tag along, too."

"Great. You have an address on Blount, right?"

"Yep. One forty-three. We'll meet you down the block from the house. We'll do a drive-by just to check things out first. I'll call you on your cell phone."

"Okay, but don't go in until we get there. I don't want to miss any of this."

Hager hung up the phone and sprang back into the hall. Lloyd was coming out of his office and they almost collided head-on. He held a single piece of paper.

"I got a faxed photo of this mutt," Lloyd said, showing Hager the paper.

He looked at the photo. Cherner was white with plain facial features, dark eyes, and thinning dark hair. That was about the extent of a black and white driver's license photo. Vanessa's limited description of her attacker matched.

"Come on," Hager ordered. "We're hittin' the house. Brick and the others are going to meet us there."

CHAPTER

45

BLOUNT STREET was scattered with cars parked along the curb on both sides of the one-way street. From what Hager had remembered, the area was notorious for its street drug trafficking. For a late summer afternoon, the street seemed desolate, absent of children playing and cars passing. It seemed the entire neighborhood was standing in vigil, waiting for the show to begin.

The heat wasn't nearly as unbearable as days before with temps in the mid 80's under partly cloudy skies. The humidity had also lessened as the day progressed, giving more of a reason to venture outdoors.

When Hager turned off Jones Road, they almost collided with a black Volvo that cut the corner too closely, causing Hager to veer sharply.

Having seen the driver, Lloyd said, "A white guy in a Volvo in this neighborhood? We know what he's up to, huh?"

Who drives a black Volvo?

The car looked familiar, but Hager couldn't recall from where he knew it. His cell phone brought him back to the task at hand.

It was McLendon—his voice was low, almost a whisper.

I'm doin' a walk-by right now. I'm almost in front of the house. I'll let you know how it looks.

As excited as he was—the anticipation of the thrill of the arrest—Hager suddenly became worried. With the phone to his ear, he spotted two unmarked Fords parked adjacent to the curb and McLendon's Taurus about a hundred feet further and closer to the house. He could hear the detective's voice as he spoke to his comrades over the radio. A sinking feeling punched Hager in the stomach.

Although they couldn't locate any criminal records on Cherner, he was wanted for murder; therefore, he should be approached with extreme caution. Witnessing McLendon's antics up to this point, Hager believed the detective was outstretching his capabilities and endangering himself unnecessarily.

Hager spoke into the phone. "Brick, look. Don't move in yet. Let everyone get into position before you get close." There was no response. He kept open the connection so McLendon could communicate with him.

"What the hell is he doing?" Lloyd asked.

Hager told him and Lloyd growled. "Shit, don't he know this ain't the movies and he ain't John Wayne?"

"Apparently not," Hager said and added a little pressure to the accelerator.

He pulled the car alongside one of the Fords. Two detectives, Larry Phillips and Alan Erickson, were seated in the car. They didn't look happy.

"What the hell is Brick doing?" Hager asked.

Erickson was sitting in the passenger seat. He rolled his eyes and answered. "Doin' what he usually does. He thinks he's a black Rambo. We tried to get him to wait, but he said he wanted to do some re-con before y'all got here."

Hager heard more whispering over the radio. Phillips picked up the portable and turned up the volume. "There he is now."

I'm moving up to the driveway now. Everything is clear. The suspect's Toyota is here.

A minute of silence followed. Hager made the decision to go ahead and approach the house instead of waiting for McLendon to return from his *mission*.

"Let's go ahead and hit it. Tell Brick to stay put and cover the front perimeter."

Phillips spoke into the radio, relaying the order. McLendon didn't respond. He put the radio down and shrugged his shoulders. "What the fuck. I guess he heard. Let's go," he said, pulling the car into gear.

Hager moved his foot from the brake to the gas. Just as he was about to apply pressure, he heard a frightening scream over the detective's radio. It was McLendon and he was in trouble.

Suspect attempting to leave. He's going for the car. All units respond.

A few seconds elapsed as Hager stepped on the gas, thrusting the Crown Vic forward. They were about a hundred yards away and right behind Phillips' Ford. Both cars screeched to a stop and to their right, a black flash appeared. It was a Toyota shooting down the driveway, McLendon riding the hood.

In a glimmer of a second, the black mass of metal carrying the detective crashed into the Ford, catapulting McLendon screaming through the air and slamming him into the Ford's windshield directly facing Phillips. The windshield cracked and caved in as McLendon's face and chest tore through the glass. He wasn't moving.

The Toyota backed away from the destroyed Ford, and with a smoking squeal of tires, cannoned down the road.

Hager's first instinct was to pursue the Toyota. Instead,

he chose to run to McLendon. Both Erickson and Phillips were injured from the pulverizing crash—their heads and hands bleeding. Erickson was screaming into his portable requesting an ambulance.

Keith Moreland, who was in the other unmarked car, was out and already at the driver's side of Phillips' car. He waved at Hager and yelled, "No, go after him! I've got it under control here. Go!"

Hager jumped back into the Crown Vic; Lloyd was pulling the seat belt strap over his chest. Slamming the car into gear, Hager stomped on the accelerator, the Ford's engine roaring. Lloyd flicked on the blue light and siren, and the car blared its way down the street.

Cherner had a few seconds lead with the delay, but Blount Street was one-way and there was a stretch for about a quarter mile where no streets intersected. It was simply a matter of horsepower. Hager caught the Toyota quickly, moving perilously close to the bumper.

The Toyota veered sharply to the right onto a cross street. Hager had to brake in order to make the turn. Accomplishing the turn, he gunned the engine and quickly caught up to the Toyota. Hager checked his speedometer—it read 55 miles per hour. Lloyd was on the cell phone calling for assistance. Raleigh PD, Highway Patrol, and county sheriffs would respond to the chase.

The Toyota made another quick left, Hager right on its butt. To the right of the road, a parked car's door opened and was just as quickly sheared off at the hinges as the Toyota passed. Hager checked his rear-view mirror, seeing the door topple end-over-end into a yard. Lloyd stretched his neck to see if the driver was okay.

"He's all right," Lloyd said. "He's out of the car. He's lucky his arm didn't go with it. Keep going."

"Damn! This son-of-a-bitch is crazy."

Cherner made another quick right; this time his speed was too high and he crossed over, sideswiping a parked car. He careened off, a bit out of control, straightened and kept on going. As they passed the car, Hager looked to see it empty — thankfully.

The Toyota accelerated, increasing its lead, and two blocks later, Cherner turned left. When Hager made the turn, he saw an incredible sight. The Toyota had done a 180° turn and was heading directly for them.

"He wants to play chicken!" Lloyd shouted and leaned back in the seat bracing himself for a head-on crash.

The Toyota approached fast. Hager kept his speed, maintaining a straight path. The cars grew closer and closer; now feet separated them. "Awwwww Shit!" Hager yelled.

Inches away, the Toyota bore down on them. Like a bolt of lightening, a flash of black soared past Hager's window, smashing his door, caroming off, sending the Ford into a spin. Hager turned into the skid, the rear wheels catching, tossing their seat-belted bodies across the seat.

Hager stepped on the pedal again, but nothing happened. He looked forward, seeing the Toyota make a quick right onto the same street from where they had come. "What the fuck is wrong with this thing?" he shouted, stomping his foot.

"The engine's off, Clark. Start it up again."

Hager pushed the lever into park and turned the key, jamming it back into drive. With a thrust, the car jolted forward and back into the chase. Despite having collided with several cars, the Toyota was holding its own and still speeding down the road. Hager stopped at a cross street. Lloyd pointed to the pavement.

"Look, anti-freeze! It goes to the right. He's losing coolant. That piece of shit will quit soon."

Hager jerked the wheel to the right and floored it again. The siren noise was deafening. A left turn later, he glimpsed the black car blazing down the street. Hager quickly overtook the Toyota as it turned onto Wade Avenue, a more open four-lane road. Hager increased his speed to seventy. He looked at the sign in front of him — *To I-40.*

"He's heading for the highway," Lloyd said.

"If he makes it that far."

Surprisingly, Hager heard the phone ring over the din of the siren. Lloyd answered. He looked up. "We're on Wade Avenue approaching forty. We think he's going for the highway." A moment of silence followed by Lloyd saying, "Damn. Okay, I'll tell him."

"Tell me what," Hager asked as Lloyd disconnected.

"McLendon's dead."

"Shit."

They were on the Wade Avenue/I-40 interchange traveling west passing the construction site for the new sports arena. Hager's speedometer read 90 miles per hour. He shook his head at the Toyota's longevity despite leaking anti-freeze.

"When is this car gonna quit?" Hager asked. "It's like the Toyota from *The Terminator.*"

"I think it's time to crash him, Clark."

Hager stepped on the gas, closing the distance between them and the Toyota. They were approaching the ramp for I-40, and this would be a good location to try the maneuver. The Toyota sped up, but the Ford had too much power. Just as Hager closed in, the Toyota jerked abruptly to the left onto the grass median.

"Shit!" Hager shouted.

Hager immediately hit the brakes. He watched the Toyota cross the median, throwing the front end of the car upward as it entered the east bound lane of I-40. The car went airborne, landing on its side wheels, violently sliding. The two remaining wheels touched ground, bouncing once before the car righted itself.

"He's going the wrong way!" Lloyd cried. "What the fuck are we gonna do?"

Traffic in the east bound lane skidded, dodged, and sharply slid out of the Toyota's way as it crossed the four lanes and finally reached the shoulder where it continued speeding up the road.

"He's driving on the shoulder! There's an exit ahead—

he's gonna get away!" Hager declared, pulling the wheel hard to the left.

Lloyd clamored, "Clark, what in the hell? Oh, shit!"

Cars were still moving, but slowly as they watched the maniac booming down the left shoulder. Hager's blue light stopped a few cars, but others were paying more attention to the Toyota.

Dodging passing cars, Hager zipped across the highway and stepped on the gas, trying to prevent the Toyota from reaching the exit. His speed was near 100 and he was gaining fast. The exit ramp was a half-mile away; the Toyota was a quarter-mile in front of him.

With all his strength, Hager pushed on the pedal, the speedometer reaching 125, the cars flying by like flashes. Now a hundred feet separated them. The ramp was close. Cars were coming down, unaware that a speeding ton of metal killing machine was heading for them. There would be nowhere to go. Cherner would claim more victims.

Less than a hundred feet now divided them. If Hager crashed into the back end of the car at his current speed, it would catapult the Toyota right into oncoming traffic. He had to sideswipe the car from the right side and push him into the trees that lined the side of the highway. But he had to deal with the other cars on the road.

"Lloyd, see if anyone's in the right lane there."

Lloyd craned his neck to the right. "Yeah, there's one coming. After that, I don't see any more." He waited and the car passed. "Go!"

Hager veered to the right and pulled alongside the Toyota. The ramp was a few hundred feet away. A car was approaching. Behind it, the gargantuan mass of a gasoline tractor-trailer rolled at a slow speed.

Overtaking the Toyota slightly, Hager readied himself for the crash. Instead, the Toyota slammed into his side, jolting his teeth loose and careening him into a storm of oncoming cars. He jerked the wheel back to the left, barely avoiding a Chevy. A horn sounded, long and fearful.

Eye of the Beholder

The Toyota swerved again, crashing into his door. Hager pulled the wheel left to meet the blow; it was like turning into a punch. The force brought them off the ground, forcefully landing on both wheels; Hager's head spanked the steering wheel. His nose was bleeding—his vision blurred.

Hager brought the car back to the left. The Toyota entered the ramp. The car on the ramp stopped, but the gas truck kept coming. Hager stomped on the gas in one last-ditch effort to end this frightful pursuit. His front bumper made sudden contact with the Toyota. He floored it and turned his wheels.

The Toyota lost traction and spun, then flipped side over side, tumbling toward the gas truck. With a loud crash, the Toyota slammed into the trailer, ripping it away from the tractor and landing on its side.

Hager rolled up the ramp, staying a safe distance away. Lloyd was out of the car and on the phone, blood streaming down the right side of his face. His window had shattered from the collision with his head. Hager stopped the car, pulled off his seat belt and tried his door, which had caved in.

On all fours, he crawled across the seat and stumbled from the car. As he headed for the Toyota, the Beretta came out instinctively. It was then he'd realized his left arm was throbbing with pain.

The Toyota had toppled on the driver's side. Hager peered into the car and saw Cherner, or what was left of him. The roof of the car had been crushed, the windshield smashed, heaps of small glass pebbles scattered across the seats. Cherner's head had been severed from the impact and was lying on the front floor, his eyes open in horror. He'd seen death coming. The rest of his body looked like a mangled piece of clothed meat.

It was finally over.

CHAPTER
46

IT TOOK SEVEN HOURS for the entire mess to be cleaned up. Both Lloyd and Hager made trips via ambulance to Wake Medical Center. Lloyd had suffered a concussion and a laceration to his right cheek, which, although smaller, would match the scar on the left side. Hager, on the other hand, had a broken left arm and a huge bruise starting from his left shoulder flowing down to his knee.

Detectives Phillips and Erickson were also transported to Wake Med as a result of their injuries. Erickson sustained a broken leg, and Phillips had several cuts to his face from the flying glass.

At the hospital, SBI agents from the Capital district interviewed both Hager and Lloyd about the chase and the resulting death of Reid Cherner. Troopers and Raleigh PD detectives were waiting their turns to talk about the crash and the death of McLendon. Bob Maxwell arrived and assured all the investigators that whatever his agents had done was well within their legal boundaries.

Fortunately, no civilians had been injured during the attempted arrest. But with an officer killed and four others injured, positives were hard-pressed to be found.

The autopsy on Detective R.D. (Brick) McLendon determined that he died as a result of a fractured skull from the impact with the windshield. He was survived by his wife and son. He was the first Raleigh officer to have been killed in the line of duty in over ten years.

Two hours after he'd arrived at Wake Med, Vanessa and Elizabeth entered the emergency room. Vanessa still looked a little tired. With her hair pulled back in a ponytail and wearing no makeup, she looked much younger than her thirty-four years.

Elizabeth's eyes and nose were red from crying. When she saw Hager, she scampered through the door and wrapped her arms around him, careful not to aggravate his injuries. Vanessa greeted him with a loving smile and a kiss. With the three of them together, it looked like the storm had passed and life could get back to normal. Plus, there was a wedding to plan and a house to be built.

Epilogue

BECAUSE REID CHERNER had been killed before being interviewed, there were still lingering questions about his motives regarding the murder of Cynthia Craven. DNA test results, along with a bite mark comparison proved that Cherner had killed Cynthia Craven. The knife, believed to have been the murder weapon, was recovered from the crashed Toyota, and tests revealed the presence of Cynthia Craven and Marla Hill's blood.

Hager theorized that the killer initially saw Cynthia when she came into the locksmith shop to get a key copied—probably an extra key to the townhouse she'd purchased. Hager wasn't sure, but he believed Cherner followed Cynthia and attacked her after she and Lyle had parted ways.

Despite the Craven case having been closed, Hager utilized a full week to construct a complete background on

Cherner, assembling a criminal profile that would be submitted to the FBI.

The autopsy results revealed that Cherner had a large tumor in his brain. He'd undergone treatment for mental illness since he was fifteen years old when he'd attempted suicide. His mother attributed young Reid's problems to chronic drug use. After his first admission to John Umstead Hospital, Cherner had been committed seven times, but none of his treatment periods were for longer than a month. In all of those times, he'd never once had a CAT scan, which would have revealed the tumor and possibly prevented him from further deterioration.

As for the motivation to kill Cynthia Craven and Marla Hill, no one would ever know what possessed him to kill. In addition to interviews with psychiatrists who treated Cherner, Hager interviewed the owner of Mid-Town Locksmith where the killer worked as a key cutter, but only learned that the man was a loner and in the owner's words, "a little off."

Cherner's mother, with whom he lived, could only point to his mental illness and drug use as the cause for her son's crimes. Hager's profile, already tainted by his prior knowledge of the killer, painted a picture of a mentally ill man suffering from schizophrenia and obsessive/compulsive disorders.

In a search of Cherner's bedroom, Hager discovered three sets of keys. Two of them were confirmed to have belonged to Cynthia Craven and Marla Hill; the other is still a mystery. Cherner had also amassed a collection of books from the library, which included famed serial killer David Berkowitz's biography, *Confessions of Son of Sam*. A book about John Wayne Gacy called *Buried Dreams: Inside the Mind of a Serial Killer*, and *Catching Serial Killers: Learning from Past Serial Murder Investigations*.

It appeared Cherner was more aware of his crimes — in a mental capacity — than Hager believed. The mere fact of having these books meant that Cherner was trying to learn

Jeff Pate

more about himself and how to prolong his activities.

Along with the books, Cherner had written poetry. Most of them appeared unfinished, but one stood out among the others as a true insight into the mind of this monster.

Life is almost over
I fear the end is soon
My anger swells inside me
There's nothing left but doom
I see red, then black
The colors fade
I see so many eyes looking at me
With a fear so lovely
I listen to their last breath
As they cling to precious life
What are they trying to tell me
As I drive inside the knife?